CUM
LAUDE

Cecily von Ziegesar is the author
of the Gossip Girl novels

CUM LAUDE

Cecily von Ziegesar

HYPERION

NEW YORK

Copyright © 2010 Cecily von Ziegesar

Permissions on p. 262 represent a continuation of this copyright page.

Library of Congress Cataloging-in-Publication Data has been applied for.

ISBN: 978-1-4013-2347-9

Hyperion books are available for special promotions and premiums. For details contact the HarperCollins Special Markets Department in the New York office at 212-207-7528, fax 212-207-7222, or e-mail spsales@harpercollins.com.

Design by Chris Welch

FIRST EDITION

10 9 8 7 6 5 4 3 2 1

SUSTAINABLE FORESTRY INITIATIVE — Certified Fiber Sourcing — www.sfiprogram.org

THIS LABEL APPLIES TO TEXT STOCK

We try to produce the most beautiful books possible, and we are also extremely concerned about the impact of our manufacturing process on the forests of the world and the environment as a whole. Accordingly, we've made sure that all of the paper we use has been certified as coming from forests that are managed to ensure the protection of the people and wildlife dependent upon them.

For my teachers

CUM
LAUDE

Considering the lack of direction in the world, it seems as though many people get through college and beyond without really questioning who they are.

—Preface, *The Insider's Guide to the Colleges*, 1992

College is for lovers. At least, this one was. Looming up out of the trees on its hilly pedestal, Dexter College looked so strikingly pretty and at the same time so quaintly academic, it was almost as out of place in its rural setting as some of its students. The campus was fortified on all sides by forests of ancient conifers, tall birches, and dense maples, so that only the proud white spire of the college chapel was visible from town. Homeward Avenue, the road that led uphill to campus from Interstate 95, continued down the hill to the blink-and-you'd-miss-it town of Home, Maine, which consisted of a Walmart, a Shop 'n Save, the Rod and Gun Club, and a few mom-and-pop shops frequented only by locals.

Shipley Gilbert would have sprinted up the hill to campus if she could, but her family's Mercedes was loaded down with a semester's worth of freshman essentials, so she had to drive. At least her mother wasn't with her. Shipley had insisted on that.

She steered the car into one of the temporary parking spots in front of an imposing brick building with the word "Coke" engraved in marble over its black double doors. The parking area was a busy place. Students carted wheeled suitcases and cardboard boxes, dads reined back dogs on leashes, little sisters twirled their skirts, little brothers shot at birds with their fingers cocked, moms fanned the humid air. The sky was blue, the grass green and freshly shorn, the brick red and clean. A gaggle of tie-dyed T-shirted boys played Hacky Sack on the sprawling lawn. A handsome young English professor sat cross-legged as he read aloud from Walt Whitman's *Leaves of Grass,* trying to inspire a thirst for something other than beer in the twitching semicircle of incoming freshmen seated around him. Three girls in matching pink Dexter T-shirts jogged toward the field house.

Dexter College was exactly as advertised.

Shipley stepped out of the car, releasing the scent of Camel cigarettes and Juicy Fruit gum into the sun-burnished air. Never a gum chewer or a smoker, she'd decided to cultivate both habits on the drive up. A late August wind rustled the maple trees that stood between the car and the quad—that long expanse of grass at the center of Dexter's campus. On either side of the quad, red-brick buildings with massive white columns challenged each other to do better. The pristine white clapboard chapel stood at the peak of the hill at one end of the quad, and Dexter's new glass and pink stucco Student Union stood at the other end, a perfect juxtaposition of tradition and modernity.

"Tradition and Modernity" was the college's most recent motto, indoctrinated during the Student Union's ribbon-cutting in June. The Dexter College bookstore even sold a pair of wind chimes with the word "Tradition" printed on one bulky brass chime and "Modernity" on its slim stainless steel mate. Of course the Dexter College letterhead still bore its original Latin motto—*Inveni te ipsum* ("Find yourself")—but very few students knew or bothered to find out what it meant.

Shipley inhaled the clean country air and imagined kicking up the maple leaves this fall when they were red and crisp and covered the ground. Bundled into her favorite cream-colored cable-knit sweater, she'd stroll along the stone walks with a group of new friends, drinking hazelnut-flavored coffee from the Starbucks café, discussing poetry and art and cross-country skiing, or whatever people talked about in Maine. Eager to get on with it, she popped open the trunk and grabbed the handles of her largest duffel bag.

"Want some help?" Two boys appeared at her sides, flashing eager, helpful smiles.

"I'm Sebastian." The taller of the two reached for the duffel bag and then ducked into the car for another. "Everyone calls me Sea Bass." He tossed the second bag at his friend, whose dense thicket of hair could only be described as a Greek afro. "That's Damascus."

Damascus clasped the duffel against his burly chest. His knuckles were meaty and tan. "We're totally harmless," he assured her with a mischievous smile.

Shipley hesitated. "I'm on the third floor. Room 304. I guess that's kind of a hike?"

"Fucking A!" Sea Bass crowed, the corners of his mouth spreading so wide they nearly touched the tips of his carefully sculpted sideburns. "That's right next to us!" He dropped Shipley's bag on the ground and threw his arms around her, hugging her with such force that her feet left the ground. "Welcome to the first day of the rest of your life!"

Shipley took a startled step backward and tucked her long blond hair behind her ears, blushing furiously. She wasn't used to being hugged by friendly, boisterous boys. She'd gone to the same girls school—Greenwich Academy—since kindergarten. It had a brother school—Brunswick—and she'd sung in choir with boys and even had a male lab partner in AP Chemistry. But because her father was of the mostly absent variety and her older brother was strange and remote and had been away at boarding school almost since she could remember, she remained unsure of herself around boys. She walked around the car and opened the door to the backseat, where she'd stowed her goose down pillow and her portable CD player, wondering if she would take to fraternizing with males as easily as she had taken to chewing gum and smoking.

"Okay." She tucked the pillow beneath her arm and slammed the door closed. "I'm ready."

"So why'd you choose Dexter?" Sea Bass asked as she followed him up Coke's dark and winding back stairs.

Shipley shrugged her shoulders. "I don't know," she answered vaguely. "My brother went here." She paused. "And I didn't get into Dartmouth."

"Me neither," Damascus replied from behind her. "I guess that's why we all end up here, huh?"

Shipley followed Sea Bass down the hallway. Dexter provided a dry-erase board on the door of each room so that students could leave messages for one another. Yesterday, the staff from the Office of Student Housing and Campus Life had marked each board with the names of the students who would occupy each room. The names "Eliza Cheney" and "Shipley Gilbert" were written in loopy cursive on the board outside room 304.

The room itself was small and plain, with two single wooden beds pushed up against the white walls. A wide wooden desk stood in front of the only window, with a chair on either side and a lamp in the middle. Across from the desk stood a built-in set of drawers with a large rectangular mirror and an electrical outlet for a hair dryer or curling iron on the wall above it. The drawers were framed by two shallow, rectangular spaces fitted with wooden rails for hanging clothes. The white walls were freshly painted, but the wooden furniture and orange linoleum floor were scratched and pen-marked, bestowing the room with a gloomy institutional charm.

Shipley sat down, claiming the bed nearest the door. Sea Bass and Damascus hovered in the doorway.

"You want beer?" Sea Bass asked. "We ordered a keg."

"Funnels!" Damascus whooped.

Down the hallway Shipley could hear the sounds of parents calling out their last good-byes. "Don't we have to leave for orientation soon?" she asked.

Freshman orientation was a Dexter tradition. Incoming students spent a night camping in the woods with their roommate and five or six other freshmen, under the guidance of one of the professors.

"Nah." Damascus ran his hands over his chubby stomach. "We're juniors. Been there, done that. We just got here early to party. Hardy."

Sea Bass went over and pushed open the window as far as it would go. He perched on the window ledge, stretching his long legs out in front of him. The knees of his jeans were split open like giant paper cuts. "They give all the freshmen the tiniest, shittiest rooms. Ours is like a palace compared to this." He watched as Shipley fluffed up her pillow and tossed it onto her mattress. "So what class was your brother in?"

Shipley hadn't given any thought to how she'd respond to such a question. Four years ago, she'd come with her parents to drop Patrick off at this very dorm, in a single room on the first floor. He'd sat on his bed with his jacket on, his carefully packed trunk at his feet, and waved them cheerfully away. Two months later, the college had called to complain that Patrick rarely went to class and often left campus for days. A month after that, they'd called to say he'd disappeared entirely, leaving behind his un-packed trunk.

Traces of Patrick appeared on credit card bills. He'd been to bars, motels, and diners all over Maine. Then there were the police reports. He'd broken into empty houses to get warm and slept in parking lots, campgrounds, and on beaches. He'd stolen a brand-new bicycle. Then there were the emergency room bills. He'd had pneumonia, frostbite, and poison ivy.

Shipley's parents tried to leave word for him to come home or at least call, but he never did. Long after dinner was over and Shipley had wandered up to her room to finish her homework, they would sit at the dining room table, drinking in silence. Sometimes her mother cried. Once, her father broke a plate. Eventually they canceled Patrick's credit card and gave him up for lost.

"At least we've got Shipley," they'd said.

"He didn't graduate," Shipley explained now, fanning herself with her hand. Despite the open window, the air in the room was thick and hot. "He left," she clarified. "No one really knows where he went."

"Freaky," Damascus remarked from the doorway.

"*Excusez-moi?*" A girl with razor-straight black bangs popped her head up over his shoulder. "Talking about me already?"

"Sorry." Damascus stumbled into the room and attempted to shove his hands into his hip pockets. His brown corduroys were stretched so tight at the waist it was more like a finger dip.

The girl wore black denim cutoffs that were so short the frayed white insides of the pockets showed. "I'm Eliza." She pointed her finger at Shipley. "Hey, you're sitting on my bed."

Shipley jumped to her feet. "I don't have to have this bed," she stammered.

Eliza rolled her eyes. She was used to scaring the shit out of people—it was her specialty—but if she didn't want her new roommate to hate her instantly she would have to make an effort to be nice. "I was kidding. I was just trying to make you feel stupid. I'm sorry. Now I feel stupid. And I got into Harvard."

"No shit," Sea Bass whistled. "What are you doing here then?"

Eliza shrugged her shoulders. She'd chosen Dexter over Harvard because the girl who'd given her a tour of Dexter's campus had worn old-fashioned roller skates with yellow pom-poms on the laces and had skated backward in them the entire time. That was all she remembered about the tour. It seemed to her that at a small, boring, vaguely crunchy New England liberal arts college like Dexter, the eccentrics really stood out, whereas at a place like Harvard no one would notice them. And she wanted to be noticed.

"I don't know." She shrugged her shoulders. "I heard the food was better?"

Her drab green army duffel—the only bag she'd brought with her on the bus from Erie, Pennsylvania—blocked the hallway like a dead body. She dragged it into the room. "This one is fine," she told Shipley, attempting to modulate her bitchy tone as she sat down on the bed against the far wall. She turned to Sea Bass, still perched on the windowsill. "And you live where?" she asked, the bitchiness coming back. It was obvious the boys were only hanging around because Shipley was beautiful and blond. She also seemed weirdly shy, which was a good thing, because Eliza herself was anything but. They'd get along swimmingly. Two peas in a pod. Two pumpkins in a patch. Two hens in a peck, or whatever the fuck you called it. "Because I really need to count my tampons before orientation starts."

Sea Bass stood up quickly. Damascus was already gone.

"Remember there's a keg waiting for you when you get back!" Sea Bass called before slamming the door.

Looking for something to do, Shipley unzipped the smaller of her two bags and pulled out her new Ralph Lauren sheet set. She could feel Eliza staring at her as she ripped open the plastic and removed the bottom sheet from its casing. She'd spent a long time at the Lord & Taylor in Stamford, picking out new sheets. They were the first she'd ever bought for herself and she wanted them to be right. Something about this pattern, with its dark purple, navy blue, and hunter green swirling paisleys seemed just rebellious enough to say "college," while still being Ralph Lauren.

"Nice," Eliza commented. "Those are really nice sheets," she clarified. "Really."

"Thanks." Shipley couldn't tell if her new roommate was entirely sincere. She stretched the bottom sheet over the mattress, tucking it in where it draped at the sides. "I told those guys I didn't get into Dartmouth, but actually I did." The fact that she and Eliza had both chosen Dexter over an Ivy League school gave them at least one thing in common. "Just like you, I decided to come here instead." She smoothed the wrinkles out of the sheet. The room looked better already.

"How come?" Eliza unzipped her duffel bag and pulled out a collection of books—*The Bell Jar, Flowers in the Attic, Interview with the Vampire*—and a giant white rabbit's foot on a little gold chain. Kneeling on the mattress, she thumbtacked the chain to the wall so that the rabbit's foot hung over the head of her bed. She sat back and smiled, delighting in its perverse mix of tackiness, gore, and desperation.

Shipley shook out the top sheet. Her parents were annoyed when she'd even applied to Dexter. When she'd decided to go, they'd almost stopped talking to her. Of course they blamed the school for not keeping a closer watch on Patrick. And what exactly was Shipley trying to accomplish anyway? Dartmouth was a far superior school. But Shipley was eighteen now, and she was tired of doing the right thing in the shadow of the brother who'd always done the wrong thing. To her, Dexter represented a sort of backless wardrobe, a gateway to a far more interesting life than the one she'd led thus far. Patrick had come here and then—gloriously—*disappeared.*

Someone knocked. "Shipley Gilbert? Eliza Cheney?"

Eliza went over and opened the door. "Who wants to know?"

A tall, lean person with spiky golden brown hair, a square jaw, a prominent Adam's apple, and long earlobes decorated with two tiny gold studs blinked coldly back at her. Eliza studied the baggy shorts, loose-fitting Dexter T-shirt, and brown suede Birkenstocks. Male or female? It was impossible to tell.

"I'm Professor Darren Rosen, your orientation leader. It's time to head out. Don't forget, you're in Maine. Bring something warm to wear tonight."

Eliza grabbed the first sweater she could find, a magenta-colored acrylic V-neck she'd bought at JCPenney. Magenta was like a big, loud fuck-you to light pink, a color she absolutely loathed. She wadded up the sweater and tucked it under her arm, watching as Shipley pawed through an array of pretty sweaters until she settled on a cream-colored cable-knit cardigan with pockets and tied it around her waist. She looked like a model in one of those clothing catalogs Eliza's mother always threw out because "Penney's has everything."

They followed Professor Rosen downstairs and outside the dorm. Most of the other freshmen had already left for orientation, and the temporary parking lot was quiet now.

"Oh no!" Shipley cried. "My car!" She sprinted over to an elegant black Mercedes sedan with Connecticut plates. A neon yellow parking ticket was tucked beneath one of its windshield-wiper blades.

"Hurry up!" Professor Rosen barked. "The main parking lot is across the road. We'll wait for you in the van."

Eliza's roommate assignment hadn't mentioned that Shipley would be beautiful or blond, or that she would drive a black Mercedes with tiny windshield wipers on its headlights. It hadn't mentioned that Shipley's trim, suntanned legs looked great in white shorts, especially when she ran, which she did now with the effortless grace of a Thoroughbred. Eliza didn't know how to drive, her legs were shapeless and pale, and the only shorts she owned were the butchered black denim ones she'd worn today. It was growing increasingly difficult not to be envious of Shipley, and even not to ever so slightly hate her.

Professor Rosen slid open the door to the waiting van, a beat-up maroon Chevy with Dexter's logo of a single green pine tree emblazoned on it. Eliza couldn't help thinking that Harvard probably had a whole fleet of Mercedes.

Inside, the van was musty and crowded. Professor Rosen, who was in fact female, tapped her fingers impatiently against the wheel while Eliza squeezed into the very back seat, next to three girls wearing matching powder pink cap-sleeved Dexter T-shirts. This particular feminine cut of T-shirt was new this year and had proven to be a hit with incoming students. The bookstore had already sold out of them.

In the second row of seats, directly in front of Eliza, Tom Ferguson and Nicholas Hamilton waited impatiently for Professor Rosen to start the engine and crank up the AC.

"Freaks," Tom muttered under his breath. Freaks in their wool hats and Birkenstocks. Even the professor in charge of their orientation trip, the one behind the wheel with the spiky brown hair and gold earrings. Mr. or Ms.? He had no freaking clue.

"Why am I even going to this place again?" he'd asked his dad that morning in the car. Tom's parents had given him a new Jeep Cherokee for graduation. His father rode with him while his mother followed them in the Audi.

"Because you're a legacy, and it's the best place you got into," his father reminded him. "Hey, don't knock it, kid. Dexter's my alma mater and look how I turned out: ma—"

"Yeah, Dad. I know, I know. Manager of your own fund, happily married to a beautiful woman, two boys in good colleges, big house in Bedford, beach house on the Cape."

Tom smoothed his dark hair back with his hands—what was left of it anyway. He'd wanted it cut short for the Westchester triathlon, but his dad's barber didn't get what he was asking for and had given him a crew cut. He glanced at his father. His gray, neatly trimmed hair was flawless. His skin was flawless. His white shirt was flawless. He looked like the fucking "advertisement of the man" to quote *The Great Gatsby*, the only assigned book Tom had actually finished and enjoyed. But he hadn't always looked like that. Tom had seen pictures of his dad in college. A hippie with bad skin—long stringy hair, stoner smile, zits all over the place, even on his eyelids.

His father gazed out the window and nodded his head with that annoying parental mix of knowing and nostalgia. "Dexter will surprise you."

"*How* will it surprise me?" Tom demanded, pressing the gas pedal to the floor. He thought maybe his dad was going to tell him about Dexter's underground secret society, where the men were weeded out from the boys and the women wanted one thing and one thing only.

But his dad just clapped him on the shoulder and grinned cluelessly. "I have no idea."

The van's windows were down. Tom stared at the grassy lawns—so green it hurt—and listened to the birds singing their heads off. He'd always noticed stuff like that—the ambient background of what was going on. He really dug that shit. He turned to the guy seated next to him, his new roommate. They'd met briefly in their room before he and his parents had taken off to grab some lunch.

"Nicholas?" Tom addressed the wool-flap-hat-wearing freak. "Is that what you go by?"

The guy pulled his earphones out of his ears. Dirty blond curlicues of hair fell down over the collar of his oatmeal-colored embroidered freak shirt. Actually it was more like a tunic, since it came down almost to his knees.

"I prefer Nick."

Tom jiggled his legs in annoyance. If Nicholas wanted to be called "Nick," why didn't he just put "Nick" on his registration forms the way Tom had put "Tom" on his? No one called him "Thomas," not even his great-grandmother.

"Hey, Professor," he called to the guy behind the wheel. "Any chance we could get moving soon, dude? This van could really use a little air circulation."

"*He's a she*," Nick whispered. "Professor Darren Rosen. She teaches a senior seminar called Androgyny. I read about her in one of those college guides."

"Jesus." Tom wondered if it was too late to transfer to a school with fewer freaks. He glared out the window, his gaze scanning the vast wasteland of dingy woods, muddy farms, and depressing shit-ass towns scattered around the hill the college was perched on. "Mud, grass, and trees. Mud, grass, and trees," he muttered.

One of the girls behind him kicked the back of his seat. "Come on, dude. This is Maine—*vacationland?* People come here for the scenery. You should feel honored."

Tom turned around to glower at the girl with short dark bangs and a permanent snarl.

"Nice to fuck you, too," Eliza added, acknowledging his glare.

"I was thinking of camping out on campus. You know, while the weather's still warm? Maybe build a yurt?" Nick mused aloud, oblivious to Tom and Eliza's little repartee.

Nick was one of the happy people, Eliza could tell. He wore the standard boarding school hippie uniform, and his perma-grin was probably pot-induced, but she bet he smiled like that even when he wasn't stoned. A guy as happy as he was drove her insane. She wanted to devour him or molest him, or both.

Nick stuck his headphones back into his ears. Eliza was right, he was happy. Never happier than when he was listening to one of his favorite albums: Simon and Garfunkel's *The Concert in Central Park.* His mom had taken him to the concert when he was seven years old, just the two of them. She'd shared a joint with the people dancing in the grass next to them and had even let him take a hit, just for fun.

After four years of boarding school, Nick should have been used to being separated from his mom and little sister, but he was already homesick. He'd spent the entire summer in the city with them, listening to records and eating picnics in the park. The bus ride up to Dexter had been lonely indeed. He'd even forgone a Subway sandwich with Tom and his parents so he could call home. His mom was at work and Dee Dee was at day camp, but it did him good just to hear their voices on the machine.

"So what's a—what did you call it? A yurt?" Tom asked him now.

"Huh?" Nick kept his headphones on, trying to tune out the fact that his new roommate was going to kill him and eat him before school even started.

"A yurt." Tom spoke up. "What the hell is it?"

Nick brightened. Maybe Tom would lighten up if he received enough good vibrations. "Oh, it's like a big, permanent tent. I'm going to ask the college if I can build one and sleep in it sometimes, you know, so I can commune with nature?"

Laird Castle, a senior at Nick's boarding school when Nick was a freshman, had built a yurt behind the science building and lived in it until he graduated. Laird was supposed to have gone to college at Dexter, but his tent pole was struck by lightning on a camping trip in the Berkshire Mountains, killing him instantly. Nick hadn't really known Laird, except to admire his collection of hand-knit earflap hats, the "Meat Is Murder" bumper sticker on his beat-up Subaru, and the constant plume of pot smoke emanating from the air holes in his yurt. But he had taken it upon himself to carry on Laird's legacy at Dexter. He liked to think of Laird as Yoda, the hobbling, green centuries-old Jedi master from *Star Wars*, and himself as the young Luke Skywalker. In order to master the force, a Jedi knight in training needed a safe hideaway in which to hone and perfect his skills. The yurt would be that place.

Nick sneezed violently and wiped his nose on the back of his hand. Then he sneezed again.

"Jesus, man," Tom exclaimed in disgust.

"Sorry," Nick apologized. "Allergies."

"Bless you," Eliza murmured from the back.

Tom loosened his canary yellow belt a notch and shifted away from Nick. Obviously his sneezy new roommate couldn't wait to invite him camping. They could have a gay old time in their tent or yurt or whatever, drinking hot toddies and wiping each other's nose and rear-ending each other. Damn it to hell, why couldn't school just start already so he could get the next four years over with and start working for his dad? He didn't need any stupid orientation. He was already pretty fucking oriented, and all compasses pointed toward four long years of mise-fucking-ry, starting with an entire year rooming with this allergic twat from Manhattan.

Professor Rosen started up the engine. "Here comes our last passenger—finally. Scoot over, boys."

Shipley had smoked another cigarette while she looked for a parking space. She wasn't even sure if she was smoking correctly, but just imagining what her mother would think if she saw the car's ashtray stuffed with old butts gave her a singular thrill.

"There were no spots left so I had to park in the grass," she told the professor. "Hope that's okay." She tucked her hair behind her ears and contemplated where to sit. Eliza was all the way in the back, squashed between three girls wearing matching pink T-shirts.

"Sit here!" Two boys parted ways, clearing a more than adequate place for her between them. One of the boys wore the same oatmeal-colored J. Crew beach tunic she'd bought as a swimsuit cover-up last summer. The flaps of his wool hat barely covered the headphones of his Walkman. The other boy wore blue seersucker Bermuda shorts and had to crouch to keep from hitting his closely shaved head on the roof of the van.

Shipley sank into the seat as the van eased out of the parking lot and down the hill toward town. Warm wind whipped in through the open windows, blowing her blond hair backward.

"That breeze feels so good!" one of the girls in the back cried.

"Amazing!" her friend agreed.

"Awesome!" the third one chimed in.

"Listen, I'm Tom." The big preppy boy thrust his right hand at Shipley. "From Bedford," he added with the implied assumption that Shipley would know what he was talking about. And she did. Bedford, New York, was Greenwich, Connecticut's smaller kissing cousin. It was hunt country, as in horses and hounds. Shipley had ridden in pony trials in Bedford almost every weekend when her old pony was still sound. "And that's Nick over there." Tom glanced at the other boy. "Don't even try calling him Nicholas. I did and he almost bit me in the sac."

"Oi!" Professor Rosen shouted from behind the wheel.

Eliza snorted and kicked the back of Shipley's seat. Nick grinned. "I'm Nick," he said in a loud voice. He pulled his headphones off and leaned toward Shipley. He smelled like basil, sort of. "You know the person driving, our anal leader?" he whispered.

Shipley giggled. "What about him?"

"He's a *she*," Tom murmured in her other ear. "But she seems like kind of a dick anyway."

"Her name is Professor Darren Rosen," Nick continued. "I'm pretty sure she teaches Freshman English."

Eliza stared out the window as she eavesdropped on their conversation. She'd actually seen Tom's and Nick's ears perk up when Shipley got into the van. They'd pointed, like horny bird dogs. Her father used to have two springer spaniels that he used for hunting ducks. She knew pointing when she saw it.

The van paused at a stop sign and a pale, skinny jogger ran by, his maroon Dexter basketball jersey flapping loosely against his limbs. He reminded Tom of Salvador Dalí's famous painting of dripping clocks. He'd been running so long, he was melting.

"Pay attention, folks!" Professor Rosen announced. "We're about to cross the Kennebec River. Two miles downstream is our camp. If anyone has to go pee-pee, find a spot *away* from the river. It's ramen noodles for dinner. You'll be eating a lot of ramen this winter, so why not get used to it now?"

"*Ew. Yuck!*" The three pink-T-shirted girls moaned a chorus of dismay from the back.

A farm flashed by. A trailer home. A dilapidated barn. More clover, more daisies, more buzzing bees. Motionless cows blinked at the van, insects hovering over their heads in clouds.

"Damn. Did you see that? This whole geographic region is freaking depressing as hell," Tom complained.

"Hey, man," Nick countered. "People live here. And they probably hate us, you know? Rich city kids turning up to go to college in their town? Littering on their farms? Driving up the price of bacon or coffee or whatever."

Nick could feel his earlobes flush a deep, hot pink. He tugged on the flaps of his hat and glanced self-consciously at Shipley, who was busy pretending to gaze dreamily out the window while secretly admiring Tom's bulging triceps. Eliza continued to glare at the back of Tom's meat-headed skull, while Tom marveled at the way in which the sunlight reflected off the tiny blond hairs on the tops of Shipley's thighs, causing them to sparkle. The van turned onto an old logging road that led directly into the woods. It barreled over a pothole, tossing its passengers together as the trees enveloped them.

2

The relationship between town and college is often fraught with tension. The town would like to think it doesn't need the college, however pretty, to draw visitors. After all, the town has its old mill, its tannery, its rushing river, its dramatic dam. Elm Street is still almost postcard-perfect despite the blight of Dutch elm disease. The pizza and pancakes aren't half bad. The high school wins the regional championships in both basketball and hockey nearly every year. And the townies are friendly, for the most part.

"Of course you don't have any money," Tragedy snapped at her brother. She manipulated her ever-present Rubik's cube, scrambling it up so she could solve it again. "Neither of us does. And we never will, unless we get the fuck out of Dodge."

Adam and Tragedy Gatz were not related, but they were brother and sister nonetheless. Tragedy was adopted, and she never let anyone forget it. Their parents, Ellen and Eli, were hippie subsistence farmers and crafts fair vendors. They had both grown up in Brooklyn and had dropped out of Dexter their junior year after taking too much acid and missing too many classes. They got married and, with their parents' help, bought a dilapidated horse farm right there in Home. Instead of horses, they raised sheep. Ellen spun wool and Eli welded hand-wrought oversized fork, knife, and spoon-shaped fireplace tongs. They ate their own grass-fed lamb and pesticide-free organic vegetables. They baked their own bread and made their own sheep's milk cheese and yogurt. And they gave birth to a son, Adam. When Adam was four years old, Ellen and Eli adopted the infant daughter of Hector Machado, a Brazilian sheep trader who'd died of a heart attack right on their doorstep, or so the story went. As he lay dying, Hector asked the Gatzes to take care of his baby daughter, whose mother had already died in childbirth. The baby had been named Gertrudes Imaculada, after her mother. The Gatzes renamed her Tragedy, after their favorite Bee Gees song, and they raised her as one of their own.

Right now Adam and Tragedy were sitting in Adam's battered white Volkswagen GTI on the shoulder of the road leading through campus, directly opposite Dexter College's new Student Union. They were arguing about whether or not to try and finagle some free coffee. Of course Tragedy would be the one to do the finagling; she always was.

"I don't see why you can't just make coffee at home," Adam said, trying to be reasonable.

But Tragedy was never reasonable. "Doesn't taste the same. Especially not with ewe's milk." She set her Rubik's cube down on the dashboard. "A feta-cheese-fucking-cino?" She stepped out of the car. "No, thank you," she added and slammed the door.

The freshmen had left for their orientation trips, and registration for the upperclassmen wouldn't begin until the day after tomorrow. Except for the few older students who'd arrived early, the campus was quiet. Adam watched his sister cross Homeward

Avenue and stride purposefully up the walk to the Student Union, her waist-length ponytail bobbing behind her.

It was Tragedy's fault Adam had graduated from high school virtually friendless. Over the course of his senior year, Tragedy had grown six inches taller in as many months. Her hips and chest developed at the same rapid rate, forcing her to switch from junior misses to women's sizes. "Your sister is ridiculously hot, man," Adam's classmates would protest. "How can you stand it? After all, you're not even related." Then someone seeded the rumor that Adam's relationship with his sister was more than brotherly, and instantly both he and Tragedy became social outcasts.

Of course nothing had ever transpired to justify the rumors, but Tragedy kept right on developing, and for the population of Home High and the town of Home itself, that was justification enough. The irony was, Adam didn't see it. He didn't see what was so ridiculously hot about his sister. She was simply his little sister—annoying, confrontational as hell, impossibly demanding, constantly around, and because beggars can't be choosers, his only friend.

Tragedy studied the menu board on the wall of the Student Union's new Starbucks café, trying to make sense of the ridiculous Italianate lingo. Tall was small, grande was bigger, and venti was the biggest. A few Starbucks had opened in Maine's larger towns—it had been reported that the chain was growing at a rate of one new outpost per day—but this was Home's first, and her first time ever inside one. It was very clean and orderly, definitely a step up from Boonies, the greasy muffin shop littered with old newspapers and overflowing ashtrays and equipped with the most disgusting bathroom in New England.

The pimply guy behind the counter stared her up and down. He was probably wondering why he'd never laid eyes on her before. She was kind of hard to miss.

"I only have a dollar," she told him boldly. "But I don't want to spend it." She was fond of getting away with murder. It was her favorite sport.

"That's okay," the guy responded, staring moronically at her chest. He dragged his palms across the green fabric of his apron. "What can I get for you?"

She glanced up at the board again, searching for the most expensive beverage they offered. "I'll take a venti mocha cappuccino thingy with lots of whipped cream and chocolate powder and a couple extra shots of espresso. And give me one of those chocolate biscotti cookies too, please. Oh, and make sure you use fair trade coffee."

The guy's pimply cheeks turned pink. "I'm not sure what you mean by 'fair trade.' It's okay if you can't pay for it."

She stared at him, enraged. How hard was it to know what was going on in the world? How hard was it to use your mind? "You sell coffee but you don't know what fair trade means?" she demanded with disgust. "And they call this a *liberal* arts college. Who grew that coffee? Who picked it? Who's profiting here?" She blinked her feathery black eyelashes angrily. "I'm still in high school, but I can guarantee you that I'm going to college someplace where people know what's what. Maybe not even in this fucking country!"

The boy blinked mutely back at her, obviously depressed that he'd dropped so miserably low in her supreme estimation. "Do you still want your mochaccino?" he asked timidly. "I'll throw in an extra biscotti."

"Fine. Sure." Fair trade or not, she really did want the coffee.

She turned her back as the guy fussed with the machinery. Afternoon sun flooded into the Student Union through a giant wall of glass facing the road. Adam tooted his horn and she waved at him, waggling the fingers of her left hand to indicate that she'd be back in the car in five minutes, tops.

Adam was such a loser. In two days he'd be starting college at Dexter as a day student. Dexter, of all places! So what that it gave Maine residents discounted tuition? So what that it rated up there with the Ivies and had a brand-new Starbucks café? So what that it had been selected as 1992's Prettiest New England College by both *USA Today* and *Yankee* magazine? Adam could have gone to California or Colorado or Florida or the Sorbonne, in France. Even U-Maine Orono—where most of Home High's college-bound graduates went—would have been ten times more interesting. Orono was far enough away that he would have had to live in a dorm. He would have been able to eat nonorganic, artery-clogging, delicious dining hall food. And she could have left Home to visit him.

Dexter prided itself on being part of the community and encouraged Maine residents to apply. Because Adam had graduated from high school with honors, Dexter had given him a free ride, but due to the housing squeeze, it had fallen short of providing him with a room. He would be a day student and continue to live at home. This was fine with him. He hadn't even signed up for the freshman orientation trip, claiming that it was too expensive. "I know where I am," he'd insisted. "I don't need any orientation."

In truth, Adam had no idea where he was. He was eighteen years old and bursting with potential. He liked to read and play tetherball. He could pick a shitload of blueberries. He could weld. He could shear a sheep. But he'd lived every one of his eighteen years with a sense of detachment that frustrated him. When would he start to *live*, full throttle? When would he begin to engage with his surroundings? Even the Dexter College campus,

which had existed prettily in the background throughout his entire life, felt strange and menacing. He felt as if he were seeing
it for the first time. The buildings were pristine. The grass was
green. The chapel was as white as his car had probably been
when it was new, long before his time. He was about to spend the
next four years of his life here, patrolling these green lawns, attending seminars in these immaculate brick buildings, or concerts and lectures in the quaint white chapel, but right now he
was too terrified to even get out of the car. Tragedy was right, he
was a pansy.

Adam tapped lightly on the horn, but he doubted his sister
could hear him. The glass walls of the new Student Union were
incredibly thick, built to withstand the frigid temperatures of
the long Maine winter.

The guy behind the counter was still grinding, filtering, and
steaming. Tragedy was about to inform him that she could have
flown to Guatemala, picked her own coffee, milked a fucking
cow, and baked a batch of biscotti herself by this time, when the
door to the bathroom swung open and a guy with a blond beard
wandered into the café. He wore a black parka, maroon Dexter
sweatpants, and old work boots. A thick book was clutched in his
grease-streaked hands. He looked young and old at the same
time, as if he'd been through a lot and didn't want to talk about it.

"Shit," he muttered as he walked by.

"Hey!" the guy behind the counter called out. "Hey man, I
told you yesterday. You're not supposed to use the bathroom unless you're a student or a customer."

Ignoring him, the bearded man pushed open the glass door
and stepped out into the sun.

"How do you know he's not a student?" Tragedy demanded.
"He's wearing Dexter sweatpants."

The guy placed an enormous cup of coffee on the shiny black countertop, squirted a dollop of whipped cream on top, and sprinkled it with cocoa powder before securing the lid.

"We only opened a few days ago and that guy's been in here every day to use the bathroom. He never buys anything. He's always wearing the same clothes. He always looks a little dirty and acts a little weird. He's no student." He slipped a cardboard sleeve around the cup and handed it to her. "One venti mocha cap with two shots and two biscotti," he announced, pushing the cellophane-wrapped cookies across the counter. He winked. "No charge."

The coffee weighed a ton. Tragedy grabbed the cookies and tucked them into her back pocket. "You tell your bosses the next time I'm in here I want to see some fair trade fucking coffee," she reminded him.

The bearded man was sitting on a bench in a sunny spot outside the Student Union, reading his book.

"Hey," she greeted him. "I'm Tragedy. What's your name?"

He looked up, his gigantic light blue eyes staring without seeing. His face and hands were dirty, and he was younger than she had first thought, but older than her brother was. His parka had a feather-oozing gash in the chest and must have been hotter than hell. The book in his hands was *Dianetics*, by L. Ron Hubbard. She recognized the erupting volcano on its cover from a *60 Minutes* episode she'd watched one Sunday night. The report was all about why Scientology was so appealing to celebrities, who tended to have "lifestyle problems." The Church of Scientology encouraged fucked-up people to delve into their pasts and "audit" their shitty memories or "engrams" to get "clear." The thing was, you had to *pay* them to do the auditing because, goodness knows, delving into your past is not something you should try on your own at home. Just another totally wack concept brought to you by the modern world of Planet Starbucks.

The guy was still staring at her. Or staring through her. She didn't mind. At least he wasn't staring at her boobs.

"Patrick," he said finally. "Pink Patrick."

"Here." She offered him the mochaccino. As with everything, now that she had it, she didn't really want it. "Take this too," she said, handing him a biscotti. "Sorry, the other one's for my brother."

Pink Patrick tore open the wrapper with his teeth and devoured the biscotti.

"Fuck it," she said, and handed him the second one. Adam wasn't hungry, not like this guy. The dude in the café was probably right. He wasn't a student.

Adam observed the proceedings from across the road. He didn't like the guy's ripped parka or how he was talking to his sister without looking at her. He didn't like his beard or his dirty boots. He didn't like how she'd given him all her food, especially not after she'd taken so much trouble to procure it. He tooted the horn again.

The bearded guy shot to his feet and lunged toward the car. "Hey! What's your problem?" he shouted as he stormed across the road. "Is there a problem?"

Adam locked the door. His window was wide open, but he didn't want to roll it up for fear of pissing the guy off even further. He started the engine, revving the gas pedal with what he hoped was a menacing roar. There were crumbs in the guy's beard and his blue eyes were round and fierce. He looked like Kris Kristofferson on crystal meth.

"Don't worry about him," Tragedy called out as she sauntered across the road to the car. "That's just my brother, Adam.

He's harmless." She opened the passenger door. "Hey, want a ride?" she asked the bearded guy.

"Jesus." Adam let his head fall back against the headrest, resigning himself. The guy was either going to hurl that huge cup of steaming hot coffee in his face, scarring him for life, or he was going to get into the backseat and ride with them for a mile or so before bashing their heads in with his boots.

"No thanks." The guy turned abruptly and walked up the road, away from town.

Tragedy got in and pulled her door shut. She picked up her Rubik's cube and swizzled it around. "I got you a cookie but I gave it away. Guy was fucking starving. I don't think I've ever seen anyone that hungry."

Adam let the car coast in a free fall down the hill toward town. Twenty, twenty-five, thirty, thirty-five, forty, forty-five, fifty. "Guy was nuts," he said.

Patrick carried the coffee into the parking lot across the road from his old dorm. Even though it served no actual purpose, Buildings and Grounds kept the grass surrounding the lot neatly mowed. He circled the tidy, green perimeter, headed for the depression in the lot's far corner, one of his favorite resting spots. He liked to stretch out in the sun in that particular grassy dimple, obscured from the road and the rest of campus by the cars in the lot. But today a black Mercedes sedan was parked at an awkward angle, half in the lot and half in the grass. The car bore Connecticut plates and a Greenwich beaches parking sticker. It was the car he'd learned to drive on, and it was in his spot.

"Shit," Patrick swore, about to turn and run. After all these years they'd finally come after him. Then he noticed the pack of cigarettes on the dashboard. His parents hadn't smoked when he lived at home, and it was doubtful they'd taken it up since then. He moved closer to the car and put his nose up against the driver's-side window. Gum wrappers and cassettes littered the passenger seat, along with a rumpled white Greenwich Academy sweatshirt.

The door was unlocked. Patrick slid in behind the wheel and put his coffee in one of the cup holders between the seats. Closing the door, he sank back into the cushiony tan leather. The car smelled stale and sweet. He touched the steering wheel with his fingertips. It was hot.

Shipley had been nine years old when he left for boarding school. Whenever he got kicked out, he'd return home for a brief stint before moving on to yet another school. But even as the years passed, he still thought of his sister as that nine-year-old girl, dutifully setting the table, a headband in her blond hair. Her fingernails were clean, she chewed with her mouth closed, she wore a tutu. How could anyone be that good all the time? She was fourteen when his family dropped him off at Dexter. She wore braces and dangly earrings, but she was still good. And she seemed frightened of him, as if his complete disinterest in pleasing anyone else would somehow rub off on her, cause her to miss the school bus.

Was it possible that Shipley was now at Dexter?

He removed a cigarette from the half-empty pack and lit it with the little yellow lighter that was tucked inside.

The summer he was sixteen, he'd gone on an Outward Bound hiking trip in the Canyonlands of Utah. The group consisted of seven kids between the ages of thirteen and sixteen, three other guys, three girls, plus two trip leaders who were both male and in their twenties. He was the only kid whose parents had paid for the trip. The others had been sent as an alternative to juvenile detention or drug rehab, and their tuition was subsidized. His sister was up in Vermont at sleepaway camp, learning to ride horses and shoot a bow and arrow. She'd begged their parents to go. He hadn't made any plans at all. So there he was, in Utah.

"Let's gather around in a circle," one of the leaders said on that first morning, after a van had dropped them off in the middle of some dusty nowhere and they'd strapped on their packs and hiked for a few miles. Except for the provisions that had been distributed evenly among them, Patrick's pack was empty. Outward Bound had sent a list of what to bring, but he'd left his bag on the plane. He was totally unequipped. He didn't even have a toothbrush.

"We're going to do a little get-to-know-you exercise," the leader explained. He wore a pair of Smith ski goggles on his head even though it was summer.

"Just say your name and then the first thing that comes into your head," the leader continued. "We'll start with you first." He smiled at a skinny girl with bruised shins.

She squirmed around a little before speaking up. "I'm Colleen. I steal."

The leader nodded like that was good news. He pointed at the next kid.

"I'm Roy. I'm jonesing." Roy had a red mohawk.

The leader pointed at Patrick.

"I'm Patrick." He told them. "Pink Patrick."

The entire group howled with laughter, leaders included.

"Motherfucking faggot!" Colleen shrieked, covering her mouth with her gold-ringed hands.

After that he was Pink Patrick for good. On the second night of the trip, he hitched his pack onto his shoulders and started walking. No one followed him. They were too busy playing I Spy and Concentration.

He walked through the desert for an entire night and all the next day without eating or drinking anything. It was hot. He was wearing jeans. His eyelids and tongue were swollen and heavy. Finally he reached an Indian reservation—a group of trailers and RVs with pieces of Astroturf cut to fit around them like lawns. An overweight Indian smoking a cigarette in a plastic lawn chair outside an RV stood up and handed him his half-empty can of Tab. Patrick gulped it down, feeling it burn the lining of his stomach with its fizzy brownness. He waited on the piece of Astroturf while the Indian went inside. He came out and handed Patrick a package of Oscar Meyer thick cut bacon. And that's what he ate that day—raw bacon and Tab—until he made it back to Moab and got a bus home.

His parents were on a cruise in the Greek Isles, so he hid out in Greenwich for a whole month, lying beneath the sprinklers out on the lawn, letting the water tickle his tongue. When they came home, they didn't want to know anything about what had happened. All they knew was his dirty laundry was all over the floor, he'd drunk everything in the liquor cabinet, and the kitchen was a disaster. His sister came home from camp looking happy and suntanned, with a wristful of lanyard bracelets. Soon after that he'd left for another boarding school. He was never home much.

Patrick reached for the warm coffee and took a sip. It tasted like a hot fudge sundae made with coffee ice cream. It was blended heaven, better than anything he'd ever tasted.

Dexter's overnight orientation trip had been much the same. He'd introduced himself as Pink Patrick just to see how everyone would react. Of course they laughed, and then they avoided him. He'd requested a single in Coke, so when they got back to campus he kept to himself. Those first few weeks he tried to go to class, but he couldn't see the point. He felt like he was standing outside a fish tank watching a busy school of fish. They just kept on swimming.

Since leaving school he'd been as far as Miami, but he always circled back to Dexter again. He liked Maine's extreme weather, its rugged shoreline, its endless greenery, and its relatively tolerant population. No one minded a loner like him. Plus, it was always easy to find food or grab a shower and some clean clothes on campus. But he always had that nagging feeling that he was waiting for something.

He took another sip of the warm, sweet coffee. Maybe this was it.

Shipley and Eliza put themselves in charge of setting up camp and sent the boys to collect firewood. Tom was really jacked up about it. He snapped a thin twig in half with his hands and tossed it onto their measly pile. "Come on, man, before it gets dark."

Nick wasn't at all sure he would survive the night, let alone a whole year, living with this brute. He sneezed four times in quick succession and wiped his nose and eyes on his shirt. "Any special wood we should be looking for?" He assumed Tom knew all sorts of manly stuff about which wood burns the longest and the cleanest.

"Fuck if I know." Tom peeled a skinny green branch off a nearby bush. "I'm from Westchester."

Nick pressed his lips together in a determined half smile and tried to maintain his usual sunny outlook. Life at boarding school often fosters a hunger for philosophical exploration. The Berkshire School in Massachusetts, from which Nick had graduated in June, went so far as to offer a course called Adventures in Eastern Philosophical Concepts. *The Tao of Pooh* and *Zen and the Art of Motorcycle Maintenance* were required reading. "Everything is an analogy." "When you discard arrogance, complexity, and a few other things that get in the way, sooner or later you will discover that simple, childlike, and mysterious secret: Life is Fun." It was Nick's favorite course.

"I think we'll need some big stuff if we're going to use the fire to cook with." Nick patted the trunk of a huge half-dead spruce, as if he just so happened to have in the pocket of his embroidered tunic the chainsaw they'd need to cut it down. They didn't even have a hatchet. He looked up, examining the upper branches of the tree. He'd come to Maine for its natural beauty. Well, here was his first opportunity to commune with nature.

3

It's often said that the best way to strengthen a relationship is to go camping. The simple tasks of choosing the campsite, unpacking the supplies, setting up the tent, gathering firewood, preparing and cooking the food, and washing the dishes allow each person to demonstrate their strengths and encourage teamwork. At the end of the day, when the coals are dying and each member of the group is snuggled up in their warm sleeping bag under a starlit sky, they can congratulate each other on a job well done, feeling grateful that they were not alone to conquer the elements.

"Keep looking," Tom commanded as Nick scrambled around on his hands and knees. Before leaving them to fend for themselves for the night, Professor Rosen had split the group in two. The three girls in pink Dexter T-shirts were on one side of the river while Tom, Nick, Shipley, and Eliza were on the other. As soon as she'd dropped them off, Professor Rosen had disappeared into the woods with her sleeping bag, promising to come back for them at daybreak.

Tom watched in awe as Nick let out a wild-boy yelp and hurtled himself through the air and into the arms of the tree, desperately straddling its wide, sturdy trunk.

"Jackass," Tom chuckled admiringly. "Jesus. Watch your balls, man."

Nick could feel his eyes water and his hands break out in a rash as he shimmied clumsily up the trunk toward the next set of branches. He turned his head to the side so as not to breathe in too much of the tree's noxious, hive-inducing fumes.

"Take it slow, monkey nuts," Tom warned.

The tree tolerated Nick's scraping and kicking like an old horse that is used to abuse. How had he done this as a little kid without castrating himself? The rough bark tore up the skin on the insides of his knees and bruised his crotch. There were splinters beneath his fingernails and he'd already skinned both elbows. Ten feet off the ground was a thick branch around ten inches in diameter that had been stripped of its bark by a porcupine. If he hung on long enough, jiggling his weight up and down just a bit, maybe gravity would work its magic and the branch would snap. He released his grip on the tree's trunk and swung, Tarzan-like, onto the branch.

"Dude!" Tom crowed. "You're a fucking kamikaze!"

Nick flailed at the branch, but before he could even wrap his fingers around it, the base of the branch came away from the trunk, splintering wetly. He crashed to the ground face-first. The rotten branch thudded against the back of his head.

"Ouch." Tom approached his fallen companion. "Did you break anything?"

"Ow," Nick moaned pitifully. "It hurts."

"Wood's rotten as shit, man," Tom observed standing over him. "I could've told you that."

Nick clambered to his knees and swiped at his face with the

backs of his hands. Blood smeared his knuckles. He touched the stinging space between his eyebrows and his fingers came away bloody. He could still see though. He was fine. And now he had a war wound.

He reached for the splintered branch and used it as a crutch to stand up. "Think it'll still burn?" he asked, holding the branch out for Tom's inspection.

Tom liked to think he was tough, but not around blood. During rest time in preschool he used to have to lie down next to Wallace White, who suffered from chronic nosebleeds. He threw up every time.

"Oh shit." He clapped his hand over his mouth. "Dude, you're bleeding." He staggered off toward camp, retching. "I'm going back."

Nick wiped his hands and face on his shirt. The blood was tacky, like red paint. "What about the wood?" he shouted, but Tom was already out of sight.

"He's fucking bleeding!" Tom crashed through the woods like a rabid bear and threw up a few yards away from the tent that Shipley and Eliza had just managed to pitch, no thanks to the boys.

"Who? Nick?" Shipley dropped the dented pan they were expected to cook ramen in, denting it even more. "What happened? Is he okay?" Her heart beat hard and fast in her chest and she could actually feel her light blue eyes turn a deeper shade of blue. College was already so exciting.

Eliza emerged from the tent holding a box of Kraft macaroni and cheese. "Look what I found. It's probably twenty years past its sell-by date, but who cares? It's better than ramen. Hey, where's our wood?" she demanded of Tom.

Tom's face was ashen. He sat down cross-legged beside the

fire ring that Eliza and Shipley had only just finished assembling out of sturdy rocks. There was no fire because there was still no wood. "I'm not feeling well."

"Excuse me?" Eliza responded, about to lay into him.

"Something's happened to Nick," Shipley interrupted. "Stay here," she told them importantly. "I'll go."

Just then Nick himself strode out of the woods, a parcel of sticks cradled in his shirt. "I fell out of a tree!" he announced. "I'm okay though."

Shipley hurried over to help him with the wood. She touched his cheek. "Your face is bleeding. Come on, there's a first aid kit in the tent."

"Fucking fuck!" Tom exclaimed. He lunged forward and puked directly into the fire ring. "Please get him the fuck out of here," he gasped.

"Poor baby." Eliza tsked unsympathetically. Camping out with these three was like watching the Westminster Dog Show on TV. *The first dog in our terrier group is the Bedford Terrier, known for its loud bark and tiny penis. This is number 44, Tom Ferguson, Bedford Terrier. Next is the Boarding School Terrier, known for its shaggy coat and perma-grin. This is number 33, Nick Hamilton, Boarding School Terrier. And finally, the Florence Nightingale of Greenwich Terrier, known for its lovely blue eyes and willingness to hump. This is Shipley Gilbert, number 69, Florence Nightingale of Greenwich Terrier.*

"Come on." Shipley led Nick into the tent and rummaged around in the Dexter-issued orientation pack for the first aid kit. "Sit down. I'm just going to get you cleaned up, and then we'll make a nice dinner." She knew nothing about first aid or cooking, but she liked the idea of playing nurse. She daubed an alcohol swab on the torn-up skin between Nick's eyes.

"Yeesh!" Nick gasped through clenched teeth. Tears streamed down his dirt-smudged cheeks. It stung so badly he wanted to kick her.

Shipley lifted her hand away, but only for a second. The wound was dirty. She had to get it clean. "I'm sorry. I know it hurts," she murmured, swabbing it determinedly.

There is probably nothing more painful than rubbing alcohol on an open wound. Nick shivered from head to toe and forced a smile to his face, trying to remain zen. "As long as you're the one hurting me, I can take it," he told her through gritted teeth.

Shipley blushed. She was aware that he was flirting with her, but she had no idea how to respond. She selected a round Band-Aid from the first aid kit and pasted it over the cut. It looked a little silly, but it would have to do.

Eliza ducked into the tent. "The Cowardly Lion is resting and replenishing his fluids. I moved the fire to a nice, vomit-free spot and put a pan of water on to boil. I just came up with a great invention though: a battery-operated camping microwave. Imagine the millions I could make on that." She dug around in one of the packs in the tent and then glanced at Shipley and Nick, kneeling only inches away from each other. "You guys done playing doctor?"

Shipley sat back on her heels. The round Band-Aid wasn't very professional-looking, but it would be too painful to take it off and put on a new one. "I did my best," she said apologetically.

"It feels better, thanks," Nick told her gratefully, even though he could feel the Band-Aid's adhesive trying to adhere to the wound itself. It wasn't a good feeling.

Eliza could practically see his tail wagging happily through the back of his tunic. "I'm looking for some pepper or maybe some garlic powder or herbs," she explained, still rummaging. "Something to spice up the mac."

"But that's my bag!" Nick protested.

Eliza removed a Ziploc bag full of clumpy dried green leaves from Nick's backpack. She opened the Ziploc and sniffed its pungent contents. "Is this pot?"

Nick crossed his arms over his chest. He'd wanted to introduce the pot after dinner as a sort of get-to-know-each-other aperitif. "Yeah, it's pot. I brought it for all of us."

Shipley stared at the Ziploc bag. Her brother was sent to boarding school for the first time because of pot. He got kicked out of Brunswick for breaking into the school after hours and stealing pot from another student's locker. Pot was illegal. It did things to you. She was terrified of it. And she'd always wanted to try it.

Eliza watched in fascination as her new roommate's eyes grew very round and took on a silvery blue glow. She looked like Alice in Wonderland falling down the rabbit hole.

"Can we smoke it now?" Shipley demanded.

Nick stood up and retrieved the bag of pot from Eliza's hands. "Come on. I've got rolling papers in my pocket." He led the way out of the tent.

"Hey, wake up." Shipley crouched next to Tom's prone form and whispered into his ear. "Nick has pot!"

"Just what I need," Tom mumbled. He sat up anyway, more aroused by the sensation of Shipley whispering in his ear than by the thought of getting high. The fact that he'd managed to puke repeatedly his first day at college was more than a little embarrassing. But pot was known to alleviate nausea and cause short-term memory loss. Maybe it was just the thing. "I want my own joint though. You should hear this guy sneeze," he told the girls. "Dude's got freaking TB."

They gathered around the campfire, sitting cross-legged as Nick rolled four perfect joints and distributed one to each member of the group. The campsite was in a small clearing a few hundred yards from the riverbank. They'd followed Professor Rosen there on foot from the logging road, fifteen minutes through pathless woods. Tall trees surrounded them in a huddle, offering their silent and unbiased protective service. Nick removed a burning stick from the fire and lit the tip of each joint. They smoked wordlessly for a while, interrupted only by a choking first-time cough from Shipley and Nick's incessant sneezes.

"Six years on the rugby team and now I'm smoking up like a total douche-bag," Tom reflected before taking another hit. His eyes were trained on the strands of Shipley's hair, set aglow by the firelight. They were gold, platinum, bronze, and rose. Auburn, plum, violet, and lemon. And . . . peony. "Christ, I'm already wasted."

Eliza smoked her own joint with a great deal of skepticism. She'd only gotten high a couple of times, taking hits from bongs at parties when no one else was looking. She liked how relaxed she got, but she hated how stupid it made her feel. Why would anyone want to feel that stupid on a regular basis? Plus, getting high made you want to eat, which made you fat. It was a no-brainer, literally.

Nick was glad he'd brought the pot. Everyone was mellow now. It was like they were all meditating on the same theme. Twilight had set in, and every atom and molecule swirling around them seemed to glisten. Across the river the girls were singing "Yellow Submarine." Their voices sounded very far away.

Shipley wished she could just eat the pot instead of smoking it. Her lungs ached after a day of smoking cigarettes, and the rolling paper stuck to her dry lips. But it was all so naughty, which was what made it all the more fantastic. Her nostrils were buzzing. Her ears were buzzing. She could feel Tom staring at her, and it felt nice. If he wanted to kiss her right now she would let him. She'd run her hands over his bristly head and lick his muscular neck.

She took two more hits and then rose unsteadily to her feet. "I have to pee," she announced and walked toward the woods. Maybe Tom will follow me, she thought as she stepped out of the clearing and into the darkening forest. Tree trunks rose up around her like the legs of giants. This was what it felt like to be a small child walking among adults.

She'd never peed in the woods before. Up ahead was a clump of young fir trees that looked like a promising private toilet. Squatting down behind the bushy trees, she watched in stoned fascination as her pee streamed out of her, making a little hole in the earth. A mosquito stung her thigh. She swatted at it, spun around, and attempted to pull up her shorts at the same time. There were other bites but she wouldn't notice them until tomorrow.

No one had followed her into the woods. Her stomach rumbled hungrily as she started back. She could eat a Dunkin' Donuts cruller. She could eat a dozen of them. She paused and glanced around, unsure of the way. The light between the trees appeared to be less dim in one direction. She headed that way, walking and walking for what felt like a long time. She wondered what Professor Rosen would do when she found out Shipley had disappeared in the night. Would they send out a search party? Dogs? Her mind was preoccupied with wondering what breed of dog was most commonly used to find missing persons and whether dogs liked to eat donuts, when she ran headlong into the maroon Dexter van, parked on the shoulder of the old logging road.

Professor Rosen had left the keys on the front tire, just like Shipley's dad did with their old station car, in case someone else needed the car while he was at work. Shipley climbed behind the wheel and started the engine, invigorated by her own daring. This certainly was a day of firsts. She turned on the radio. Guns N' Roses blared from the speakers.

"We abandoned the fire," Nick complained as he followed Tom and Eliza into the woods to look for Shipley. She'd been gone for more than fifteen minutes—longer than she needed to do her business.

"Oh, Shipley, dear?" Eliza called in a hoity-toity voice. "It's time to get thine ass back to camp, darling."

"Yoo-hoo," Tom cupped his hands around his mouth. "Where are you?"

"We haven't even eaten dinner," Nick complained. He always got a little whiny when he was high, especially after the munchies kicked in. His mom's vegetarian three-bean chili. He could eat three helpings of it right now. With cornbread.

Twilight was fading and the air was cool and still. The ground beneath their feet was damp and alive. Eliza wished she'd put on her sweater.

"Did I ever tell you guys about the time I actually saw a werewolf and almost died?" she asked. Of course they hadn't heard her story before. She'd never seen these people in her life before today.

"I was ice skating on this pond out behind our house and it got dark but I kept skating because I used to be really into it and yeah so fuck me I was the blind girl in *Ice Castles*. Anyway. All of a sudden the wind starts howling in the trees and there's lightning and it's the whole Great Lakes effect storm system coming in and my mom is yelling for me like Aunty Em."

She was talking extra-fast to make up for the fact that her tongue felt like a waterlogged hot dog. It was hard to tell if either of the boys was listening.

"So I realize I can't find my boots in the storm and I have to walk through the snow back to the house in my skates, which is pretty fucking impossible if you've ever tried it, and of course I fall down. What I don't realize is that I hit my head when I fall down and I get knocked unconscious. I wake up when something is licking my face, and okay that would be totally harmless if we had a dog, but we don't. So I sit up and there's this like dog-slash-man werewolf dude with yellow eyes in front of me. You know, complete with drooly fangs and raw meat stew bad breath? I scream and he scampers off, and then I crawl back to the house and my mom puts me to bed and feeds me bouillon with a teaspoon. I was thirteen. I got my period the next day."

"Jesus." Tom gagged at the mention of blood and kept walking. "Almost died," he snorted disparagingly as he struggled to regain his composure. "You probably just got a concussion and dreamt the whole thing."

Eliza glared at his back. Asshole.

"Maybe it was just hormones," Nick inferred from behind her. "Because of—you know—what happened the next day?"

"Shush!" Tom stopped. "Do you hear that?"

The sound of Guns N' Roses' "Sweet Child O' Mine" echoed through the woods.

"Come on." Tom broke into a run. The way he ran, dodging the trees, reminded Eliza of horror movies. *Freshman Orientation: The Haunting.*

Up ahead, Tom could see the old logging road. Then he saw

where the music was coming from. Shipley was behind the wheel of the van, doing slow figure eights in the road. It looked like she was giving herself a driving lesson of sorts. The radio blared obnoxiously. She spotted them and pulled up. Her pale blue eyes glowed in the half-light.

"Anyone up for Dunkin' Donuts?"

4

The sheep were out grazing and the house was quiet. Ellen and Eli Gatz had gone out west to a crafts fair in Stanley, Idaho, and left Adam and Tragedy in charge. The sheep could take care of themselves. It was Tragedy who needed stewardship. If left to her own devices, she would have pawned every pawnable object in the house and hitchhiked to Rio by now. She would have drunk all the wine and burned the house down. Not that she was irresponsible. Quite the contrary— her teachers often said that she was fifteen going on fifty. But she was easily bored, and, as she liked to remind everyone in the family on a daily if not hourly basis, she couldn't wait to get the fuck out of Dodge. Her bedroom was filled with travel guides.

Tonight they watched reruns of *Scooby Doo* while Tragedy played "Global Fashion Charades," a game she'd invented. She tried on every odd article of clothing in the house—flippers, long underwear, fishing waders, snowmobile suits, beekeeping hats, sunbonnets, snowshoes, hunting vests—and Adam had to guess what sort of international fashion disaster she was dressed as.

"What am I now?" she asked, jigging noisily across the living room in her mother's wooden clogs and a white bikini, a fringed green and yellow plaid blanket tied at her waist. Tragedy could tell Adam was nervous about starting at Dexter tomorrow. She was trying to make him laugh. So far it wasn't working. Adam was wound way too tight.

"Loud?" Adam replied. "Annoying?"

"I'm a Scottish hula dancer," she declared, stomping her feet and undulating her arms like a deranged octopus. "I'd play the bagpipes, but we haven't got any."

Adam picked up the discarded red flannel shirt from her Australian kanga hunter costume and tossed it at her. "Please put your clothes back on," he begged.

His sister seemed to forget that she was no longer five. She seemed not to realize that clogging in a too-small bikini top in front of her brother was entirely inappropriate. If only she had friends who could tell her what was okay and what wasn't, but the girls from school all hated her. Her legs, eyelashes, and hair were all longer than theirs. She'd started wearing a bra in fifth grade. She was their nemesis.

"*Scooby dooby doo, where are you...?*" Tragedy kicked the clogs off her feet and removed the blanket from her waist as she sang.

Adam averted his eyes and sighed. His life thus far had been full of these bored, tiresome moments, but at least it was quiet at home with their parents away. The Gatzes never ceased shouting. Not because they were angry, they simply preferred to shout. And the more Tragedy riled them up, the louder they shouted. The house was almost peaceful with them gone, although still not peaceful enough for him to really *think*. Not with Tragedy around. She never shut up.

"*...the way you shake and shiver...,*" Tragedy sang. She

dropped the plaid blanket on the floor and tied a white chef's apron over her bikini. She knew she should have put on a pair of shorts and maybe a shirt, but it wasn't like they were expecting the queen mother or anything.

Adam crossed and recrossed his legs. He kicked his sister's flip-flops across the room. He pulled a string out of the weary gray sofa. His mind paced restlessly. Tomorrow he would register for courses at Dexter, and the day after that classes would begin. Shouldn't I be doing something to prepare? I don't even know what college is *for,* he thought morosely. But at least it was something.

Tragedy ran up to her room and came back downstairs with a small blue teddy bear stuffed into the front pocket of the apron and a pair of sweatpants pulled on over her bikini bottom. She retrieved a Yankees cap from the hall closet and put it on. "What am I now?" she asked, standing in front of Adam with her hands on her hips.

Adam just scowled at her.

"I'm a baseball mom from Florida, although it really should be a Marlins cap. Or maybe I'm the head chef for the Yankees." She stuffed her feet back into the clogs.

Adam didn't respond.

"I guess you're not playing anymore." She bounced onto the sofa next to him and picked up her Rubik's cube. "Bet you I can do all the yellow and all the green before the next commercial."

The country road was deserted. There weren't any streetlights. There weren't even any cows. The van plowed through a four-way stop and eased down a hill.

"How do you know where you're going?" Eliza demanded. She crouched between the two front seats, gazing anxiously out the windshield like the family dog. Tom sat in the passenger seat. He kept turning up the volume on the radio and then turning it down again.

Nick knelt sideways in the backseat, clutching the door handle. "I knew this was a bad idea," he complained.

"I'm sure if we keep driving we'll come upon a town eventually," Shipley mused. She wasn't driving very fast. The van's steering column was out of alignment and she could barely reach the pedals. It felt scary topping twenty.

Off in the distance a blue light glowed on the tip of a tall church spire. All of a sudden the road wasn't deserted anymore. A white shingled farmhouse loomed up ahead, its windows blazing with cheery light. Puffs of gray smoke rose from the chimney, and a yellow rocking chair stood on the porch. Behind the house was a red barn, and behind that a white-painted fence surrounded a hilly pasture dotted with fluffy white sheep. It looked like Santa and Mrs. Claus's summer home.

"Let's stop there," Tom suggested. "I'll ask someone for directions."

"Just be careful," Eliza warned. The countryside was beginning to creep her out. Axe murderers and serial killers lurked behind every tree.

"Watch out!" Nick cried as Shipley steered the van toward the house. She ignored the driveway entirely, veering off the road and into the yard.

A yellow light flashed through the window. The twin beams of a car's headlights bounced across the yard toward the front porch.

"Hello, psycho drivers?" Tragedy rushed into the kitchen and threw open the screen door. "Hey, slow down!" she shouted, waving her arms. "There are kittens around here! Kittens and lambs!"

Adam followed his sister, throat dry and knees stiff. Nothing truly exciting ever happened in Home, but he was pretty sure something was about to.

A maroon van pulled up directly in front of the steps leading up to the porch. Adam could just make out the Dexter College pine tree logo printed on the side. A blond girl in white shorts got out from behind the wheel. Her pale blue eyes seemed to glow in the dark.

"Yowza!" Tragedy exclaimed. "Holy guacamole!"

Adam gripped the screen door's dinky metal handle. The passenger door opened and a huge, muscular guy emerged. He wore preppy Bermuda shorts and a bright yellow belt. Behind him tumbled a tough-looking girl with black bangs. The back door slid open and a guy wearing a wool earflap hat poked his head out, like a groundhog checking to see if spring had sprung. All they were missing was a big, slobbery Great Dane.

"Hey." The guy in the hat jumped down from the van. He wore a gray Patagonia fleece vest and looked exactly like everyone else at Dexter except for the Band-Aid in the middle of his face. "Sorry about the lawn. She . . . We . . . got lost?"

The blond girl's lips parted. Her blue eyes shone up at Adam with luminous intensity. "We're not lost," she insisted.

"Hello, Dolly! Well, hello, Dolly . . . !" Tragedy belted out ridiculously. Any excuse to make as much noise as possible. Adam wanted to smack her.

"Can we help you?" he greeted the visitors.

"We were looking for Dunkin' Donuts," the girl with the bangs explained. "You're probably going to tell us they don't even have Dunkin' Donuts in Maine."

Adam was disappointed. He was hoping their van had broken down or their orientation leader had had a heart attack. Something dire. "The nearest one is in Augusta, I think."

The big guy chuckled. "That may mean something to you, but not to us. Can you draw us a map?"

"Hold on."

Adam was about to go inside and get a piece of paper and a pencil when Tragedy shoved him aside. No way was she going to pass this up.

"Hey, why don't you guys come in? Our parents are away and we're so friggin' bored. We have beer and wine and fresh sheep's milk. It tastes like ass, unless you add a whole shitload of Quik. Then it's not bad."

Pot did wonders for Shipley's shyness. She took a step forward, placing her right flip-flopped foot on the porch step. The wood creaked. "I'm sorry. I'm a terrible driver. You're lucky I didn't run over your dogs or whatever." She glanced around, looking for signs of animals. She thought she'd seen a cat scamper beneath the porch.

"I'm Adam," the lanky redheaded boy introduced himself with a freckle-faced smile.

"And I'm his little sister, Tragedy," the tall, olive-skinned girl standing beside him explained, hands on the hips of her white chef's apron. She wasn't wearing a shirt, just a white bikini top and a Yankees cap. A blue teddy bear peeked out of her apron pocket. She was obviously a sports fan. "Let's hope you didn't fuck up our lawn or my dad will nail your ass to a tree. He's completely anal about his grass."

"Do you have any food?" Tom asked, barging up the steps. "We're starving, so if you have anything to eat at all, we'd really appreciate it." He knew he ought to have been more polite, but all that vomiting had left him feeling pretty hollow inside. If he didn't get a ham sandwich, quick, he was going to pass out.

"Of course. Definitely." Tragedy held the screen door open wide. "Please, come on in."

Shipley glanced behind her to see what Nick and Eliza were up to. Nick stood on one foot like a flamingo, looking hesitant and uncomfortable with that ridiculous Band-Aid pasted between his eyebrows. "And then we'd better get back," he mumbled. "Otherwise they'll think we got eaten by bears or something."

Eliza stuffed her hands in the pockets of her cutoffs and approached the porch. "As long as they've got food," she agreed with stoned reluctance.

The four newcomers sat stiffly at the kitchen table while Adam and Tragedy dug around for food and drink. The house was topsy-turvy, with books and clothes and tools for gardening or welding or fixing cars scattered all over the place. A woodstove hunkered in the corner of the kitchen. It seemed to be the only available cooking device.

"Is this really where you live?" Shipley asked incredulously. She meant was this where they lived all the time; it wasn't just a country house where they pretended to be farmers while most of the time they lived someplace urban and modern like Los Angeles.

"I was even born here in the house," Adam admitted.

"Mom doesn't believe in doctors," Tragedy elaborated. "She and Dad are from a place called Park Slope, in Brooklyn. They met at Dexter, but they dropped out to start this farm. They grow vegetables and raise sheep for wool and milk. And they make these totally useless fireplace tools. That's where they are now—at a crafts fair, selling their stupid tools."

Adam put four brown bottles on the table. "Dad makes his

own beer. It's kind of cloudy and it tastes a little funky at first, but once you get used to it it's pretty good."

"I'll have wine," Eliza said.

"Me too," Shipley agreed.

"A wise choice." Tragedy arranged this morning's batch of chocolate chip cookies on a plate and presented it to her guests. She liked to bake. It helped relieve the boredom. "Let me guess. You guys are freshmen and you bagged the overnight?"

"Kind of." Hat Boy shoved a cookie into his mouth. "I'm Nick." He pointed at the beefy guy seated across from him. "That's Tom." Then he pointed at the blonde. "That's Shipley." Finally he pointed at the girl with the bangs. "And that's Eliza." He swallowed the cookie and reached for another one. "Sorry if we're acting wacko. We're pretty stoned."

So that was their problem. Tragedy removed the blue teddy bear from her apron pocket—a weird accessory, even for her. Then she grabbed a tall Coca-Cola glass and filled it to the brim with red wine. "Adam's going to be in your class." She handed the glass to Shipley and poured another one for Eliza. "He was too cheap to sign up for orientation though."

Adam uncapped a beer and took a gingerly sip. "I would have had to pick $150 worth of blueberries to pay for it," he told his sister. He noticed Shipley was staring at him and instantly regretted any mention of picking blueberries.

"That's a lot of blueberries," Tom observed with his mouth full of cookies. He'd never eaten anything so good in his entire life. He could actually taste the cocoa beans in the chocolate chips. He could taste the sunshine that had shone down upon the heads of the chickens that had laid the eggs that were in the batter. The cookies were life-changing.

A large gray cat swaggered lazily through the kitchen, licking her chops. Yellow fly tape hung from the ceiling like an ornament, festooned with dead flies. The air smelled of blueberry jam and freshly baked cookies.

Shipley sat directly opposite Tom, sipping her wine with rhythmic precision. She was glad she'd already peed.

Eliza bit the rim of her glass. Any minute now she'd hear the roar of a chain saw and heads would begin to fly.

"Hey, we should play a drinking game or something," Tragedy suggested.

"Please, no," Adam groaned. Tragedy always had the worst ideas.

They played Bullshit with two decks of cards. Tragedy called "bullshit" every hand, which was annoying, but meant that they all got very drunk. Six bottles of wine and a case of beer later, Shipley lay on the living room sofa with her head in Tom's lap and her feet in Adam's, watching Tragedy and Nick dance to the Gatzes' collection of Bee Gees albums. The operatic wails of the brothers Gibb sounded almost futuristic, even though the music had come out almost two decades ago. Eliza knelt on the floor next to the coffee table, staring at the pieces of a jigsaw puzzle. The *Scooby Doo* marathon continued to play on the muted TV. Scooby and Shaggy tiptoed around a deserted amusement park, their teeth chattering noiselessly. It was two o'clock in the morning. The sheep would be waiting for their grain at six.

"Plum," Tom said, gazing down at the side of Shipley's head. "That's what color I'd start with if I were going to paint your hair. Everyone thinks blond hair is yellow, but it's really not."

"Mmm." Shipley had never been this intoxicated. She'd long given up trying to speak. Way down at the other end of the sofa she could feel Adam's knuckle brush against her bare foot. She closed her eyes.

The next song was a slow one. Rather than attempt an awkward promlike slow dance, Tragedy and Nick knelt down beside Eliza to help her with the puzzle.

"It's from the Mensa Society," Tragedy told them. "I joined just for fun. It's a picture of the first landing on the Moon and it's got eighteen hundred pieces—eighteen hundred and only four corners. I've been doing it for almost a week and I lost the cover of the box with the picture on it so now I'm really screwed." She grabbed the piece Nick had just picked up. "Hey, gimme that. That's Neil Armstrong's thumb." She pressed the piece into place. "One small step for womankind!"

Another slow song came on, and even as their bodies continued to participate with what was happening in the room—talking to each other, moving puzzle pieces around, pretending not to fall asleep or stroke a foot or a lock of hair—their minds were elsewhere. Each of them in his or her own way was marveling at how they'd gotten there, to this particular house in Maine, this wee-hour moment together, when at breakfasttime they'd been in their own houses, in their own hometowns, with no inkling of this whatsoever.

"Life is like an hourglass. Consciousness is the sand." Nick repeated a phrase he'd memorized from a book of Taoist meditations, or maybe it was another one of Laird Castle's bumper stickers. His mom had been putting away money to send him to college since he was in utero, and here he was, throwing it all away on the very first night. It was only a matter of time before they got caught, and then they'd be in deep shit.

Eliza weighed her own propensity for violence. In the last twelve hours she'd seen five guys fall under the spell of Shipley's infuriating white shorts—their neighbors in the dorm, the injured Nick, puke-faced Tom, and now this farm boy. If the serial killer never showed, she would have to murder Shipley herself.

Tom was having second thoughts. When he'd filled out his pre-registration forms, it was all about Economics and Government. But Shipley's hair was an inspiration. Tomorrow he'd sign up for painting. Even if he sucked, it would probably be an easy A.

Tragedy had just realized that she did not own a single book about space travel. After she'd visited every destination she'd marked up in her travel guides, she'd start saving for the Moon, Mars, or your anus—*gotcha!*

Adam was also dreaming of an extraterrestrial existence. If this were *Star Trek*, he thought, boldly taking hold of Shipley's drowsy bare foot, I'd beam everyone back to the ship except for her. We'd start our own civilization on some abandoned planet, and I'd set up some kind of force field around her so nothing bad could ever happen to her. Even if keeping up the force field meant sapping power from the planet, or losing contact with Earth or the mother ship, I'd do it. I'd even die for her. All at once, his life was imbued with meaning.

But in the fecund forest of her imagination, Shipley had already yielded to another boy's charms. The wood creaked as Tom carried her upstairs, the gray cat butting ahead of them like a nosy chaperone. He laid her down on a bed. The comforter was purple and blue Ralph Lauren paisley and the walls were decorated like a diorama at the Museum of Natural History. Ducks skated across icy ponds, the tips of their wings touching. A rabbit crouched, sniffing the air as it held up its injured foot. The branches of a willow tree wafted over a burbling brook. Sheep grazed on a grassy hilltop. A wolf looked up from its prey, its fangs dripping. Tom kissed her and their clothes fell away like onionskins. The animals stood watch while they made love.

Tragedy picked up her Rubik's cube. "Who wants to time me?"

Like jigsaw pieces that had been cut to fit but until now had roamed randomly disassembled in the box, the six of them were now inextricably linked. Of course the puzzle was largely unfinished—it would take a lifetime to complete, or at least four years.

The screen door banged in the kitchen. Shipley bolted upright on the sofa, relieved to find that she was still wearing her shorts.

Here we go, Eliza thought morbidly. Cue chain saw.

"If you're in there, I want your rear ends back in the van!" It was Professor Rosen. She sounded winded, like she'd been running hard. "I'm taking you back to campus. Obviously you can't be trusted on your own in the woods."

5

College has a break-in period. First there is the unfamiliar task of sleeping in a strange bed in a noisy building with a virtual stranger sleeping across the room from you. Your roommate might be an early riser who, after snagging the first shower, is fully dressed and blow-drying her bangs by seven. The roar of the hair dryer hurts your head. When you get up, you will probably have to wait outside the bathroom down the hall to use the toilet or shower or sink. You might be hungover after staying up most of the night doing funnels with the upperclassmen next door. Then there is breakfast in the dining hall, a confusing combination of preschool cereal options and tiny cups of weak coffee.

Next is registration, a madhouse in the field house. Professors of unpopular courses like Geology or German try to hawk their syllabi like door-to-door salesmen, while the line to sign up for Creative Writing or Film Studies goes out the door. You remember what your high school guidance counselor said about taking a variety of courses your first two years of college. By dabbling in every subject you will open up more options as to your major and complete your core requirements so you can focus on the courses you really want to take. Besides the required Freshman English, you sign up for Intro to Geology to fulfill your science credits, Intro to Psychology to use up your social science credits but also because you think the class consists of lying on a couch and talking about yourself, Music Comprehension (aka Clapping for Credit), The Romantics because it sounds romantic, and Creative Writing: Poetry because Fiction was full and poems are shorter and therefore require less work.

For the first week of school you cling to the people you met on orientation, not because you have anything in common, but because you don't know who else to talk to besides the guys in the room next door who are both majoring in their favorite subject: beer. You enjoy your classes and lectures this first week because they are among the faculty's best performances, their chance to win you over so you won't drop the course before Friday's add/drop deadline. Since most of the students are still in the process of buying their books, the workload is light, a false representation of what it will be like later on.

Cut to Friday, the end of the first week.

Just like all the other freshmen, Shipley, Eliza, Tom, and Nick remained clustered in their orientation clique, eating together in the dining hall, studying together in the library, watching TV together in their respective dorms, not because they liked each other particularly, but because they were being punished.

"The punishment must fit the crime," Professor Rosen had said before giving the four miscreants "roaming restrictions," which meant that for the first week of school they could not leave campus.

By Friday morning, Shipley had had enough of that. Dexter's

welcome BBQ picnic was tonight, and she needed cigarettes, insect repellent, and if she could muster up the courage to buy them, condoms. She'd never even seen a condom out of its wrapper, but it seemed to her that every self-respecting college girl, however virginal, should have condoms on hand just in case the guy she'd fallen for during orientation stopped bickering with his roommate and started noticing her. Her first class didn't start until eleven, and there was a gas station with a convenience store only just down the hill. The week was almost over. Surely Professor Rosen wouldn't mind if she roamed to the edge of town for just a minute.

The car should have been right where she left it, nose in the shallow dip of mown grass in the rear corner of the lot, tail sticking out onto the pavement, keys on the left front tire as was her family's habit. She circled the perimeter of the lot, glancing back across the road at her dorm to make sure she was in the right place—the student parking lot across from Coke, where she'd left her car last Saturday. There were very few black cars in the lot at all, and the only Mercedes was an ancient beige convertible. Her car was gone.

Shipley folded her arms across her chest and bit her lip. Who could she tell? Not her parents, and definitely not her advisor, who happened to be Professor Rosen. She'd seen a Campus Security car patrolling the road at night, but it seemed to be a one-man operation, and she wasn't sure how to contact him. Perhaps it was best not to tell anyone. The car would turn up eventually— maybe. And it might be a good way to get to know people, having to ask for rides. Tom had a car, and she definitely wanted to get to know him. Blushing to herself as she played out a little fantasy of losing her virginity to Tom in the backseat of his Jeep, she traipsed down the hill toward town, flip-flops scuffing the loose stones on the shoulder of the road, early September sun baking her bare arms. It wasn't long before a white Volkswagen pulled over to wait for her.

Adam couldn't believe his luck. He'd been looking for her all week. In fact, he'd seen her several times—at registration, buying coffee at Starbucks, in the library, in the computer lab—but she was never alone, and there was such a rush of blood to his extremities every time he saw her, he was afraid of what he might say. Tragedy wasn't with him, but it was her voice he heard yelling, *Stop, you wussy, stop! Pull over!* So he mustered up his courage and stepped on the brake.

"Need a ride?" he called out through the open window.

It was the boy from the farmhouse. "Oh, it's you," Shipley said, embarrassed that she couldn't remember his name. "I was just going down the road to buy cigarettes. I lost my car," she explained, opening the VW's passenger door.

"Here. Sorry." Adam swept the pile of books and caseless cassettes from the front seat to the back so she could get in. "Do you want to file a report with the police—for your car, I mean?"

Shipley yanked her denim miniskirt down over the tops of her legs. "Police? No, that's all right. I just want some cigarettes."

The car careened down the hill toward town. Monday had been Labor Day, and summer's warm breath was already tainted with the chilly afternote of fall. Soon the leaves would turn and the woods around campus would echo with the sounds of gunshots. Hunting was big in Home.

"Are you going to the barbecue tonight?" Shipley asked brightly. "I heard there's going to be a band and everything."

Adam turned on the radio and quickly switched it off again, unsure of what to do with his hands besides change gears and rotate the steering wheel. "I would go if . . ." His voice trailed off. Why had he begun the sentence that way? If *what*? If she went with him and held his hand? If she promised to go home with him afterward? If she let him kiss her?

Shipley didn't seem to mind that he'd left a blank for her to fill. "Well, we're going. Me and my roommate, Eliza, and Nick and Tom." She cocked her blond head. "We've been hanging out all week."

Adam bristled at the mention of Tom, his apparent rival, and abruptly changed the subject. "How long have you smoked?"

"I only just started." Shipley laughed. "It's not like I'm addicted or anything. I'm just trying it out."

Adam squeezed the button that dispensed windshield wiper fluid onto the windshield and switched on the wipers. They flapped wildly back and forth before he could stop them again. Scummy blue fluid dripped into the open windows. "Sorry," he muttered, annoyed with himself.

The gas station was just ahead. "You can drop me off here," Shipley told him. "I don't mind walking back." She was about to get out of the car when she saw Professor Rosen pumping gas into a white minivan.

"Shit!" she cursed, ducking down in her seat. "I'm not supposed to be off-campus." She glanced at Adam and smiled, her cheeks flushed. "Do you mind just sitting here until she leaves?"

Mind?

Adam switched off the engine and slipped down in his seat so their heads were at the same level. It was very romantic. Or it would have been if he could think of something to say. Instead he just stared at her. He could stare at her all day. *Don't talk. Just kiss her!* Tragedy's disembodied voice shouted. And even though he wanted to—oh, how he wanted to—he thought it might be wise to become friends first.

"Are you liking Dexter so far?" he asked.

Shipley shrugged her shoulders and nodded her head in a

so-so sort of way, obviously bored by his boring question. She glanced around the car for something with his name on it, feeling stupid that she still couldn't remember. "You didn't get into any trouble, did you?"

Adam shrugged his shoulders. "My parents were kind of surprised to find all that beer and wine gone, but they didn't really mind. And I don't think the professor knew I was a student."

It was becoming increasingly apparent that as a day student Adam would not get the full college experience. His mother still made his eggs and did his laundry. His father still helped him with his car and whistled while he was trying to read. He still had to take out the trash. He still had to endure Tragedy parading on the porch and belting out show tunes while she watered the geraniums. He never had to wait in line for the shower in the morning, and he would never have to pull an all-nighter in the library to keep from waking his roommate. If he wanted to get to know his fellow students and become a member of the Dexter community, he would have to put himself out there—join sports clubs, try out for plays, become politically active. But he was not a joiner by nature. Even the idea of attending Dexter's welcome BBQ made him break out into a nervous sweat.

He glanced at his watch. He was about to miss his second Intro to American Studies class. His professor, Dr. Steve, was one of those great old lecturers who could talk about anything—lighthouses, Civil War battles, coal mining—and make it completely fascinating. But it was worth missing class just to be able to sit beside Shipley and breathe the same stale car air that she was breathing. Maybe he'd even invite her home for lunch.

On the other side of the pumps, Patrick sat behind the wheel of his family's black Mercedes, watching his old English teacher pump gas into her minivan. She had been his advisor when he was a student at Dexter. When he missed his first scheduled advisor meeting and the first month of classes, she'd shown up outside his dorm room with a tin of Toll House cookies and a copy of *The Catcher in the Rye*. Patrick took the cookies but told her he'd already read the book, which was a lie. So many shrinks and guidance counselors had given him the same book that he could guess what it was about: alienation, loneliness, lack of interest in school, breaking the rules. People assumed that reading the book might somehow change his life. Maybe he'd feel less alone. Maybe it would give him perspective. Maybe he'd realize that his experience was not so unique. He preferred nonfiction.

It was great to finally have a car. He'd spent the last few days cruising the old dirt roads and sleeping in the backseat. He'd driven to the shore and swum in the ocean. He'd been to Baxter State Park, where he saw a brown bear, and Moosehead Lake, where he saw a whole family of otters. Now there wasn't much gas left in the tank, and he couldn't risk pumping and driving away without paying, because there was a Home Police Department patrol car parked outside the convenience store. He'd been to jail twice—once in Miami for sleeping on the beach and resisting arrest, and once in Camden, Maine, for breaking into an empty condo during a hailstorm. Miami kept him for four months. That's when he'd discovered *Dianetics*, by L. Ron Hubbard. He'd read it twice. Maine let him out after five days.

He started up the engine, deciding to leave the car in the Dexter parking lot exactly where he'd found it last Saturday. Before turning onto Homeward Avenue, he eased up alongside a white VW parked near the curb with its windows rolled down. The people in the front seats looked like they were kissing. All he could see was the tops of their heads. One of the heads was very blond like his sister's and one of them was very red. He recognized the car. It belonged to the asshole who'd gotten all uptight outside of Starbucks the other day. He revved the gas pedal and laid hard on the horn as he pulled out onto the street.

Reluctant to give up the car and the easy freedom that came with it, Patrick took the long way back to campus, driving through town, past the Walmart and the Shop 'n Save. Home High School was just up ahead, across from the on-ramp to Interstate 95. A girl stood beside the road with her thumb out. He slowed down and lowered the passenger-side window. It was the girl from Starbucks.

"I'm out of gas," he told her, "but I can take you up the hill to Dexter."

"Fuck that." It was the first day of Tragedy's sophomore year of high school and she'd left the building during homeroom, already bored to tears. She rested her elbows on the window frame. "I was thinking Texas, or maybe Mexico." She squinted at him. Patrick was still wearing his ripped parka and dirty Dexter sweatpants. They were the only clothes he had. "Hey, you're that guy. Where'd you get this schmancy car?"

"Found it," he said. "Do you want a ride or not?"

"Nah." Tragedy removed herself from the window. "I'm holding out for Texas." She planned to get as close to the border as possible, then stroll on into Mexico. She'd get a job making tacos or training donkeys.

Patrick pulled away and eased the car up the hill toward campus. The gas light had been on all day. He pulled into the parking lot across from Coke, did his best to emulate his sister's terrible parking job, and left the keys on the tire.

Shipley squirmed in the front seat of Adam's car while Professor Rosen disappeared inside the convenience store to pay for her gas and stock up on Pringles and Oreos, or whatever else sustained her.

"I can't believe I've only been here a week and my car was stolen," Shipley fretted. "My dad's going to kill me."

"Are your parents pretty strict?" Adam asked, only because his parents weren't.

"They're not, not really," she mused. It was she who was strict, with herself. How could she screw up when her brother had screwed up enough for the both of them? She was about to tell Adam all about Patrick and the tense silences between her parents at dinnertime, when Professor Rosen's head loomed large in the open window.

"Shipley Gilbert, do the words 'roaming restrictions' mean anything to you?" she demanded. There was no way for Shipley to know this, but roaming restrictions as a form of punishment had been put in place during her brother's tenure at Dexter.

Shipley sat up and glanced at Adam. His face was very red. "I'm sorry," she stammered. "This isn't his fault. My car was stolen. I thought the week was pretty much over, and I needed some bug repellent for tonight."

Professor Rosen frowned and turned her attention to Adam. "Maine plates" she observed. "You live around here?"

Shipley decided not to remind her that she'd already been inside Adam's house.

Adam wondered if he was in for it now too. "Just a few miles away. River Road, toward China."

Professor Rosen's eyes lit up. "No kidding. We're on River too, the Homeward end." She squinted at him for an awkward minute. Her hair was pretty, Shipley noticed for the first time, light brown with natural reddish blond highlights that reflected the sun. "I have to ask," the professor continued. "You don't happen to have any acting experience, do you?"

Acting in front of an audience was not something Adam had ever considered. In fact, the idea terrified him. "No, not really. Sorry."

"Well, I'm putting on a one-act play. I do one every year. This year's *The Zoo Story* by Edward Albee. Know it?"

Adam shook his head.

"There are only two parts, Peter and Jerry, and you're just right for Peter."

"Okay." Adam nodded politely, even though he had no intention of ever acting in the professor's play.

"What's your name, anyway?"

"Adam. Adam Gatz."

"All right, Adam. Think about it." Professor Rosen rapped her knuckles on the roof of the car, directly above Shipley's head. "Now, be a good kid and drive her back to campus where she belongs."

6

Dexter was an earnest place. Eliza had been waiting all week for something ironic to happen—a deadly hailstorm of Hacky Sacks, or a Birkenstock-induced foot fungus requiring amputation—with no luck. And the student population was dead-set on being *into* things—the Woodsmen's Team, football, the election, beer—that she simply could not get excited about. If she wanted to enjoy the next four years she would have to amuse herself. Which was fine. She was used to that. And there was certainly plenty of fodder.

"It's nice to know you're not ashamed that your mothers still dress you," she greeted Nick and Tom outside her dorm. The boys lived in Root, on the opposite side of the quad from Coke. Tonight Tom wore a pair of navy blue shorts with little green dogs stitched all over them, a yellow Lacoste shirt, a kelly green cotton webbing belt, and Docksiders without socks. Eliza thought it took courage not to be influenced by all the crunchiness around him. Nick, on the other hand, wore a strategically shredded purple T-shirt with a picture of a yellow gummy bear on it, a pair of ancient brown corduroys, and his trademark earflap hat. "How's married life?" she asked them.

The boys shrugged their shoulders uncomfortably. Obviously neither one was too pleased to be rooming with the other.

"Any luck in the employment office?" Nick asked, changing the subject.

"Yeah," Eliza said. "You?"

"I did okay," Nick responded carefully. He'd been waiting for Tom to tear into him for needing a campus job at all. The less said about it, the better.

Eliza and Nick's tenure at Dexter was contingent on financial aid, and their financial aid package was contingent on their keeping a campus job. The best-paying jobs were in Dining Services and Physical Plant, but the upperclassmen usually snagged those while the freshmen were at orientation. Other jobs included assisting professors with their photocopying and filing, mail room detail, helping students with their papers in the Writing Center, shelving books in the library, operating the audiovisual equipment for films or lectures or performances, or modeling for Studio Art: Portraiture classes.

At a big public university you could get away with a modeling job without the fear of being constantly recognized, but not at Dexter. It was a small school, and after a few months there were no new faces. A model for any of the studio art courses could count on the fact that by graduation half the campus would have seen her naked. This did not deter Eliza. It was way better than skinning and filleting raw chickens, a restaurant job she'd had in the past.

Nick had taken a job in the audiovisual department. He liked the idea of getting to watch movies from a little booth in the back of the theater, and he already knew how to use a slide projector. Back at home he often got out the carousel full of slides of his mom smoking pot on the beach while pregnant with him, or of his dad digging sand castles. That was before his dad went to California for business and met a yoga instructor from Santa Cruz, home of the most captivating women in the world. They hadn't had much more than a postcard from him since.

"Where's Shipley?" Nick demanded.

Eliza made a face. "Who cares?" She'd gotten into the routine of hating Shipley. She even hated her underwear, which looked like it was dry-clean-only, and her jeans, which she hung up on hangers. Her jeans! "I think she already went to the barbecue. She said she'd meet us there."

The sun hung low and hot. The Grannies, Dexter's Grateful Dead cover band, were tuning their guitars on a small makeshift stage beside the Pond, the impressive man-made lake on the edge of campus. It was an all-male band, but each of the Grannies wore the type of flowing Indian-print skirt bought from vendors in the parking lot at Dead concerts. Throngs of students milled around on the grass eating hamburgers and hot dogs cooked on smoking charcoal grills provided by Dexter Dining Services. A few students browsed the literature stacked on tables set up along the banks of the Pond, one table for each of Dexter's special interest groups: the Women's Group; the Bisexual, Gay, and Lesbian Group; the Woodsmen's team; the Chess Club; Dexter Recycles; the Dexter Republicans; the Dexter Democrats; Dexter ROTC; the Dance Club; the Drama Club; the Ultimate Frisbee Club; Dexter Vegetarians; the Knitting Circle. Some of the upperclassmen sipped from plastic cups of Busch near a cordoned-off keg manned by a security officer holding a sign that said, "Please provide ID." Professor Darren Rosen stood on the fringes of the crowd drinking beer with a group of sleep-deprived poetry majors wearing woolen cardigans despite the heat.

Nick spotted Shipley almost immediately. She was registering to vote at the Dexter Democrats table, aided by that redheaded guy from the farm.

"Democrat, Independent, or None?" Shipley wondered aloud. "My parents are both Republicans." She wasn't sure about her brother. Probably he didn't vote.

"None," Adam advised, wishing he could touch her hair. His parents had driven him to Augusta to register on April 10, the day he turned eighteen. They were both registered Democrats, but they'd told him not to register for a party unless he was sure who he wanted to vote for in the primaries, and how could he know that if he never bothered to read the paper or listen to NPR? They had both been gaga for Jerry Brown, and had helped him win the Maine caucuses, baking brownies for fund-raisers and cheering him on at rallies, but they didn't seem to mind that Bill Clinton had won the Democratic nomination. "Clinton gives a fabulous speech," his mom would say. "Plus he dodged the draft. And," she'd continue, raising her voice, "he has *gorgeous* hands!"

Tom surprised himself by not liking the sight of Shipley and Adam standing so close to each other, especially not near a table with Bill Clinton's smiling face pasted to it. His parents were both Democrats, which he thought was hypocritical as hell. His dad had gotten very rich during the Reagan years, and Bush had won the Gulf War, pretty much. Didn't he deserve some appreciation?

"Good to see you again, man." Tom clapped Adam hard on the back. "All set to vote?"

Shipley wasn't sure how much longer she could continue to discuss the election. Her political knowledge began and ended with the Gulf War was bad news, George Bush was old and boring, Ross Perot was old and crazy, and Bill Clinton was relatively young and handsome and played the saxophone and didn't seem to mind that both his wife and his daughter had terrible hair. She'd only followed Adam over to the Dexter Democrats table in the first place to distract herself from the note scrawled on the dry-erase board outside her room. *The keys are on the tire*, the note read. She'd run across the road to check, and sure enough, the car was there, right where she'd left it.

"I'm sorry." The man seated behind the Democrats table offered her a sheet of white paper crammed with voting information. "You can't use a college post office box as an address to register. You're going to have to register in your home state and request an absentee ballot that you can fill out anytime before the election."

"Thanks." Shipley took the sheet of paper and stuffed it into her bag. "You'll never guess what happened to me today," she gushed to Tom and the others. "First my car disappeared and then I got in trouble with Professor Rosen for going to the convenience store down the hill."

"I gave her a ride," Adam piped up importantly.

Nick tried to think of something interesting to report. "I got a job in AV."

Tom hitched up his shorts. "What's that stand for anyway? Actually still a Virgin?"

Nick glared at him. "No. It's the audiovisual department. I set up the slide projectors and VCRs and show movies in the auditorium. I even get to do the lighting for plays."

"What's wrong with being a virgin?" Shipley said, blushing.

The three boys stared at her with barely concealed excitement. Shipley was still a virgin?

"Hey, you know that blue light on top of the chapel tower?" Tom said. "Well, I heard there's this Dexter myth that if a virgin ever graduates, the light goes out." He nudged Nick in the arm. "Dude, we got to get you laid."

Shipley smiled. "Me too, I guess."

"I'm sure that won't be a problem," Tom said, grinning.

Adam pretended to be distracted by the music. Nick scowled down at his shoes.

Eliza's eyes were glazing over. Listening to Shipley flirt with every guy in sight was even more excruciating than watching her hang up her jeans. Eliza had done away with her virginity at the ripe old age of fourteen with Fabrizio, her neighbor. He was sixteen and skinny, and spoke no English, having just arrived from Genoa. Fabrizio went on to impregnate Candace, one of the cheese girls at his father's pesto business. They married, had twin girls, and were now obese.

As far as the election was concerned, no matter what the Dexter Democrats wanted Eliza to believe about Bill Clinton, Ross Perot already had her vote. He was a fucking renegade badass who was going to revolutionize the whole fucking process. Not everyone fit in the box. In fact, she'd had an interesting run-in this morning with someone who definitely didn't. She was in the room alone, studying cross-sections of a smiling chimpanzee's brain in her Psychology textbook, when the door to the room started to rattle and shake. She thought maybe it was a tremor—she'd read somewhere that even Maine had tremors—but nothing else was shaking. She decided it must be Sea Bass and Damascus, throwing their beer guts around next door as they polished off another keg. She got up and opened the door.

A guy stood in front of her, dry-erase pen poised. Despite the sweltering late summer heat, he wore a dirty black parka with a leaky tear in the chest, dirty maroon Dexter sweatpants, and dirty work boots. His long blond hair was matted and his beard was flecked with bits of grass and other miscellaneous crap.

"What are you doing?" she demanded.

"Leaving Shipley a note," he told her gruffly.

"Figures," she said, and slammed the door.

"The band's starting," Eliza observed now with a yawn. "Let's get some food."

Adam followed the group to the food line. When he and Shipley had arranged to meet at the barbecue, he'd hoped the others would stay away. But wasn't this what he wanted? Friends? A life? His sister had practically drop-kicked him out the door. "Get the fuck out of here," she'd said. "And don't come back till you've gotten some action."

The Grannies were playing "Sugar Magnolia." Clouds of charcoal smoke drifted through the warm air. A group of girls with bells tied around their ankles danced in a ring, flipping their long hair from side to side, their eyes unfocused and their wrists limp. Professor Rosen lay on the grass while someone read her palm. She appeared to be a favorite among the older students. A group of freshman girls who looked about thirteen kicked off their flip-flops and dangled their feet into the lake, arms around each other's shoulders as they swayed in time to the music. Beyond the lake and the smoky chaos surrounding it, Dexter's brick buildings stood poised and resolute.

Shipley tried to take everything in, but there was too much to process. With a total population of only nineteen hundred, Dexter was a small college in a small town, but it still felt overwhelming compared to high school.

She pressed her lips against her roommate's ear. "Sea Bass and Damascus are going to finagle us some beer."

"Good for them." Eliza sounded unimpressed. She resented it when boys waited on girls. She was trying to turn Shipley into a feminist.

"They're just being polite," Shipley would argue. "They were taught to do that by their own mothers."

"Yes, but don't you see?" Eliza would point out. "The more

they wait on us, the weaker we are. It's how they keep us *down*!"

Shipley didn't have an answer for that. She knew she could push a door open herself, but it sure was nice when a guy opened it for her.

They loaded their plates. Two cheeseburgers with everything on them, a corn dog, and a huge pile of potato chips for Tom. Nick filled up a bun with potato chips, tomatoes, cheese, lettuce, pickles, mustard, and ketchup—a vegetarian's delight. Eliza selected a foot-long hot dog, which Shipley was sure she was only eating because it was shaped like a penis. Shipley chose a bleu cheese burger with tomato. Adam got a hot dog with ketchup just to see if he could taste the rat testicles his mom insisted they were made with.

"She's got everything delightful,
she's got everything I need.
Takes the wheel when I'm seeing double,
pays my ticket when I speed ... !"

The singer's dirty blond hair hung over his shoulders in matted dreadlocks. His voice was raspy, his blue eyes wide and excited. Tom stood to Shipley's right, wolfing down his food. Shipley was glad she'd taken the time to brush her hair and change into her pretty white sundress from Martinique. She loved how soapy and clean Tom smelled most of the time, and how big he was. She felt safe with him. Since his arrival at the barbecue she'd paid no attention whatsoever to Adam, who stood to her left, quietly munching his hot dog.

Nick had run out of pot. He ate his condiment-filled bun with forlorn sobriety, pretending not to care that Shipley's attention was being monopolized. If Shipley were to choose either one of the others, Nick preferred Adam, but he could tell by the way she kept looking up at Tom between her long blond eyelashes that she was smitten with him. How she could like a guy who could eat a whole sausage pizza between dinner and bedtime and burp the national anthem he simply could not understand.

"This music sucks," Eliza noted to no one in particular. Mustard dripped down her chin, but she left it there on purpose.

"I like it," Shipley told her defiantly.

"You would," Eliza shot back.

"Brewski anyone?"

Sea Bass and Damascus danced over to them and passed out plastic cups full of Busch beer. A yellow bandanna was tied around Damascus's unruly black curls. His wobbly stomach poked out above the waistband of his jeans. Sea Bass had done something to his sideburns. Their shape was more severe now, like sled runners zooming across his cheekbones toward his nostrils.

"Marry me?" Sea Bass asked as he handed Shipley a beer.

"Sorry, but she's already spoken for." Tom reached for a cup and downed most of it in one go. It had taken him all of a week to notice what everyone had seen from the start: Shipley was the best-looking girl on campus. And it wasn't like they had to spend a lot of time getting to know each other. They were practically from the same town. They even went to the same dentist—Dr. Green, in Armonk.

I'll be damned if any of these clowns is going to nab her first, Tom thought. It would only be a matter of days before she'd be burning patchouli incense out of her belly button and dancing around topless in the grass. He could think of better things to do with her topless. He dropped his plate on the ground and slipped his arm around Shipley's waist, claiming her before anyone else could.

"Tom?" Shipley demanded. "What are you doing?"

Tom pulled her toward him. He liked how small she was, how neat her waist felt under her thin dress. He yanked her plate out of her hands and dropped it on the grass. The fact that Damascus and Sea Bass and Nick and Adam and Eliza and half the campus were staring at him enviously increased the size of his balls. "Kissing you," he announced before kissing her.

Shipley had been kissed a few times during party games in ninth and tenth grade, but as she got older and more concerned with propriety—in the face of her brother's impropriety—she'd stopped going to parties. She kissed Tom back eagerly, even daring to press her fingernails into his back. Tom smelled so manly. Kissing him made her feel like the star of a movie, except it was better than a movie because it was real. Her first week of college and she already had a boyfriend.

"Look how cute they are together," Eliza commented with disgust. "I heard while I was waiting on line in the employment office today that some insane number of Dexter students wind up marrying each other. Like sixty percent. Guess there's not much else to do here besides fall in love." She retrieved the dirty plates from the ground and stalked off to dump them in the trash.

Adam sipped his beer without tasting it. He shouldn't have come. He certainly wasn't going to get any "action," as his sister so aptly put it. Not that he'd wanted any. He just wanted to talk to Shipley, and maybe hold her hand.

"And it's just a box of rain, I don't know who put it there. Believe it if you need it, or leave it if you dare...." Nick sang out loud so as not to notice that Shipley and Tom were still kissing.

"I'm totally not marrying you now," Eliza told him when she returned.

The Grannies finished the song and put down their instruments. Nick thought he saw one of them exchange money with another student. Scoring some pot was crucial if he was going to have to watch Shipley and Tom kissing in the next bed for the rest of the year. Even more crucial was his idea of erecting a yurt out in the woods somewhere. He would need a place to go, an escape pod, a zen retreat. He might even get credit for building it.

"Welcome to Dexter." Darius Booth, the first Home-born president of Dexter College, took up a microphone in his frail hands and beamed at the crowd. He was eighty-two years old and had started as a janitor at the school, slowly working his way up the ranks and to the front page of the *New York Times* on his inauguration day. It was just the kind of small town story the *Times* liked to report during the summer when there wasn't much newsworthy news and most of the writing staff was in the Hamptons or on Cape Cod. Mr. Booth was beloved by the college faculty and staff for his devotion to Dexter and for his steadfast, by-the-book leadership. The consensus among the students was that he was a bore. "This is the second or third or even fourth barbecue for some of you, but for our first-year students this night is very special. Why don't we lead them in a round of 'Bravo, Dexter, Bravo'? They're going to have to learn it sometime. I'll give you a hint, boys and girls," he said in his hokiest Maine accent. "The tune sounds a little bit like 'O Little Town of Bethlehem.' "

The Grannies dutifully picked up their instruments and played an intro to the college's corny anthem. As long as they humored their dotty old president, he'd never bust them for doing and dealing drugs, or stealing ether from the chemistry lab.

"*Upon this hill, through winter's chill, Dexter so divine. Snow swirls round our heads, trees wrapped in its glistening glory. Brave men and women write their own stories. Bra-vo, Dexter. Bra-vo.*"

Everyone was so busy trying to learn the song or mock the lyrics, no one noticed the tall, beautiful, dark-haired girl stride across the grass on the opposite side of the lake. It was Tragedy, looking like she'd gotten lost somewhere between Rio and Bangor, in a yellow bikini top, a flippy white miniskirt, and bare feet. She'd come to spy on Adam and the blonde from Connecticut, getting busy, and was disappointed to find Tom getting busy with the blonde instead. Adam held up his hand, signaling her to wait. He left the group of singing, dancing, kissing freshmen and circled the water, glad to have talked to Shipley for a little while at least. Maybe she'd think of him in November, when it came time to vote.

7

And so it went. Shipley lost her virginity to Tom that night. It was a Friday night, and Root's halls and walls thrummed with music and general insouciance. Tom's room was in the basement, near the dorm kitchen, and the air smelled perpetually of curry. Two windows at ground level faced the woods behind the dorm. Nick had decorated the white walls on his side of the room with trippy tapestries made from the same sort of cloth as the Grannies' skirts, and the window ledge nearest his bed was strewn with candles and incense burners. The walls on Tom's side of the room were bare. Beneath his bed was a pile of balled-up dirty socks. The bed was made up with the plaid flannel sheets his mother had had shipped directly to him from L.L.Bean. Nick's bed didn't have sheets, just a red nylon sleeping bag on top of the ticking-striped mattress, and a pillow in a plain white case.

"I've never done this before," Shipley murmured as Tom slipped her white dress over her head.

"That's okay," Tom said. "I have."

Some girls might have been grossed out. They might have begun to imagine Tom with other slutty, possibly diseased girls. They might have imagined that Tom was an egomaniacal player, roving from girl to girl, always hungry and never satisfied. Some girls might have had a creeping fear that he would use them and then toss them out. But Shipley was not like other girls.

She slipped beneath the covers while Tom lit one of Nick's candles and put on his favorite Steve Miller Band tape. Then he tore off his clothes, threw them onto the floor on Nick's side of the room, and grabbed a Trojan from his toiletry kit.

Shipley lifted up the covers to welcome him in. "I knew you were the right man for the job," she giggled nervously as Tom took her in his arms and began the quick work of deflowering her. As is the way with all rites of passage, it seemed to be over almost as soon as it had begun. It was inelegant, thrilling, and routinely monumental.

Afterward, they fell asleep in each other's arms. They were sleeping still when Nick crept in around one in the morning, eyes strained from reading up on yurts in the library, grateful for the cozy warmth of his sleeping bag.

Cut to October. The air was nippy and the foliage was on fire. Dexter College had never looked finer, a shoo-in for every prettiest college campus award in the country. So far no one had fallen from an upstairs window after taking too much acid, or driven into a tree. No professor had molested a student. The president of the college hadn't had a stroke, or been arrested for being drunk and disorderly at a saloon downtown. Not a blade of grass was out of place. The errant black Mercedes with Connecticut plates did occasionally disappear from the parking lot, but it was always returned, albeit with an empty gas tank.

Most nights, Shipley slept in Tom and Nick's room. She even kept a few outfits in Tom's closet to avoid the morning Walk of Shame back to her dorm. There was nothing shameful about her and Tom. By now they were practically married.

Nick was well on his way to finishing his yurt. He'd researched the construction carefully. Hundreds of pamphlets on yurt-building had been published on the World Wide Web, and scrolling through them had actually been fun. One yurt builder extolled the virtues of yurt dwelling in such a seductive way that Nick was sure he was onto something:

"On clear nights you can lie inside the yurt and see the stars through the open crown. In poor weather there is plenty of room for you and your friends to sit comfortably around a warm stove, listening to the storm rage. From outside, the yurt radiates a welcoming glow. . . ."

It didn't have to be big. Just big enough to lie down in and entertain a visitor or two. And the smaller it was, the easier it would be to erect. Nick was no carpenter. The most complex structure he'd ever put together was a balsa wood airplane.

At last he discovered an outfitter in Colorado who sold yurt kits with the timber cut to size, the screw holes already drilled, and a weighted wax canvas cover and flap door that Velcroed on and off. The company claimed it would only take six hours to put it together. Nick ordered the fourteen-footer—the smallest and most inexpensive kit they offered. He used his mom's credit card number, promising to pay her back with the earnings from his AV job. Three days later, the giant box arrived via Federal Express.

He'd borrowed a stepladder and tools from the guys at Buildings and Grounds, found the perfect building site bordering the woods behind Root, and followed the kit's simple instructions. Six days later, it was still a wobbly work in progress and his hands were blistered from hammering, but he was determined to get it done. Once it was complete, he could sleep there instead of staying up late reading in the library or watching TV in the common room until Shipley and Tom had finished fooling around and gone to sleep.

This was just such a night. From outside the door, Nick could hear Steve Miller Band's "Fly Like an Eagle" playing on repeat, a good sign that Tom and Shipley were still naked. Nick wandered down the hall to Root's ample kitchen, where Grover, Liam, and Wills, the juniors who made up the Grannies, were making curry. Unlike the residents in Dexter's other dorms, Root residents could opt out of the meal plan and cook for themselves. This was particularly attractive to students with special diets, like the Grannies, who were vegan.

"All right, man?" Wills greeted Nick.

Nick had met the Grannies in person a few weeks before when he'd missed breakfast in the dining hall and wound up in Root's kitchen, foraging for cereal. Most of the food in the kitchen belonged to the Grannies, and they were generous with it. They were also generous with their pot. They'd already given him a Ziploc bag full of it for $20, way less than it cost in the city. Nick had only just finished smoking a joint out behind his unfinished yurt. Now he was starving.

"Brewtarski?" Wills opened the fridge, pulled out a can of Busch, and handed it to Nick. Tonight Wills wore a red tiered skirt with black cats batiked all over it and a red and black plaid wool shirt. His platinum blond hair was plaited into messy half cornrows, half dreadlocks that pattered against his shoulders as he stirred the enormous pot of curry simmering on the electric stove.

Nick cracked open the beer and pointed at the curry. "Hey, you guys mind if I have some of that?"

Wills grimaced. His bloodshot eyes rolled around dramatically. "Aw, man, we just chucked in a gigantic eggplant. Stuff's raw. Plus, we need more tasty vegetable ingredients. Wanna come divin' with us?"

"Diving?" Nick wasn't sure he'd heard right. The nights were already cold, and the coast was at least an hour away.

Grover hitched up his blue-and-white-striped OshKosh B'Gosh train conductor overalls and stuck a wad of chewing tobacco in his bearded cheek. Nick had heard that Grover was from Bethesda, Maryland, an affluent suburb of Washington, DC, but he dressed like someone from the Deep South at the time of the Great Depression.

"Dumpster diving," Grover explained. "We hit the Dumpsters out behind the Shop 'n Save. Stuff they throw away you wouldn't believe. Last week I found a perfect pineapple. The best pineapple I ever tasted." Grover ran his hand over his shaved head. Most of the time he wore a red bandanna tied like Aunt Jemima's, but tonight he was going commando. "Come with us. You'll see. Best food you've ever had, completely free. And the store doesn't care cuz they're throwing it out anyway."

Nick frowned. He liked the idea of free food, but it seemed like more trouble than it was worth. Was there some profound philosophical point being made by rooting around in Dumpsters for your food? After all, the tuition at Dexter was pretty high. The Grannies could probably afford groceries. But it seemed like something Laird Castle would have done.

"Let's hit it!" Liam jangled his car keys. His orange and gray wool flap hat was pulled down so far that his murky hazel eyes were almost completely obscured. Nick flipped up the flaps on his own hat in an effort to distinguish himself.

Moments later he sat in the back of Liam's red Saab, listening to Phish sing "Proud Mary." The road into town was dark and the air was chilly. Nick thought he might have even seen a stray snowflake.

He wondered if Shipley and Tom had finished having sex. The sight of her in Tom's bed depressed him. He didn't like Tom to begin with, and the fact that Shipley had chosen Tom over him or even that redheaded local boy made him question her judgment. Tom ate meat three times a day, he was totally unspiritual, he snored and farted loudly in his sleep, he'd signed up for the expensive laundry service instead of washing his own socks and underwear in the laundry room down the hall, and he wanted to major in Economics with only a concentration in Studio Art. Tom also refused to address Nick directly except to say, "See you later, man." Tom was a dick.

We are all one and connected, Nick reminded himself. I am you, you are me. Your good fortune is my good fortune. Your misfortune is my misfortune. If Tom is a dick, then I am a dick. Hopefully Tom's redeeming qualities would reveal themselves in time.

Shop 'n Save bore a giant neon orange sign and seemed to be the only place open in town. Even so, the parking lot was nearly empty.

"Shhh," Wills whispered as they clambered out of the car. "Be werry, werry quiet."

"Hey dude, you knit?" Liam whispered, tweaking Nick's hat as they approached the Dumpster.

"Nah," Nick responded. It occurred to him that the Grannies might be a harmless-looking Grateful Dead cover band by day and torturous psycho killers by night. Had they brought him here to stuff his mouth full of brown bananas so he couldn't scream while they took turns scalping him and pulling out his toenails? He pulled the flaps of his hat down over his ears again, steeling himself.

The Dumpster was gigantic and black and stank of rotting cabbages. The Grannies were experts. They had their method down pat. First Grover got down on his hands and knees. Then Liam climbed onto Grover's back and got down on his hands and knees. Then Wills climbed aboard and did the same, his red and black skirt draping elegantly over Liam's shoulders.

"Come on," Wills called to Nick. "You go first. You gotta experience a virgin dive."

Nick climbed the human ladder, careful to distribute his weight evenly. When he was up on Wills's back, he peered into the blackness of the Dumpster.

"Go on, get in there," Liam urged.

The sickly sweet smell of rotten fruit was so powerful Nick could hardly breathe. He closed his eyes and, using Will's back as a springboard, somersaulted into the depths of the Dumpster.

"Cannonball!" Grover shouted as Nick dropped down into the garbage.

His back hit something hard and he rolled away from it, pain shooting down his spine to his coccyx. Before he could orient himself, a harsh light shone in his eyes. Fuck! Was Shop 'n Save Security after him already? Nick blinked, making out a pair of pale blue eyes behind the flashlight's beam. The furry-faced creature brandishing the flashlight held up a heavy book with an illustration of an erupting volcano on its cover.

"Hello," Nick said cautiously. He sneezed. "Sorry to disturb you."

The blue eyes blinked and a voice mumbled something complicated about the survival of a unit of life.

It was Sunday. Patrick had been reading his book inside the Dumpster for over an hour, waiting for the bakery staff to throw out all the out-of-date bread, a regular Sunday night Shop 'n Save ritual. French bread, Tuscan farm bread, kaiser rolls, and bagels.

Sometimes there were muffins and donuts too. He'd fill the trunk of the Mercedes and live on the stuff all week. The last thing he wanted was to share his cache with a bunch of stoned Dexter idiots.

Trembling, Nick took an unsteady step forward on the stinking heap of garbage. A grapefruit swelled and then gave way beneath the sole of his Birkenstock, bursting with the sweet, acrid odor of overripe citrus. He squinted into the harsh ring of light, trying to get a better look at the guy. Maybe he was just another Dumpster diver, who, without the comradeship of the Grannies, had gotten lost along the way.

Nick took another wary step and sneezed again. "We're just looking for some . . . tasty raw vegetable ingredients? For our curry?" he told the guy, feeling stupid.

"Hey!" The flashlight swung toward him. "Get the hell away from me!" The stranger's voice was throaty and vicious. "Leave me alone!"

"Okay, okay. Sorry." Sheepish and terrified, Nick backed away. "Guys, can you help me? I want to get out!" he called out to the Grannies. He didn't care how many perfect pineapples he left behind. He jumped up and clawed helplessly at the Dumpster's inner wall before toppling back inside it again.

"Get anything good?" Wills asked, dangling his arms inside the Dumpster. He spotted the flashlight, still pointed at the back of Nick's frightened head. "Holy shit! Come on, man." Wills flapped his hands at Nick urgently. "What the hell? Who is that?"

Nick grabbed his hands and Wills heaved him out of the Dumpster. The other two Grannies were still in their two-tiered Ringling Brothers formation, but the force of Will's heaves and Nick's extra weight sent them crashing.

"Aw, ya broke it! You broke my neck!" Grover screamed, writh-ing around on the pavement. The other three boys crouched on the chilly asphalt, breathing hard, the orange Shop 'n Save sign glowing above their heads.

Liam giggled. "Dude, you're not dead, right? If your neck was broken you'd be way dead."

"Jesus," Nick muttered, rubbing his sore hands together. "Hey, can we go now? There's someone creepy in there." He stood up and started for the car, wanting to run, but fearful of looking like a huge chicken.

"Someone's in there? Holy cow!" Grover exclaimed. He leapt to his feet and sprinted toward the car.

"Damn, why didn't you say something?" Liam chased after him.

"Yeah," Wills agreed, falling into step with Nick. "We can go diving another time. Maybe try a different Dumpster, like the one behind the natural food store down in Camden."

"Or maybe you should just go to the store and buy stuff like everyone else," Nick snapped in annoyance. "A head of cauli-flower costs what—a buck?"

"Dude, that's not the point," Wills reminded him. He low-ered his voice. "Hey, who do you think that was with the flash-light anyway?"

Nick opened the door to the Saab and scooted into the back-seat next to Grover. "I don't know. Nobody, I guess."

Nick returned to the site of his yurt, leaving the Grannies to finish their curry without him. He would have invited them in, but the roof wasn't covered and the Grannies were loud. He'd only managed to convince the Office of Student Housing and

Campus Life and the Dean of Students Office to permit him to build the yurt by claiming it was for "spiritual purposes." It was no party pad.

The yurt was supposed to be built right on top of the ground, but he'd cheated and built a platform out of plywood and cinder blocks scavenged from a pile behind Buildings and Grounds, hoping to add some distance from the earth come spring when the mud thawed and the rains came. It was rumored that Dexter's campus had been erected on top of an old turkey farm and in the March–April mud season, the whole place stank of turkey shit. Right now though, his yurt smelled of freshly cut wood.

From his dorm room window the yurt looked like a tiny circus tent. It was a good eight feet high, and once he'd installed the waxed canvas cover, the crown of the roof could be rolled back to reveal the sky or to provide ventilation for a stove or fire. He had to be very careful with fire in the yurt. There was an entire booklet on it in the kit, covered in bold exclamation points and the word "WARNING" in red. Without proper ventilation, the whole thing would go up in a matter of minutes, since it was basically made out of twigs.

Eliza was huddled on the rough plank floor, reading his book of daily zen meditations. She looked up. Nick's headlamp shone from her forehead. "Do you really believe all this shit?" she demanded.

Ever since Shipley had virtually moved into Tom's room, Eliza had tried to enjoy her roomy single. Studying at the desk beneath the window, she would flick booger bombs onto Shipley's unwrinkled Ralph Lauren sheets. What a shame to have such nice sheets and never sleep in them. Sometimes she fantasized that the bearded guy in the ripped parka would return and either befriend her or stab her in her sleep. Her own solitude had become oppressive, and he seemed like someone who was used to being

on his own. Maybe he could give her a few pointers. To her surprise, college was even lonelier than high school. At least in high
school she'd had her parents to blame for the lousy state of things.
It seemed to her that at college you had to be in love not to be
lonely. You had to have someone to hold hands with while walking to class and someone to eat with in the dining hall. You had
to have someone to lie down with on the lawn and kiss, or someone to sleep with, packed like sardines in a narrow single bed. If
you didn't have someone, if you weren't in love, you felt like an
asshole.

What Eliza and so many of her classmates were discovering
was that living on a small college campus in the middle of the
woods was like being trapped in a snow globe. The best way to
interrupt the tedium of student life—the to-and-fro from classes
and meals, the reading and studying, the occasional private talk
with or great lecture by an inspiring professor, attending a
semi-decent film or play, getting drunk or stoned on Saturday
night and sleeping in on Sunday—was to fall in love and have
as much sex as possible. Otherwise life could get pretty lonely,
especially after winter set in.

"It's not really a matter of believing." Nick sat down beside
her and picked up the zen meditations book. "It's like learning
an instrument. I'm not very good at it yet, but if I practice
these . . . these simple truths, they'll eventually become part of
my everyday existence, and I'll achieve zen."

Eliza rolled her eyes. "Good luck with that."

Nick pulled his bag of pot and Zig-Zag rolling papers out of
his pocket, sneezed five times in succession, and rolled himself
another joint. He was still starving, but he'd just have to make
do with getting high. "So, what do you think?" He sneezed
again and gestured at the yurt's bent wood walls. "Like it?"

Eliza lay on her back with her head in her hands and gazed

up at the yurt's half-finished roof. She flipped the hood up on her wool army jacket to keep the spiders out of her hair. "You need something to sit on, like a futon or at least some pillows. And it might be nice to have one of those little cooking stoves, and a cooler for food. I don't know about you, but all this fresh air all the time has really fucked with my metabolism. I should just attach a bag of Cap'n Crunch to my gut and keep it pumping all day, like a reverse colostomy."

Nick licked the joint and tamped down the ends. "Soon as I get the roof done, I'll bring my sleeping bag out here." He lit one end of the joint and offered it to Eliza, but she waved it away.

"Did I ever tell you about my toilet seat back home?" she asked when she realized the yurt did not have a bathroom. She didn't wait for Nick to answer. Since Shipley and Tom had paired off and Nick had started building his yurt in earnest, their little orientation gang had entirely dispersed. Nick didn't know any more about her than what he'd learned the first week of school.

"My mom has a Disney fetish. Anytime they have a sale at Kmart or Penney's or Sears, she'll buy anything with a princess on it. Our whole house is like a Disney shrine. My toilet seat is yellow with light blue flowers on it, and when you put up the lid, it sings that song from *Snow White*, you know: '*Whistle while you work!*'

"My parents have an office over the garage. They rent real estate in beautiful Erie, Pennsylvania, where no one in their right mind would want to live. When I was little, like, before I could go to school, they'd park me in front of a Disney movie and head out to the garage. When the movie ended I'd tap on the window and one of them would come back inside and flip me a Rice Krispie treat or a fruit roll-up and stick in another video. I didn't fucking care. Kids get molested and abused at day care. I always was a little scared of that toilet seat though. Sometimes I'd pee in the bathtub just so I didn't have to listen to it."

Nick continued to smoke his joint, unsure of what to say. Eliza's story was sad and he was pretty depressed already. He tried to remember what the guy in the Dumpster had said about cells just wanting to survive. Then he tried to think of an uplifting zen meditation to lighten the mood. But his mind was a blank.

Eliza continued her depressing monologue. "I almost offed myself once, when I was around eleven. Or no, I guess I was thirteen. I think I was just lonely, and I'd been reading a lot of Sylvia Plath. I drank a whole bunch of aspirin and Scope and sat in the kitchen with the oven on. My mom came over from the garage to get a sweater and wound up taking me to the hospital to have my stomach pumped. I probably wouldn't have died anyway. I would've just shat bluey green for about a month. Anyway I was okay once I discovered sex—not that I've had any lately." She shot him a meaningful glance. "But at least I've got my lucky rabbit's foot."

Nick wondered if he should hug her. She sounded like she needed a hug. "Shit happens and then you die," he said, and immediately wished he hadn't. He sneezed. "Hey, did you hear about that huge meteorite?" Yesterday a giant meteorite had fallen out of the sky in Peekskill, New York, and smashed a Chevy Malibu.

"You can kiss me now." Eliza propped herself up on one elbow, waiting.

"Huh?"

"Or we could have sex," she said hopefully.

Nick took another hit off his joint, holding the smoke in until his face turned pink and his lungs were about to burst. He really liked Eliza. He didn't want to hurt her feelings. He just didn't feel like kissing her or anyone else right now, unless maybe Shipley walked in and threw him down on the ground and ripped off her clothes and insisted that he kiss her.

"I'm kind of saving myself for someone," he told her as he exhaled.

Eliza stared at him through the cloud of smoke. Her eyes were tearing up and she couldn't see for shit. She tossed the headlamp at him and stood up to go. "Aren't we all?"

8

At college you are free to do as you please, almost. You can—if you so choose—eat Doritos for breakfast, not comb your hair, wear the same jeans for a month without washing them, sleep all day, cut your classes, and stay up all night. You can not floss. You can take up a dangerous hobby that would terrify your mother, such as hang gliding or collecting wild mushrooms. But absolute freedom is a scary concept. Without some sort of sympathetic authority, chaos reigns. You need to know that someone is paying attention and that you will be chastised, if not punished, for slacking off. That's where the advisor comes in.

Every professor embraces the role of advisor in a different manner. Some invite their advisees over to dinner with their families. Some treat their advisees to ice cream and mini golf on Friday nights. Some take them to a folk music festival to drop acid. Professor Rosen preferred to meet with her advisees the old-fashioned way—in her office.

Shipley's advisor meeting was right after Eliza's. Shipley sat on the wooden bench outside Professor Rosen's office, listening to the shrieks of laughter that emanated from within. The hallway was narrow, windowless, and plain, embellished only by the flyers, sign-up sheets, and other miscellany with which the English staff had decorated their office doors. A portrait of Shakespeare. A flyer advertising a screening of the film *Halloween* in the Student Union. A sign-up sheet for pumpkin carving at a professor's home—*BYO pumpkin. Knives provided.*

The three girls from Shipley's orientation trip emerged from the office next door to Professor Rosen's, wearing matching pink hooded Dexter sweatshirts. Elli, Nina, and Bree. Or was it Briana, Kelly, and Lee? They shared a triple in Sloane, the only all-women's dorm on campus, and had recently formed the Dexter Spirit Club to replace the now-defunct Dexter Cheerleading Squad, which had lost its funding in the late seventies.

The girls paused in front of Shipley, smiling giddily, their arms linked.

"Poor you," one of them said. "Lucas is our advisor." She lowered her voice. "He's so amazing."

Professor Lucas Weaver was one of those handsome young English professors who toys with the hearts of his female students by wearing his hair just long enough to hang in his eyes, asking them to call him by his first name, reading aloud from Molly Bloom's sexy monologue at the end of *Ulysses*, and placing just so on his desk a picture of himself hugging his terminally ill wife. So sensitive and charming and trapped in a loveless marriage to an invalid! Lucas—as he was known—was even more crushworthy than the average handsome young professor because of his adorable Tennessee accent and his tendency to moonwalk into class.

"Oh my *God* is he cute," one of the other pink-sweatshirted girls agreed. "He's like Bill Clinton, but younger and thinner and with better hair."

"He's reading ghost stories aloud in the chapel on Friday night for Halloween," the third girl chimed in. "We're going to dress up."

"The guys in our class are going to be Ghostbusters," the first girl explained. "And we're going as sexy ghosts."

"Wow." Shipley was only half listening, distracted by something thumbtacked to Professor Rosen's door. It was the sign-up sheet for *The Zoo Story*, Edward Albee's one-act play. Professor Rosen was directing. *First Year Students Only!* the sheet read. *Extra Credit!* A single signature was scrawled across the sheet in green ink—Adam Gatz, it read.

"Aren't you dressing up?" one of the girls was asking. "There's going to be a party in the Student Union with a haunted house and everything."

Shipley blinked. She was aware of the fact that by holing up with Tom in his room she was missing out on most of Dexter's social offerings. Did Adam go to these things? She hadn't spoken to him since the welcome barbecue. Would she have seen him dancing at Oktoberfest or pounding hard cider during Apple Cider Week had she not been with Tom? Maybe he even had a girlfriend by now—the Apple Cider Queen.

Eliza stepped out of Professor Rosen's office. "The professor will see you now," she announced, sounding absurdly formal. "Hey, are you guys, like, planning a pajama party?" she joked. "Thanks a lot for not inviting me."

The three girls rolled their eyes. "See you later," one of them told Shipley before stalking off down the hall with her two friends in tow.

Eliza rolled her eyes in return. She hated those girls and

their pink sweatshirts so much she hadn't even bothered to learn their names. She was pretty sure they hated her too. It occurred to her that if the Office of Student Housing and Campus Life had placed Shipley in that same triple in Sloane, she'd be mincing around in a pink sweatshirt right now, shouting out dumb cheers and doing the splits during rugby games. Even if Shipley and Eliza weren't friends, the mere fact that they were roommates had opened up a whole new world to Shipley, one where light pink was evil and irony ruled.

Shipley stood up and waited for Eliza to let her pass.

"She's in a foul mood," Eliza warned, which was a lie. Professor Rosen only had one mood: bitchily condescending.

Shipley frowned. "But you guys sounded like you were having fun."

Eliza rolled her eyes again. Shipley was so gullible. "What a maniac," she said, and stepped aside.

Shipley pushed open the door and entered the tiny, crowded office, still unsure of whether Eliza was calling her a maniac or their teacher. Professor Rosen sat at her desk, thumbing through a ragged, pen-worn address book.

"Ah, Shipley," she said, looking up. She indicated the small wooden chair beside the desk. An orange fondue pot squatted beneath the chair, long forks poking out in all directions. A red Radio Flyer tricycle was pushed into one corner of the office and a cardboard model of a moose head was tacked to the wall. On the desk was a picture of Professor Rosen kissing someone dressed as an Egyptian pharaoh. "Sorry for the clutter. Have a seat."

Shipley crossed her legs and clasped her hands together. This was her chance to win Professor Rosen over. She waited patiently while the professor shuffled a pile of manila folders around until she found Shipley's. She removed a piece of paper from the folder and read it, her lips moving silently.

It was the poem Shipley had written in class last week. The assignment—write a short poem about a member of your family—had annoyed her at first. Did it have to be so personal? Why couldn't they write about the changing seasons or migrating geese or their favorite pair of boots?

"I didn't make the last name connection until I read this," Professor Rosen said. "I remember your brother. He only showed up for one class."

Shipley nodded. The last thing she wanted to discuss was Patrick. But then she shouldn't have written a poem about him.

"How's he doing anyway?" The professor sounded genuinely concerned.

Shipley wasn't sure what to say. She hadn't seen Patrick since 1988. "He's great," she enthused.

Professor Rosen frowned. "Really?"

Shipley shrugged her shoulders. "We don't really stay in touch." She shifted uncomfortably in the hard wooden chair. The meeting wasn't going the way she'd planned.

Professor Rosen studied the poem again. "It's very good," she remarked. "It shows your curiosity about him. I like the dichotomy that someone we grew up with and should know so well can be a complete stranger to us."

Shipley nodded eagerly. She hadn't thought about any of that when she wrote the poem, but what Professor Rosen was saying made her sound insightful and wise.

Professor Rosen removed a red pen from the chipped mug on her desk and scribbled a giant capital A below the last line of the poem. Then she tucked the piece of paper back into the manila folder. "You might want to think about East Anglia for your junior year. They've got a great poetry program."

Shipley gazed blankly back at her.

"It's in England. We have an exchange program."

"I haven't really thought about it," Shipley said. "My junior year." She tucked her hair behind her ears.

"No, of course not." Professor Rosen drummed her fingertips on the cover of her old address book, looking distracted. A collection of crystal prisms hung from the windowpane. The sun came out from behind a cloud, casting trippy rainbows all over the puny room. Was the meeting over? Shipley wondered. Were they finished?

Professor Rosen pursed her lips. "I didn't like that trick you pulled at orientation, but you seem like you've got your head screwed on right after all. You come to class. You do the reading. You write very nicely."

Shipley waited for the catch—surely there was one.

"While I've got you here, I may as well ask. Do you happen to babysit? Our regular sitter just got sent home with mono and we have tickets to see a play in Augusta Sunday night. I wanted to eat out afterwards."

The professor leaned forward in her chair, the waistband of her olive wide-wale corduroys stretching tight across her flat, wide hips. "I asked Eliza and she said, and I quote, 'I'm not into being nice to mutant gremlins.'" She shook her head. "What a character. But at least she was honest." She smiled at Shipley. Her teeth were long and crooked. "Don't tell me you don't like kids either. Our guy's only six months old. He's a peach."

Shipley smiled back, an image forming in her mind of Professor Rosen's charmless brick house, her nerdy clean-cut husband from the Computer Department, and their bucktoothed, spiky-haired baby, a mini version of Professor Rosen. A lot of the girls at Greenwich Academy had babysat; she'd just never been asked. The baby would probably sleep the whole time anyway. She could eat donuts and watch *Pretty Woman* on HBO.

"I could if you wanted me to," she offered.

Professor Rosen slapped her palm on the desk. "Good. We're in the directory. Just swing by around six. There's a good chance I won't be there because I'm supposed to be rehearsing my one-act. That is, if I can find someone to play the other lead. It's a pretty demanding role. Pretty far out. I don't know what it is about the boys this year, but I can't find anyone to do it."

She cocked her head, her murky hazel eyes widening.

"Hey, what about that hunky boyfriend of yours? What's his name? Timothy? He's big enough to scare the living daylights out of people." She faltered. "When he gets fired up, I mean."

"Tom?"

Obviously the play had something to do with the zoo. Shipley tried to imagine Tom and Adam flitting around onstage together wearing black unitards, their faces painted like mimes as they pretended to be tigers or gorillas or boa constrictors. She'd slink onstage wearing a black cat suit and lick her paws seductively while they fought over her, waiting to be claimed by the last beast standing.

Tom didn't seem like the theater type, but Professor Rosen was just starting to warm to her and Shipley wanted to give her everything she could give. Besides, Tom's grades were terrible. He could use the extra credit.

"Sure, why not? He'd love it."

"Tell him I want to start rehearsing as early as tomorrow if we can." The professor pulled on her earlobes and looked at her watch. "The show's at the end of term, which is a lot closer than you'd think."

Shipley stood up to leave, but Professor Rosen held up her hand. "Not so fast. We're supposed to talk about whether you like your classes or not and what you want to major in. Do you miss home, are you happy, that sort of thing."

Shipley shrugged her shoulders. "So far I love it."

Professor Rosen smiled. "You wouldn't believe how rarely I hear that."

Success!

Shipley wasn't sure how she'd done it, but she and Professor Rosen were practically best friends now. Outside the office, she scribbled Tom's name on the sign-up sheet for the play, ignoring the rush that coursed through her when her fingertips accidentally grazed the green A of Adam's name.

9

November was a curious month. Some days it was warm as summer. Some days it rained. And some days the wind ripped the leaves off the trees and scattered them mercilessly all over campus. Buildings and Grounds worked round the clock to keep the quad green and leaf-free. Weekends the leaves were burned, filling the air with pungent gray smoke. The heat had come on in the dorms and hot chocolate was served in the dining halls. There was a briskness to the student body, too. Midterms weren't far off, and after that, vacation. Of course Thanksgiving was first, but anyone who lived farther away than New York stayed on campus for the turkey buffet in the dining hall.

Now was the time when students became aware of how well they were doing in school. Tom was nearly failing Portraiture. Economics was impossible. English sucked. Geology required way too much memorization. And there was a good chance he would be replaced in Professor Rosen's one-act play, meaning that he would fail to obtain the extra credit. Today he'd decided to try something new.

"It's like this," Wills explained. He tied his long platinum dreadlocks in a knot on top of his head to keep them out of the way of the hot pink ecstasy tablets he was counting out on Root's kitchen table. "You do E every two days. On the off days you smoke pot and cook huge meals and eat like a king. On E days you chew gum—lots of it—and run around outside. Or, if you can't get any E, you steal ether from the chemistry lab. It doesn't last and it stinks, but man—you got to try it at least once. Between the drugs and the running around and the healthy food, your body stays in shape, and basically you're golden."

Each tiny pink pill had the almond-shaped outline of an eye stamped on it. Tom watched as Wills sorted the tablets into neat piles, four for each of the Grannies, and four for him. He'd agreed to purchase the E on the condition that the Grannies do it with him, in case he freaked out.

Back in Bedford, Tom had stayed away from drugs. Mostly because of sports, but also because he wasn't sure how he'd behave. Drinking was okay. His parents drank. Everybody drank. His dad was even cool with picking him up at rugby team parties at 3 A.M. when he was stark raving shit-faced with puke on his shirt. Still, he'd always been curious about drugs, and now that he was away at college, why not? Mainly he was looking for a way to loosen up.

"Dig deeper. Go nuts. Let yourself come unhinged!" Professor Rosen had screamed at him during his first rehearsal. Then she and that quiet kid, Adam, had stood there gawking at him and waiting for him to go nuts, but all he could do was talk louder and wipe his nose a lot and apologize for being such a shitty actor and forgetting his lines.

"You will never create something that is truly yours until you let go of your inhibitions," his painting teacher, Mr. Zanes, would murmur. Mr. Zanes was a whispering graybeard who padded around the studio in bare feet and was forever sucking on lollipops. "For my laryngitis," he said. Apparently his work was all the rage in Prague in the early eighties, but the only evidence of his artistry was a teetering mound of lollipop wrappers in the corner of the studio.

Of course it was nearly impossible for Tom to let go of his inhibitions when the subject of every class was Eliza in all her naked glory. Eliza sitting with her angry chin on her fists. Eliza in profile. Eliza lying on a sofa with her dark hairy crotch in plain sight. Every time Tom looked up, she would mouth "suck my tits" or "olive juice" or "blow me" while subtly giving him the finger. In retaliation Tom would turn her face into a giant oozing sore and omit her pale but rather nice tits. Now he was getting a D+ in Portraiture, which was supposed to be his easy A. And the play was a fucking disaster. Drugs were his last and only hope.

"You know this stuff is all-natural? Comes from the oil of sassafras root," Wills said. "Used to find sassafras oil in soap and root beer and all sorts of shit till the FDA got involved in the sixties and banned it. I was gonna order a big ole sassafras plant through the mail so I could make my own E, but then I was like, do I really want the FBI parked outside my dorm? Do I really want my phone tapped? Do I really want the pigs up inside my sphincter? I think not."

Tom nodded. The little history lesson was interesting and all, but he really couldn't give a fuck. Grover sat down next to him at the table, his electric shaver in hand. He turned it on and ran it over his closely shaved head, buzzing off the few filaments of brown peach fuzz that had accumulated since he'd shaved his head the day before. The kitchen windows just grazed the grassy edge of the quad. Outside a bunch of sporty-looking girls played Ultimate Frisbee.

"What you do is put it on your tongue, flip it back, and swallow it," Grover explained, pinching a tablet between his thumb and forefinger and demonstrating the technique.

Liam came over and stuck out his tongue with a lizardly flicker, waiting for Wills to place a tablet on its tip. He flicked his tongue back inside his mouth. "It goes down kind of dry, but pretty soon you'll be feeling it and you won't care."

Tom poked at one of the tablets with his fingertip. It looked like confetti or baby aspirin. "Feeling what?"

The Grannies chuckled. Wills leaned over and sucked a tablet into his mouth right off the table like a human vacuum cleaner. "Like a god," he elaborated enticingly. "Like you're all dick."

Tom liked to think that he felt that way all the time, but maybe the enhancement of his existing attributes was exactly what Professor Rosen and Mr. Zanes meant by digging deeper. He put a pink tablet on his tongue. It was bitter and wrong-tasting, like he was eating a crumb of squirrel shit off his shoe. He swallowed it down. If this smidgen of trash could get him off, he'd be pretty freaking amazed. "Now what?" he demanded. He couldn't just sit in his dorm kitchen staring at the Grannies while they waited for the E to kick in.

Wills pushed his chair back and stood up, his wraparound skirt cascading down to his ankles. "Now we go for a really long walk." He reached out and patted Tom's shoulder. "And when we get back, you'll be a different man."

Hands tucked innocently into their coat pockets, the pre-rapturous huddle of boys crossed the quad and headed for the five-mile running loop that snaked around the periphery of Dexter's pretty brick and ivy campus. Mr. Darius Booth, the frail president of the college, could be seen creeping along the loop every morning at 5:45 A.M. with his three terrifying German shepherds. Tom knew this because he'd actually woken up a few times at that hour and gone jogging himself. He'd thought he wanted to stay in shape, but all he got from running that early was a killer cramp and some serious heartburn that lasted all day.

He'd come to Dexter with every intention of joining the rugby team. After all, he'd played rugby for the Bedford school district since he was twelve. But he really wasn't up for spending weekends at away games and going through the fratlike hazing rituals of a men's team. Weekends were all about having sex with Shipley, sleeping late with Shipley, and ordering in with Shipley, not necessarily in that order. Besides, he'd heard the guys on the rugby team actually made the freshmen eat a saltine with a senior team member's jizz on it. Not exactly appealing. So he'd skipped the first practice and didn't even mention it to his dad, who'd been captain of Dexter's rugby team his senior year and had probably eaten a whole bucketful of jizz in his day.

Tom hadn't noticed before what a perfect fall day it was. The leaves were gold and crimson and hot pink, and the fading sun slid down the hill behind campus like a giant egg yolk. As they walked, the hair on the backs of his hands took on a lovely coppery sheen. Wills walked directly in front of him, his tie-dyed skirt swaying back and forth, his long platinum hair bouncing liquidly in the late afternoon light.

"Nice," Tom observed, allowing Liam to take his hand. Grover started to skip. The toes of his dirty bare feet were painted with silver nail polish. He played a cheerful Irish-sounding ditty on the harmonica strapped around his neck, accompanied by some enthusiastic chest beating and overall strap jangling.

Grover liked to make noise, which made sense, given that he was the Grannies' percussionist.

A jogger strode up behind them. His long brown hair was pulled back in a ponytail and his cheeks were sunken and sallow. A maroon Dexter basketball shirt flapped from his bony shoulders as his sinewy arms and legs pumped away. Besides the shirt, he sported a pair of those flimsy Dexter running shorts with the built-in mesh underwear that no full-grown man would ever wear, and white Asics running shoes with no socks. The thing was, this guy wasn't full-grown. In fact, he looked like he was shrinking as he ran. When they were shoulder to shoulder, the jogger turned to look Tom square in the eyes, not accusing or threatening, but penetrating Tom's very soul and mind-melding with him. A powerful chemical odor pervaded the air. If Tom weren't on E, he would've been freaked out.

"That guy eats only Granny Smith apples," Liam explained in a whisper as the jogger pulled away from them. "You know how the grocery store puts wax on the apples to make them shiny? Well, he scrapes the wax off with the file on a pair of nail clippers because he doesn't want to ingest the extra calories."

"He's very pure," Wills added from up ahead, his voice bulging with admiration. "All he does is apples and ether."

"We should hit the Pond and go for a swim!" Grover shouted gleefully, puffing on his harmonica a few times for emphasis. He stopped in his tracks and pulled a pack of Doublemint gum from the chest pocket of his overalls. "It's seriously minty," he said as he doled out pieces to each of the boys.

They continued to walk. Tom unwrapped the gum and stuffed it into his mouth. It tasted unbelievably fresh. His jaw thrilled with the act of chewing.

"Come on. Who's up for a swim?" Grover said again, skipping backward down the road.

"I'm not ready to get wet yet," Liam murmured, gripping Tom's hand even tighter. "Get wet yet," he repeated, smiling goofily.

"Neither," Tom agreed, chewing hard on the gum. They were walking faster now. He could feel it in his legs. It felt awesome, *he* felt awesome. "What I really want to do is paint something," he continued, licking his lips and quickening his stride. He didn't have to stick to what they were painting in Portraiture. He could paint the leaves if he wanted to. He could paint the sky!

"I'm burning up, son," Wills called out to Grover, who was skipping and leaping and prancing ahead of them. "A swim would be good."

A green road sign loomed up ahead. ENTERING HOME CITY LIMITS. POPULATION 9,847.

"There's no place like Home," Liam declared, rubbing the earflap of his hat against Tom's burly shoulder.

A white Dodge minivan drove by, slowing to avoid Grover's flailing arms and legs. Tom gave the driver the thumbs-up, and the driver gave Tom the thumbs-up in return. It was Professor Rosen.

The van stopped. On the rear bumper was a sticker that read *SONA SI LATINE LOQUERIS*. Professor Rosen stuck her head out. "Hey, Tom. Need a ride to rehearsal?"

Tom had forgotten all about rehearsal. He dropped Liam's hand and walked toward the van.

"Hey, what're you doing, man?" Wills demanded.

"Come on," Tom called. "She'll drive us wherever we want to go."

The boys followed him to the van. Tom slid open the back door. A blast of cooked air hit him in the face.

"Van's been parked in the sun all day," Professor Rosen explained as he slid into the seat behind her. He'd never noticed how beautiful and shiny her hair was—coppery brown, with gold flecks like mini sun rays. It was darker than Shipley's, but just as complex. Shipley's hair, Tom remembered, was what had inspired him to take up painting in the first place. It was Shipley he needed to paint, not the sky or the leaves, and definitely not Eliza. Shipley was his gorgeous golden goddess—his woman, his love, his muse!

The other boys slid into the van after him. "We went for a walk," Liam told Professor Rosen, glancing conspiratorially at his bandmates. Next thing he was going to tell her all about the E they'd taken.

"Hey, teach, what's with the bumper sticker?" Wills demanded cheerfully. "Is that like a quote from Chaucer or something?"

"It means 'Honk if you speak Latin.'" Professor Rosen glanced in the rearview mirror. "Hey, Tom, are you feeling okay?"

"Yeah, but I just *gotta* paint something," Tom said, rubbing his hands together and chewing hard on his gum. "I gotta find some paint."

"And we *gotta* go swimming," Wills mimicked Tom's urgent tone.

"Brrr," Liam agreed, rubbing his arms. "Oh man, you gotta feel this!" He offered his arm to Tom. "Here, rub it."

Tom met Professor Rosen's gaze in the rearview mirror. She had the prettiest greenish brown eyes, and skin like milk. Milk! He could drink a whole carton of it right now, a gallon even. Milk was so white and pure and cold, and all of a sudden he was extremely thirsty.

"Why don't you harness some of that creative energy for our rehearsal?" Professor Rosen suggested. "And then maybe later you can paint."

"Okay, but I'm super thirsty." Tom stuck out his tongue and began to pant. "Think we could grab some milk?"

Professor Rosen grinned. Tom appeared to have done his homework. He was coming unhinged right there in her car. "Sure, sure."

Adam was early. He sat cross-legged on the floor of the small, dimly lit studio on the second floor of the Student Union, reading through the script.

The Zoo Story had nothing to do with the zoo, and not much happened until the ending. It was all about these two lonely guys who run into each other in Central Park. Peter, the part Adam played, was just an everyday businessman, sitting on a park bench after work, watching the world go by. Jerry, the part Tom played, was this scary creep who starts talking to Peter and basically ruins his life. Peter was actually a lesser role because Jerry did most of the talking, including a giant monologue about a slobbering, mean, black dog that went on for six pages. How Tom was going to pull that off, Adam had no idea.

Professor Rosen was very passionate about the play. She said it was about the loneliness and isolation we all feel, and the ways in which we reach out to others to find meaning in an existence that is basically absurd, since we're all going to die anyway. It was actually sort of depressing. But Adam had been looking for a reason to spend more time on campus, and when Professor Rosen accosted him in the bookstore and begged him once more to try out, he gave in.

That she'd seen Peter written all over his face astounded him. When he looked in the mirror, he didn't see anything written on his face, not a thing, except freckles and a shadow of red stubble. Why hadn't she cast him as Jerry, the explosive lunatic who terrorizes Peter? Jerry was virile and alive, while Peter was robotic and uninteresting. Still, he liked the deliberateness of acting, and it was nice to be someone else for a change, even if the guy he was playing was just as lonely and lackluster as he was.

This was their third rehearsal. Tom and Professor Rosen arrived together, Tom swilling from a gallon of milk. It ran down his chin as he chugged it thirstily. Would Shipley find that attractive? Adam wondered with dismay.

"All right, boys," Professor Rosen began. "Are you both as excited as I am about the election on Tuesday?"

The boys nodded their heads dutifully.

"Good, good." The professor removed her script from her purse. "Listen, I have a date tonight, so let's make this quick. There's less than eight weeks till showtime. I'd like you to read through the entire play, from start to finish. That way you can get a feel for the buildup of energy. Just get into the groove and let the words slide off your tongues. I bet you've even memorized a lot of it already."

Adam pursed his lips. The only time he remembered getting "into the groove" was when he'd sat on his sofa at home holding Shipley's feet and fantasizing about what it would feel like to hold the rest of her.

Tom guzzled another few quarts of milk and cracked open his script. "I've been to the zoom," he read.

"It's zoo," Professor Rosen corrected him. "I believe it's been mentioned on numerous occasions that this play is called *The Zoo Story*?"

Tom ran his hands over his hair and gritted his teeth menacingly. "I've been to the zoo. I said, I've been to the zoo. Mister, I've been to the zoo!"

Adam glanced up from the script. Perhaps Tom was right for the part after all. Perhaps Tom was a more nuanced actor than he'd first thought. "You're a lucky man," he muttered.

Tom looked confused. "Am I on the wrong page?"

"Just stick to the script," Professor Rosen advised.

Adam cleared his throat and read his line. "I'm sorry, were you talking to me?"

Tom gritted his teeth. "I need more milk."

Professor Rosen sighed and handed him the jug of milk. "Why don't you finish that off and start again from the beginning."

Tom tossed his head back and guzzled the milk. He smacked his lips and wiped them on the back of his hand. "I've been to the zoo," he began, sounding even more guttural and crazy than before.

Professor Rosen clapped her hands together. Her jade earrings jangled. "Yes!" she cried excitedly. "Yes!"

"Er. Ahem," Adam coughed politely into his hand. At the end of the play he got to stab Tom in the gut with a plastic knife. He couldn't think of anything more satisfying. "Are you talking to me?"

10

Why take the job when she didn't need the money? Shipley wasn't sure how to answer that question. Perhaps it was a matter of fitting in—most of the students at Dexter had some sort of job—or maybe she just needed to do something on her own, independent of Tom. She hadn't even told him where she was going.

"Babysitting?" She could hear him chuckle as he tried to hide her clothes so she couldn't put them back on. "Fuck that."

She shivered as she headed to her car, wishing she had worn a coat. It was five-thirty and already almost dark. She wasn't due at Professor Rosen's house until six, but because it was her first time babysitting, she thought it might be a good idea to arrive early and get acquainted with the baby before its parents left.

The car was in its usual cockeyed spot, keys on the tire. The same person who'd stolen it that first week of school had kept on stealing it, but they always brought it back when the tank was empty. Shipley's father had taught her to buy gas when the tank was a quarter full, so she kept on dutifully filling it, only to see the car disappear once again. Of course she could have just kept the keys on her Dexter key chain instead of on the tire, but she was terrified of losing them, thus risking the need to call home. The years she'd waited for a car. The years she'd waited to leave home.

Sometimes the stranger left notes: *This car could use a bath. Wiper fluid!! Sorry, I smoked all your cigarettes. Left rear tire feels low.* Sometimes the stranger left a present: a particularly pretty pink leaf, a pack of Juicy Fruit, *DownEast* magazine, a Snickers bar. She liked to pretend the stranger was her ex-husband. She'd left him for Tom. Neither one of them wanted to give up the car in the divorce, so they'd decided to share it. He'd drive around, listening to her music, finishing off her old, stale coffee, missing her. And every hastily scrawled note or thoughtful little token he left behind was his way of telling her he wished he'd never let her go.

Today the note on the front seat read, <u>*Needed*</u>*: 1 pair wool socks, 1 heavy wool sweater or fleece, 1 pair warm gloves, 1 wool hat. All size Large.* Shipley stuffed the note into her pocket. The car smelled like cinnamon buns. She turned the keys in the ignition. The gas tank was so empty the warning light was on.

Professor Rosen's house was only a mile or so away from the farmhouse she'd happened upon the first night of college. It even looked a lot like Adam's house, except less quaint. Weeds grew out from under the worn porch steps, and the screen door hung from the door frame at a jaunty angle. There were no animals, only a fenced-in vegetable plot that had already been dug up and mulched for winter, and a terrifying scarecrow with red button eyes and red yarn hair. The scarecrow was dressed in a billowing white sheet, with a black trash bag cape and a black witch's hat.

Shipley mounted the porch steps and pulled open the screen

door. The wooden door behind it was ajar. She knocked on it softly and pushed it open. The kitchen table was strewn with the remains of the baby's mashed peas and brown rice dinner. Soothing strings played on a portable radio. The baby cooed in another room. A nervous lump formed in Shipley's throat and she considered leaving.

"Hello?" she croaked.

Some woman who wasn't Professor Rosen came into the kitchen with a fat baby slung over her shoulder. The baby had thick black hair, black eyes, tan skin, and wore a light blue terry-cloth zip-up footie suit. The woman was freckly and blue-eyed, with frizzy blond hair. She wore a multicolored crocheted dress and fringed suede moccasin boots.

"Shipley, thank God."

"I meant to get here early, but I had to stop for gas," Shipley explained.

"Don't worry about it." The woman put down her jam jar full of white wine. "Darren's on campus rehearsing her play. I'm Blanche, otherwise known as Professor Blanche. I teach English at Dexter too." She held the baby under his armpits and offered him to Shipley. "And this is Beetle. Beetle, Shipley. Shipley, Beetle."

"Hello."

Blanche frowned as Shipley clumsily laid Beetle down in the crook of her elbow and cradled him against her chest the way she'd held her dolls as a child. Beetle's shiny black eyes glared up at her. His fat brown face was pinched and angry. He whimpered and hiccupped and thrashed his little hands and feet.

"Um, he prefers to be upright, you know, like looking over your shoulder when you walk around?" Blanche suggested.

Shipley hiked him up onto her shoulder. He didn't feel anything like a doll. He felt like a furless, pajama-wearing puppy or a breathing bag of warm, wet sand.

Blanche stood behind her, talking to Beetle. "See? She's a nice girl," she crooned. "You big mama's boy. You big fart machine. You big whatchamacallit."

Shipley bobbed up and down, hoping Beetle wouldn't fart on her.

Blanche walked around them so she was facing Shipley. "We'll only be gone a few hours. Here's the number of the restaurant. It's in Hallowell. He's had a bath and dinner. All you need to do is have fun for about an hour, change him into his pj's, give him a bottle, and put him down. Bottle's in the fridge. It's shaped like a boob. He probably won't drink it all though, since he was such a hungry man at supper." Blanche pressed her nose into Beetle's flabby cheek and breathed in, as if she couldn't get enough of the smell of him. "Just make yourself at home with little old rubberbutt."

Shipley wanted to ask what exactly Beetle liked to do for fun and what he was supposed to wear to bed, since he seemed to be wearing his pajamas already. Wasn't that what babies wore pretty much all the time? She also wanted to ask if he still wore diapers, and how she was supposed to put him to sleep, but she didn't want to seem unprofessional. Beetle belched and she felt something warm and wet seep into the cloth of her sweatshirt.

"Whoops!" Blanche handed Shipley an old stained dish towel.

Obviously this household didn't use paper towels and recycled everything, including jam jars. It was also a household in which women lived together and adopted babies from Mexico or wherever and gave them very un-Mexican-sounding names like Beetle. There was absolutely no way for Shipley to make herself at home. She was galaxies away from Greenwich.

"Just so you know, that's regurgitated baby formula all over your shoulder, not breast milk. Can't breastfeed when you adopt,"

Blanche explained, tossing back the dregs of her wine. "So we'll see you around eleven or twelve." She gave Beetle one last kiss on his little forehead and swished out the door in her fringed boots. "Help yourself to anything in the fridge if you get hungry!"

It seemed like a lot of trouble for only $40, especially an hour later, after fun time. Fun had consisted of Shipley putting Beetle down on his feet so he could walk around, and watching him topple over onto the carpet like a badly made toy. It hadn't occurred to her that he wouldn't know how to walk. Of course Beetle had begun to cry, and he'd been crying ever since. She carried him around for a while, walking from room to room, opening cabinets and drawers, reading the spines of books, checking out the contents of the fridge and generally snooping. She learned that Professor Rosen and her partner, Blanche, liked to eat things like tahini, tempeh, and quinoa. She learned that they used something called Dr. Bronner's Magic Liquid Soap to wash everything—their dishes, their clothes, their hair—and that instead of Advil and Tylenol their medicine cabinet was stocked with little vials of homeopathic remedies with names like Nux Vomica, Belladonna, Gunpowder, and Cypripedium Pubescens. She learned that they slept on the floor, on a futon covered in natural-looking cream-colored sheets, and that they owned only six dresses between them. She learned that they used organic bleach-free tampons. There was no caffeine in the house and no television, but the pantry was stocked with case upon case of wine. Their favorite authors seemed to be Virginia Woolf, Shakespeare, and Jeanette Winterson. A Clinton-Gore banner was displayed in the living room window. They had two large Maine coon cats who ignored Shipley completely. The house was cozy, full of plants and pillows and throws and furniture salvaged from thrift stores, but it was so completely alien Shipley wasn't comfortable enough to sit down.

How had they come to live this way? she wondered as she paced the dusty wood floors with the crying baby in her arms. Were they raised in a house like this? Had they always eaten tempeh? Had they always preferred women to men? And if not, when did it happen? When did they know that they wanted to be mommies together and raise a little boy without caffeine or television or meat or bleach? How did they know they preferred Clinton-Gore over Bush-Quayle or Ross Perot? Was it something they learned in college?

She couldn't help but wonder what would happen to her after four years of exposure to such people. She might experience a slight alteration, or she might be completely transformed. Would she stop shaving her legs and using deodorant and write the word "women" with a y? Would she forgo leather and refuse to eat meat? Would she grind her own wheat and get fat and grow a mustache?

Beetle kept on crying. Finally she laid him down on his back in his crib. His face was no longer tan, but red. His diaper needed changing—it had been swelling by the minute—but she couldn't very well change him when he was so hysterical. Maybe he'd wear himself out soon and fall asleep.

But the baby continued to cry.

Shipley stared at him. She reached through the slats of the crib and poked his spongy arm with her finger.

"Hush. You be quiet now," she murmured and stuck out her tongue, as if this were only a game they were playing and her helplessness was just an act. Beetle's shiny jelly bean eyes widened and the intensity of his howls increased. She left the room, hoping he would cry himself to sleep.

Downstairs she lit a cigarette and poured herself a glass of white wine from the open bottle in the fridge. She ashed into the sink, gulping the wine between puffs. Upstairs Beetle's cries grew louder and more desperate.

A worn Home phone book lay on the kitchen counter. Shipley snatched it up and without even pausing to think, turned to G for Gatz.

"Hello? Is this the Gatz household with two teenage kids—a guy named Adam with red hair, and a pretty girl with long dark hair and a strange name that I can't remember—*Philosophy?*" she asked desperately.

"Is this some kind of poll?" the woman on the other end replied.

"No, I just . . . Is Adam there?" She and Adam rarely saw each other on campus and they never spoke. Shipley wasn't sure why, but ever since she and Tom had become a couple, she'd avoided Adam completely.

"Adam is at the college, rehearsing his play."

"And what about . . . his sister?"

"Tragedy?!" the woman bellowed, her mouth away from the phone. "Who may I ask is calling?" she said into the earpiece. "Someone named Soon Yi!" she bellowed after Shipley had given her name.

The phone clattered against something hard and then Tragedy picked up.

"Hello?"

"Tragedy? I don't know if you remember me. This is Shipley."

"Of course I remember you," Tragedy huffed. "Do you have any idea what it's like to live with Adam now? He hardly talks or eats or even looks at anyone. He's like a ghost."

"I'm sorry. I didn't know," Shipley said, wondering what all this had to do with her. "But please, I just need someone to—"

She explained the situation, her voice shuddering on the verge of hysteria. Tears spilled down her cheeks. "He won't stop crying and I don't know what to do!"

"Okay, Jesus. Calm down." Tragedy sighed impatiently. "Listen, take a deep breath and make yourself some chamomile tea or something. I'll be there in a sec."

||

n driver's ed they teach you that most accidents happen on familiar roads close to home. You relax and let your guard down.
It is then that you are at your most vulnerable. Adam thought
about this every time he drove home from Dexter. He never
seemed to drive on roads that were unfamiliar, which meant,
basically, that he was an accident waiting to happen.

"Adam!" Ellen Gatz hollered across the yard from the barn
as Adam pulled up to the house. "Your sister's in there talking
on the phone with some friend of yours named Shun Lee!"

Adam tore inside the house, only to find that Tragedy had
already hung up.

"Shipley's down the road babysitting and the kid won't stop
crying," she explained. "Why in fuck's name she called here, I
don't know, but I said I'd go over and help."

"I'll drive you." Adam lunged for the door. "Come on."

The road was a blur. The car seemed to zoom along on its own.
All Adam could think about was Shipley. She was all he'd been
thinking about for weeks.

"Hi," she said, greeting them at the door, cheeks puffy and eyes rimmed with pink from crying. "Adam, you came too?"

"Yes," Adam answered robotically. From inside the house came a piercing, forlorn shriek followed by a series of breathless choking wails. The baby sounded like it was being tortured. "I came to help," he said bravely.

Shipley backed away cautiously, as if she'd just remembered that it wasn't her baby or her house. "Well, I guess you should come in."

The kitchen stank of cigarettes. A half-empty bottle of white wine stood open on the kitchen counter. Tragedy didn't wait for the grand tour, she just headed upstairs to Beetle's room, leaving Adam and Shipley to stare at each other in the kitchen.

"How was play rehearsal?" Shipley asked. Now that he was standing in front of her, she knew why she'd been avoiding him.

"Good," Adam said. "Better than before. I think it's actually going to be good."

"Great!" She glanced at the stairs. "Maybe we should go up and see how they're doing."

"Okay," Adam agreed, reluctant to give up this moment alone together, but eager for a distraction.

He followed her up the stairs, admiring the neat sway of her trim rear end. No awkward creases or excess flab. She probably looks even better naked, he thought, forgetting to breathe.

Shipley tried to march upstairs in the least provocative way possible. If only she'd worn her favorite jeans, the ones that made her legs look longer and thinner and her waist extra slim. She sucked in her breath, hoping it would make a difference from behind.

They reached the landing, panting. Beetle's room was directly in front of them.

"He's wet," Tragedy explained, expertly picking up the baby

from his crib. She rocked him back and forth, her Amazonian body swaying with motherly grace. "Aren't you, bud? Well, I'm gonna fix it. Don't you worry. It's okay. I was a little squirt like you once. I remember how bad it sucks."

Shipley and Adam stood mutely in the doorway as she laid Beetle down on the rug and removed the legs of his terry-cloth suit. His diaper was swollen and yellow.

"Lookit all that pee," Tragedy crooned as she removed the soiled diaper and replaced it with a fresh one. Beetle had stopped crying. He smiled his toothless, goofy smile at his new adored aunty. "Lookit that little wiener. It's like a worm. Just a little worm."

"Thanks so much for coming over," Shipley said. The doorway was narrow. She and Adam were practically touching.

"It's hard to imagine how guys ever get to be guys looking at a precious little fucker like this, huh?" Tragedy zipped Beetle up into a clean terry-cloth jumpsuit. This one had orange and brown tiger stripes and four little points on the end of each of the footies, like tiger claws. "There you go, hot stuff." She kissed the tip of Beetle's nose and picked him up, flying him over her head like a human airplane. "One day I'm going to have at least twelve of these things. My own crazy crew. Babies and animals everywhere."

Shipley and Adam stared blankly back at her, both focused on the humming centimeter of space between them.

"Why don't you guys go make some coffee or something while I try to put him down?" Tragedy suggested. "Does he have a bottle?"

"Oh, I forgot about the bottle." Shipley dashed downstairs and came back with the breast-shaped bottle from the fridge. "This is what they said to use."

Tragedy took the bottle and held it against her chest. "Ha!

Mine are bigger." She sat down in the rocking chair in the corner and settled Beetle in her lap to drink his milk. She watched him drink for a while and then turned to glare at Shipley and Adam, still standing in the doorway. "Would you please get the fuck out of here?"

Adam backed away and headed downstairs.

"Are you sure?" Shipley asked, desperate to follow him.

"Uh-huh," Tragedy said without looking up.

Downstairs Adam opened and closed the kitchen cupboards. Shipley went over to the sink and flushed the mound of cigarette ash down the drain.

"They don't have any coffee," she told him. "I checked."

He opened the refrigerator door. "Are you thirsty?" he asked.

"No."

"Me neither," he said, closing it again.

It was dark outside. The house was quiet save for the rattling November wind. Shipley glanced at the radio, wondering if she should turn it back on.

"Did you see the scarecrow?" she asked.

"No. Yes. I've seen it before," Adam said. "Pretty crazy."

They stared at each other for a moment. Adam's hair was a deeper red than Shipley remembered. It was auburn. And his freckles had faded a little. He looked thinner too, and taller. "Your sister got mad when I called. She said you were . . . upset." She leaned back against the kitchen counter. "Are you . . . Is it . . . better?"

Adam watched her mouth move, reveling in the notion that it was moving for his sake. In his incessant Shipley fantasies they never did much talking, only kissing. He wasn't prepared for talking.

"I was disappointed," he admitted, pressing his back against the fridge. "Because I thought we were . . . friends."

Maybe it was the wine and cigarettes going to her head, but Shipley was suddenly struck by how very similar this scene was to the laundry room fantasy she'd had at home while packing for college.

Her mother, who dry-cleaned everything except her underwear, insisted that Shipley learn to use a washer and dryer.

"There won't be any cleaning lady at college, and you can't use the laundry service because they shrink everything. Your dorm will have a laundry room," she instructed, handing over the manuals to the household Maytags. "The best times to wash your clothes are first thing in the morning or late at night. Otherwise the laundry room will be so busy your clothes will wrinkle waiting for the dryer."

The task of washing her own clothes was so foreign to Shipley as to seem romantic. The words "gentle spin" and "tumble dry" evoked thoughts of a handsome stranger who would wander into the laundry room while she was folding her clothes.

"Let me help," he'd say, picking up her laciest bra. He'd continue folding her panties and bras until, unable to control his desire, he'd tear off her clothes, dropping them one by one into an open washer. Then he'd remove his own clothes and ravish her on top of the warm, agitating machines. It would be their secret, these late-night laundry room trysts, with the washing machine spinning so noisily they'd never even learn each other's name.

The refrigerator hummed. Shipley smiled shyly up at Adam, as if he were reading the part in her diary where she'd written about him. *He* was the handsome stranger in the laundry room. She took a step toward him, and then another. "I'm going to kiss you," she whispered as she slipped her arms around his neck. And then she did, slamming his head back against the freezer door like the uninhibited adulteress in her daydream.

They kissed in the kitchen for a long time. Adam tried to

remain calm and keep his hands quietly at her waist, but Shipley slipped her hands beneath his T-shirt, causing his heart to explode out of his chest, and then his hands were all over her.

"Is it safe to come down?" Tragedy whispered from the top of the stairs.

Adam tore his mouth away from Shipley's. "No! Keep playing with the baby."

A moment later headlights flashed through the kitchen windows. Professor Rosen and her partner were back.

"They're here!" Tragedy called.

"Shit." Shipley wiped her mouth on her sleeve and tucked her hair behind her ears. "It's okay. I'll tell them you stopped by to study," she said quickly. "They won't mind." She corked the wine and stuck it back in the fridge.

Tragedy came downstairs with the empty breast bottle in her hand. "At least he's asleep."

Beetle. Shipley had forgotten all about him. Adam just stood there with his hands in his pockets, grinning.

"Hello, hello. I see you have company." Blanche pushed open the kitchen door, her cheeks flushed from red wine and cold wind.

"How was it?" Professor Rosen asked as she came into the kitchen. "Oh, hello, Adam." She removed her jade earrings and tossed them on the countertop. Her cheeks were flushed too. "Is everything okay?"

"We had to go over something for Geology," Shipley blurted out, even though Adam didn't take Geology. "Beetle's asleep. He's fine. What an easy baby!"

"And who might you be?" Blanche smiled at Tragedy.

Tragedy didn't care for pleasantries. "Adam's sister." She pushed past them and stepped onto the porch. "Come on, Adam, the sheep are waiting."

Shipley remained in the kitchen, her ears tuned to the sound of Adam and Tragedy pulling away in Adam's car. Blanche went upstairs to check on Beetle. Professor Rosen rooted around in her purse for Shipley's pay.

She handed Shipley a wad of bills and sniffed the air. "Do you smell smoke?"

Shipley wrinkled her nose and shook her head. She was a terrible liar.

"Darren read your poem to me in the car," Blanche trilled as she came downstairs. "It's very good. You should submit it to *A Muse*." *A Muse* was Dexter's biannual literary journal. "I basically run the thing so I can tell you now we'll publish it."

"Thanks." Shipley stuffed the money into her sweatshirt pocket. Knowing that Professor Rosen had shared the poem with Blanche might have been more troublesome if her mind wasn't preoccupied with how fun it had been to slam Adam's head against the freezer door—who knew she had it in her?—and how fantastically illicit it had been to kiss him in Professor Rosen's kitchen. She considered driving straight over to his house so they could pick up where they left off.

Professor Rosen opened a cupboard door and took out two clean jam jars. "That boyfriend of yours—Tom? Wow, did he ever knock my socks off today at rehearsal."

Shipley started at the mention of Tom's name. What was she doing kissing another guy in Professor Rosen's kitchen when she already had a perfectly decent boyfriend? In one of her more recent fantasies, Tom parked his dove-gray Porsche convertible in the two-car garage of their Hamptons beach house, right next to her red one, before making love to her on the beach while the surf crashed behind them. Adam was more lawnmower than Porsche. And Tom was already hers. He was probably waiting for her in his room right now, boxers off, socks on, snuggled beneath his flannel sheets with his Economics textbook.

Blanche opened the fridge and located the half-empty bottle of wine. "Can I get you anything?" she asked Shipley.

"No, thank you." Shipley swept her bag off the kitchen counter. It was best to leave before either of them noticed the rug burn on Beetle's forehead or the smelly cigarette butts in the trash. "I have to go."

"Don't forget to vote on Tuesday!" Professor Rosen shouted after her.

Tom was not under the covers. He was just getting started on a new painting. He'd brought over a fresh canvas from the art building and was busy mixing shades of apricot and taupe, trying to achieve the perfect match for his own skin. His pulse was raging. He gnashed his teeth and tore off his shirt. He could paint himself. He could paint directly *on* himself! He selected a new brush and squirted a blob of black paint on the palette. He would paint himself to look like one of those Greek statues, with pecs like fucking Hercules.

"What are you doing?" Shipley opened the door and stared at him as he traced the outline of his godlike nipples.

Tom threw down his brush. "You! You're here! Oh, you're so freaking beautiful."

"No, I'm not," she protested.

"Come here," Tom said. "Take off your clothes so I can paint you."

Shipley went over and leafed through the finished paintings on his desk, an assortment of Eliza's outsized gory body parts in various stages of undress. She fidgeted with the zipper on her Greenwich Academy sweatshirt.

"Why don't you just do my head, with the window in the background? That might look sort of cool."

Tom came over and pulled down her zipper. He brushed her hair away from her collarbone. "I want to paint you naked," he said, kissing her neck.

Shipley stiffened. Something about Tom was different. His whole body was covered in a layer of slick, cold sweat, and his voice was throaty and hoarse. "Are you okay?"

"I took some E with the Grannies. And I knocked the balls off of play practice. I fucking ruled." Tom yanked off her sweatshirt and unbuttoned her jeans. "I want to paint you right now," he told her urgently. "Naked."

Shipley was no exhibitionist—she never even wore tight jeans. On the beaches in Martinique all the girls took their tops off. They lay on their backs in the sand, soaking up the sun in calm oblivion. But when Shipley tried it, she felt like she was being cooked. Her nipples had shriveled into raisins. She'd tied her top back on and splashed into the water, hiding her shame beneath the waves.

"Can't I just wear this undershirt?" she asked, taking a seat in his desk chair. The undershirt was white and thin. So was her underwear. She was naked enough.

"No." Tom stood a few feet away holding a white plastic paint palette. The muscles in his bare chest twitched beneath their war paint. He licked the tip of his brush. "Come on."

"Come on yourself," she joked.

He went over and pulled up on the undershirt. "It's not like I haven't ever seen you naked."

"All right." She took off the shirt and tossed it on his bed. Then she removed her underwear and crossed her legs, placing her hands, one on top of the other, on her knee.

"Too stiff," Tom protested. "Just sit the way you normally would if no one was looking."

She uncrossed her legs and allowed her knees to open a quarter of an inch. Fresh air violated the space between her thighs. She pressed her knees together again and folded her arms across her chest.

"I can't do this. I'm tired. I've got baby throw-up all over me. I need to brush my teeth." She glanced around the room, hating to disappoint him. She wanted to be a good girlfriend and she'd already let him down more than he knew.

"What if I covered my face with a fan, you know like a Japanese geisha? Or what if I was reading a book?" At least that would give her something to do so she wouldn't feel so embarrassed.

Tom dropped his palette and got down on his hands and knees, crawling around and looking beneath the beds. Shipley recrossed her legs and picked at her cuticles. Someone whistled out in the hallway. There were goose bumps on her thighs.

"Okay, how 'bout this?" Tom held up a red paper Macy's shopping bag pilfered from Nick's side of the room. He grabbed a pair of scissors and cut out two eyeholes and a little round mouth hole. It reminded Shipley of Professor Rosen's scarecrow, only more sinister.

"I don't know." She pulled the bag on over her head. Her eyes were set close together and the holes were too far apart. The mouth hole was very small. "Don't look," she added, spreading her knees. Her thighs always looked fat, no matter how thin she was. Somehow the shopping bag made them even more embarrassing. Tom was looking at her legs, not her pretty face. And he was seeing them as they really were, compact drumsticks. Even her smaller than average breasts would look disappointing, she realized. But maybe that was the point? She wasn't herself any-more, just the female form. After all, this was supposed to be art. But did it have to be a Macy's bag? A bag from Tiffany's would have been much better.

"Sit back." He came over and pressed her shoulders against the hard back of the chair.

"I feel stupid," she murmured, wondering how she'd gotten herself into this.

"Shush. You're so beautiful. Besides, no one will know it's you," Tom assured her. "I'm just going to take a few Polaroids, and then we're done." He'd bought a vintage Polaroid camera at a local yard sale. He was very proud of it.

She closed her eyes, hoping that would help. The camera flashed, an explosion of white behind her eyelids.

"Just one more." The floor creaked as he walked around.

She should have driven over to Adam's, she realized. She could be kissing him right now, instead of this, whatever this was. She reached up and tugged on the bag. It ripped as she yanked it off. "I don't want to do this anymore."

Tom wasn't even looking at her. He was tinkering with his camera. Shipley was so gorgeous, it was weird how plain her body looked without her head. But maybe he could do a series of the sum of her parts, putting her head in last. It would be like an economics equation, with the whole—head included—being the only viable commodity. Beauty is not a pair of nice tits or a cute ass or pretty feet. Beauty is the whole package. He could float the parts in on a seashell riding the surf, like Aphrodite. His Portrai-ture class was having an open studio next month. So far he had nothing he'd be willing to let the public see. This was just the thing.

"That's okay, you're done. Wow, this is going to be huge," he said, suddenly inspired.

Shipley hurried into her jeans, anxious to run back to her dorm room, take a scalding hot shower, and lie down beneath her beautiful clean sheets.

"Yum," Tom said, picking up her sweatshirt and giving it a good sniff.

She yanked it out of his hands. "I have to go do my laundry," she said and bolted out the door.

Bitter wind lashed her cheeks as she raced across the dark quad. The streetlights lining the walks cast an eerie yellow glow that was both reassuring and frightful. Beyond the stalwart bricks of Coke she thought she saw the black Mercedes pull out of the parking lot and cruise slowly down Homeward Avenue toward the interstate. If this was what Maine was like in November, then what would December bring?

12

Tuesday was Election Day. The more conscientious students hurried back to their home states to vote or had already sent in their absentee ballots. The less conscientious ones pretended to have voted by asking everyone else if *they'd* voted. And the older students (who'd accidentally established Maine residency by living in run-down, off-campus farmhouses with names like Strawberry Fields and Gilligan's Island for the past three years) voted at the high school, their first authentically local experience.

The day was filled with tension. Professors cut their classes short or canceled them entirely. Students lingered on the lawns, as if waiting for some divine directive. The library was empty. When the news that William Jefferson Clinton had won resounded from TVs and radios all over campus, a feeling of euphoria set in, and even those students who never drank on weekdays stood around kegs and toasted the dawn of a new era. Those who'd voted Democrat but had Republican parents felt particularly smug. It was their turn to rule. Sea Bass and Damascus even put speakers facing outward in their dorm room windows and played Queen's "We Are the Champions" at full volume on repeat.

When Thanksgiving came, everyone had something to be thankful for. Mr. Booth brought a live turkey to the dining hall to provoke Ethelyn Gaines, the ancient head of Dining Services, on whom he had a crush. "Oh no you don't!" Ethelyn shrieked, chasing the turkey out of the kitchen, through the dining hall, and out the back door with her cleaver raised. The vegetarians were thankful that the turkey got away.

The Grannies were thankful for Grover's satellite dish. They gathered at his house in Maryland to watch the *Playboy After Dark* rebroadcast of the Grateful Dead playing three of their favorite songs and chatting with Hugh Hefner at a party at the Playboy Mansion back in 1969. Hefner looked exactly like James Bond—all suave and cool in his tux. Jerry Garcia looked more like Juan Valdez by way of Haight-Ashbury with his long hair and woolly poncho. And Jerry was so young! It was awesome.

Professor Rosen was thankful for Progresso's tasty lentil soup. Her recipe for seitan turkey—which required rinsing seven pounds of whole wheat flour in buckets of water until it formed a stringy dough, wrapping the dough in cheesecloth in the shape of a bird, and boiling it for three hours—had not turned out, and she no longer felt like cooking.

Eliza was thankful for the Darien Sports Shop.

Shipley had decided to drive home for Thanksgiving. She needed time to think, time away from Adam and Tom, but she couldn't face going home alone, so at the last minute she'd asked Eliza to come with her. "Just to make sure I don't fall asleep and drive off the road."

No chance of that. Eliza's constant questions were like a car alarm. "Do you shave your armpits every day? Do you have any allergies? How many fillings do you have in your teeth? Have you ever thought about plastic surgery? If you could change one thing about your body, what would it be? Have you ever been to see the Rockettes? How come you're sleeping in our room now? Did you and Tom break up?"

Eliza had agreed to come for purely anthropological reasons. She needed to see firsthand the planet from whence her jeans-hanging, ironed-underwear-wearing roommate had come.

They left Dexter at eight o'clock on Thanksgiving morning and arrived at Shipley's house at three o'clock that afternoon. Greenwich was lovely and clean. The Gilberts' house was big and white and colonial, with green shutters and a red door, built on a rise with a backward C of a driveway curving in front of it. The hedges were neatly trimmed, and a pot of yellow chrysanthemums stood on either side of the front steps.

Shipley turned off the ignition, pulled down the driver's side sunshade, and peered at herself in the mirror. She removed her dangly silver earrings and tossed them into her bag. Then she pulled back her hair into a ponytail and spritzed Binaca on her tongue. Finally she tucked her white turtleneck shirt into the waistband of her jeans.

"What are you doing?" Eliza demanded.

Shipley opened the car door and stepped out. "You know how moms are."

Mrs. Gilbert greeted them with a glass of Chardonnay in hand. She was sinewy and blond and her clothes were made of silk and cashmere, in varying tones of champagne and French beige. She looked like she subsisted on white wine alone, with maybe an after-dinner mint or two thrown in. She opened her arms and pressed both girls against her skeletal chest. "I've put

Eliza in the yellow room," she said as she ushered them into the house.

The sofas were upholstered in green, gold, and cream Regency stripes, embellished with black throw pillows stitched with tiny gold pineapples. The wood floors were dark and polished, the bouquets of flowers perfectly arranged in crisp crystal jugs. It looked like a set from a horror movie. The palatial suburban wonderland—until the doorbell rings. Even Shipley's room, with its white canopy bed and pink rose wallpaper, had a sinister air of too-good-to-be-true.

"Do you have a decorator or did you do this all yourself?" Eliza asked Mrs. Gilbert politely.

Mrs. Gilbert swilled her wine. "I worked very closely with the decorator. I was even thinking, now that the children are gone, I might take a decorating course myself."

"Awesome," Eliza said. The furniture in her house had been bought in sets from Sears. The shiny cherrywood TV cabinet matched the shiny cherrywood coffee table, which matched the shiny cherrywood dining room table they never used. The curtains and the carpet, the sofa and the armchairs all matched too. Nothing in Shipley's house matched, not in an obvious way, and it definitely didn't come from Sears.

They followed Mrs. Gilbert downstairs and into the kitchen.

"Look at that fridge," Eliza exclaimed. "You could keep a pony in there."

Shipley watched for the telltale twitch in her mother's left eye, revealing her distaste for Eliza's linty army jacket and dirty red Converse sneakers, but her mother actually seemed glad that Shipley had brought a friend. She'd even prepared the food ahead of time. The butcher block island was crowded with Tupperware and bags of vegetables.

"I just have to put dinner on the hotplates to warm up and throw together a salad," Mrs. Gilbert said. "Why don't you give Eliza a tour of the neighborhood and do some shopping for a couple of hours? We can eat when you get back."

Eliza couldn't believe how shameless Mrs. Gilbert was about getting rid of them. Even her mom would sit at the kitchen table, smoking her Capris and pretending to be interested, while Eliza rattled on about the snake she'd seen at sleepaway camp or the asshole swim coach at the high school who'd been fired for being a perv. "How's college?" her mom would have asked. But Shipley's mom didn't care.

Shipley could have driven to the Darien Sports Shop blind-folded. It was her favorite store. Three floors of shopping bliss. Lacoste. Lilly Pulitzer. Ralph Lauren. Patagonia. CB. Sportswear, skis, swimsuits, shoes, ice skates, tennis rackets, golf clubs. Everything.

Eliza trailed her while Shipley found a warm wool ski hat, insulated gloves, a heavy wool turtleneck sweater, and thick wool socks for the stranger who'd been stealing her car.

"Those for Tom?" Eliza asked.

"Uh-huh," Shipley lied. She wandered into women's sleep-wear and picked out a pair of white thermal long underwear and a luxurious gray cashmere bathrobe for herself.

A saleslady came to unload the pile of clothes from Shipley's arms. "I'll just keep these at the register for you, miss." She peered at Eliza over a pair of bifocals. "Anything I can hold onto for you?"

Eliza frowned. "No, thanks. I'm all set."

Shipley hadn't noticed until now that Eliza wasn't shopping. She spied a pair of magenta rabbit fur earmuffs on a manne-quin. "Hey, did you see those? Those are totally you."

Eliza removed the earmuffs from the mannequin's head and

put them on her ears. They felt like headphones but softer. She checked herself out in the mirror. They were awesome. She took them off and examined the price tag: $224.95. "I guess not," she said, putting them back on the mannequin.

"No way." Shipley swiped the earmuffs away and tucked them under her arm. "Don't worry. My family has an account here," she confessed. "I usually get whatever I want and just sign for it. Pick out anything you like. Honestly. My parents won't mind."

Eliza hesitated. She'd been prepared to hate Shipley forever, but as the day progressed, she felt herself soften. She'd thought Shipley would be more spoiled. Sure, her house was a showcase, but there was no one in it to dote on her, not even a well-groomed Labrador. Shipley had invited her home for Thanksgiving because she couldn't face going home alone. And she was totally right about the earmuffs. Maybe Shipley knew her better than she thought. "You can't buy me," she insisted halfheartedly. "I'm not for sale."

"Oh, shut up." Shipley slung her arm through Eliza's and steered her toward the jeans. "Look. An entire shelf of black denim. Go on. You know you want to."

They tried on twelve pairs of jeans in a tiny shared dressing room. Eliza decided on two particularly flattering pairs that she would have to cut up and distress herself. Then she broke down and picked out a camping stove for Nick, an insulated sports bra for the frosty-titted Maine winter, two black turtlenecks, six pairs of black wool kneesocks, and an ankle-length black down coat that was basically like a sleeping bag she could walk in. It occurred to her that she could zip her new coat right onto Nick's sleeping bag so they'd have a double-wide in which to have hot and sweaty down-insulated sex inside his yurt. Or not.

The total came to more than $2,000. Shipley signed for it

before Eliza could see. "There, that was fun, wasn't it?" she asked as they carried their bags out to the car.

It was an unseasonably warm Thanksgiving, but Eliza wore her earmuffs and her new coat out of the store. "That was awesome."

Shipley had a closet full of clothes at home, so she hadn't bothered with a bag for the trip. Eliza had thrown her duffel bag into the backseat. And so, for the first time since she'd gone to college, Shipley popped open the trunk of the Mercedes to accommodate their large Darien Sports Shop shopping bags.

"Holy shit," Eliza said.

The trunk of the car was full of food: bagels, muffins, donuts, rolls, bruised fruit, moldy cheese, bags of crushed tortilla chips, and a battered gallon jug of water.

"What the fuck?" Eliza demanded. "Do you have an eating disorder?"

Shipley closed the trunk. The stranger must have been living out of her car, using the trunk as his pantry. She opened one of the back doors and tossed the bags onto the seat. "It's not my food. It belongs to someone else."

"What do you mean, 'someone else'?" Eliza persisted. "Who?"

"I don't know," Shipley said. "Just someone I let use my car when I'm not using it."

All that week Shipley had left the car in the Dexter lot with an empty tank to guarantee that it would be there on Thanksgiving morning when she needed it. She felt a little guilty for doing so, and even guiltier for removing the car from the premises without any explanation, but hopefully the warm clothes would make up for it.

Eliza stared at her. "You let this someone drive your car, and you don't know them?"

"Right." It made even less sense to Shipley now that she'd said it out loud. She opened the driver's side door and got in. "Come on," she said. "Grab the map out of the glove compartment. I'm looking for Oliver Road, in Bedford."

Tom hadn't gone home for Thanksgiving. Ever since Shipley had posed with the Macy's bag over her head, he'd been holed up in his room, painting. Shipley left him to it. She could have taken the opportunity to rush right into Adam's arms, but Tom was her first real boyfriend, and she loved him—she did! She loved everything about him, except for his horrible naked Eliza paintings and how hyper and sweaty he got on ecstasy and his sometimes indelicate language. Adam was handsome—in a freckly, awkward sort of way—and measured and polite, but he was basically a townie, and a timid one at that. He hadn't even come after her since their kiss in Professor Rosen's kitchen. She hadn't even seen him, not once, and his desertion baffled her. Was it just a one-off? Did he think he could use her to satisfy some horny selfish urge and then move on? Or maybe he really did want her. But how could he expect to win her when he wasn't willing to fight for her? Tom had made a play for her from the beginning. There was never any confusion with him. She was sorry she'd strayed. They were perfect for each other. Just to be sure, though, she needed to see where he came from.

Eliza was very good with the map. They took the Merritt Parkway south from Darien, getting off at the Round Hill Road exit in Greenwich. Round Hill led to Bedford Banksville and on to Greenwich Road, followed by Oliver, a country road with only a few large properties. Number 149 was all the way at the end, a stately gray colonial with a wide front porch, a pink door, and a vast green lawn punctuated by mounds of raked leaves. Elegant old trees surrounded the property. A deep flower bed skirted the house, wherein hunkered November's spoils of rhododendrons, hydrangeas, hostas, lilacs, lilies of the valley, irises, and peonies. Beside the house was a fenced-in tennis court, and behind that a swimming pool covered with a green tarp. A black Jeep Chero-kee a few years older than Tom's was parked outside the two-car garage.

Shipley eased the car around the cul-de-sac where the road ended and circled past the house again. Indiana Jones, the Fergu-sons' arthritic Bernese mountain dog, rose from his roost by the front door, gazed at them curiously, and then lay down again. A middle-aged couple and their grown-up son sat in white wooden Adirondack chairs on the porch, eating pie.

"Is this Tom's house?" Eliza pressed her face against the win-dow. "Do you think those are his parents?"

"Yes," Shipley said, barely breathing. The house was bigger and more authentic somehow than her own. She imagined the whole family played doubles tennis together, and Tom's dad had probably taught the boys to swim. Tom's mother was probably passionate about her flowers, and everyone pitched in to rake the leaves. Shipley's mother employed a gardening service staffed by migrant Mexican workers. Her family never did anything to-gether except go on an annual Caribbean beach vacation, during which they would sit in separate locations on the sand, depend-ing on their tolerance to the sun, reading books.

Eliza put her window down and stuck out her arm to wave.

"What are you doing?" Shipley hissed. To her horror, the en-tire family stood up and descended the porch steps, pie plates balanced in their hands. As they approached, Shipley recognized Tom's features in all of them. He had his mother's blue eyes, her thick brown hair, and her determined chin, but he was built like his father. His father even walked in the same floppy-footed style, like he'd never quite grown into his feet. Tom's older brother, Matt, was blond and stocky, but with the same blue eyes and chin.

"What do we say?" Shipley whispered.

Eliza was never at a loss for words. "Hi there," she called.

"We're friends of Tom's. He asked us to stop by and apologize for him not coming home for Thanksgiving."

"How nice of him to send you as envoys," Mrs. Ferguson quipped. "Would you like a slice of pecan pie? It's my great-grandmother's recipe." She cupped her hands around her mouth and lowered her voice. "Highly alcoholic."

Eliza laughed and glanced at Shipley, whose face and neck were flushed pink. "Sorry, but we can't. We're actually sort of late for our own Thanksgiving." She jabbed her thumb at Shipley. "We're having it at her house, in Greenwich. This is Tom's girl-friend, by the way. This is Shipley."

"Hi," Shipley croaked.

Matt chuckled. "So you're Shipley. I've heard a lot about you. We all have. Apparently you're the love of his life. He's going to marry you one day."

"Well, we'll see." Shipley giggled and gripped the steering wheel to steady herself.

Mr. Ferguson leaned against the car and ducked his head into Eliza's open window. He smelled like freshly laundered sheets with a hint of candied nuts and bourbon. "Are you sure you don't want some pie?"

Shipley's foot hovered over the gas pedal. She was obviously dying of embarrassment. "Thanks so much, but we're actually both allergic to nuts," Eliza fibbed.

Deep, worried creases appeared on Mr. Ferguson's forehead. "Tom's all right, isn't he? He hasn't even called today."

Eliza could have told him what she truly thought of Tom, but she wasn't an asshole. Not really. "Tom's great," she said. "He's really into this art class he's taking. And he's acting in a play."

Mr. Ferguson nodded. "He mentioned that. Any idea when they're putting it on? We were thinking about making the trip up to see it."

"It's next weekend. Saturday night. You should come! And the Portraiture open studio is totally the same weekend. I would know because I'm sort of the star of the show." Eliza winked at him. "You'll see what I mean when you see it. Anyway, we won't tell. You know, in case you want to surprise him."

Mr. Ferguson grinned. "Good idea." He stepped away from the car and pushed his hands into his khaki pants pockets. "Thanks for stopping by."

"Tell Tom he missed a kick-ass turkey," Matt called.

"Happy Thanksgiving!" Mrs. Ferguson waved as Shipley leaned on the accelerator and sped away.

Shipley didn't say anything on the way home. Tom's parents were nice and his house was idyllic. It was just as she'd thought. Tom was the perfect boyfriend. When she got back to Dexter, she'd have to work very hard to fix what she'd very nearly ruined. She would make it clear to Adam that kissing him had been a mistake, and while she was happy to be friends, it must never happen again. She would try to be more understanding of Tom's art. Artists took drugs and behaved strangely sometimes. The work required it. Besides, Tom was only experimenting. Pretty soon he'd figure out that art and ecstasy really weren't his thing. Deep down he was still her Tom. Even more so now that she'd met his parents. She could imagine planning the flowers for their wedding with Mrs. Ferguson in her sunny kitchen. She could hear Tom's brother giving a witty best man toast. *"Tom had only been at college for a week when he called me and said, 'I've just met the girl I'm going to marry....' Of course I didn't believe him, especially not after I met the girl. She was way too pretty for him."*

Dinner was already laid out on platters on the dining room table. Mrs. Gilbert was seated at one end, drinking wine. "I didn't actually cook," she admitted. "I got it at Good Enough to Eat. Everything there is so fresh."

Eliza took a seat, her new coat zipped up to her chin, and helped herself to a piece of turkey breast with blood orange and pine nut stuffing.

There were only three places set. "Wait," Shipley said as she settled into her chair. "Where's Dad?" She hadn't seen her father since she'd arrived, but that wasn't unusual. Mr. Gilbert never appeared until dinnertime.

Mrs. Gilbert took a sip of wine. Then she took another. She looked like she wanted to disappear into the glass. "Your father doesn't live here anymore."

Eliza was sorry she was present to witness this, but she was also sort of thrilled. She waited for the shit to hit the fan. She expected Shipley's hair to stand on end and for her to leap on top of the curtain rod, a major gymnastic feat in ironed underwear and flawlessly creased jeans.

Shipley trimmed the skin off her presliced turkey and took a bite. Her father wasn't the type to run off with his secretary. He worked hard and read a lot and ran in marathons and skied. He liked old movies.

"What happened?" she asked. She supposed she wasn't all that surprised.

"I meant to tell you, but you never call home," Mrs. Gilbert explained. "After you left for college, he and I just agreed that we didn't have anything to say to each other. We'd had that feeling for a while, or at least I had. Your father suggested marriage counseling, but I just couldn't see the point. He's renting an apartment in the city, near his office, and he's just bought some sort of surf shack in Hawaii. I suppose the real estate out there was a steal after the hurricane."

"Hawaii?" Shipley repeated. She was still processing the

information that her parents were no longer together. Tom's father would never leave Tom's mother. They were still in love, even after all these years.

Mrs. Gilbert poured herself some more wine. "Yes, Hawaii. He said he's going to fly you out there for Christmas. He said there's even a place out there where you can ski. Some volcano. Imagine."

Shipley cut off another strip of turkey. "Patrick would like that."

"Yes, well," her mother responded with a shrug of her shoulders.

Eliza just sat there, stuffing her face. She felt sorry for Shipley. She felt sorry for Shipley's mom. But it was still better than TV.

Shipley reached across the table and poured herself a glass of wine. She got up and retrieved a pack of cigarettes from her bag out in the hall, lighting one before she sat down.

"I didn't know you smoked," her mother said. "I didn't even know you liked wine." She watched the smoke trail into the air. "Maybe I should start smoking."

Shipley stuffed the pack of cigarettes into her back pocket, annoyed that her mother wasn't more horrified. "It's bad for you," she said, taking another puff.

Eliza waited for one of them to raise her voice, make accusations, demand an explanation, but it never happened. The silence was infuriating. She couldn't help but wonder what Shipley's mom did all day, alone in that big house. Iron her underwear? Or maybe she was secretly addicted to Nintendo or porn. Maybe she was a coke fiend. Maybe she was learning Russian or Mandarin or sign language. Maybe she had a huge dildo collection and hosted orgies or key parties or whatever kind of parties Greenwich housewives hosted.

"You know what my family usually does for Thanksgiving?"

Eliza asked. "Mom always makes two different flavors of Jell-O with those little mini marshmallows mixed in, and Dad makes turkey meat loaf with Wonder bread and catsup because neither one of them really likes whole turkeys with drumsticks and skin and everything. And sometimes I make root beer floats. It's always just whatever we feel like eating. One year we had nachos." Her voice trailed off. Her mom said they weren't even having a Thanksgiving this year without her there. They were going to a casino to watch a floor show and play the slots.

"Would you like some wine?" Mrs. Gilbert offered her the bottle. She sounded a little sloshed.

"No thanks, but would you mind if I nuked the potatoes again, with some butter maybe?" Eliza asked. "They're a little cold."

Shipley yawned her way through the meal, her mind back on Tom. Did he miss her? Was he painting her right now? She was glad she'd taken her clothes off in the end, although she sort of regretted the Macy's bag.

"I thought we could stay up and watch *It's a Wonderful Life*," Shipley's mother said. "It's on tonight. Shipley and her father used to watch it every year," she explained to Eliza. "I've never even seen it."

"Sorry, Mom." Shipley yawned again and pushed back her chair. "I can't keep my eyes open."

Eliza followed her upstairs. On the way down the hall she spotted something that made her stop in her tracks. "Wait a second. Come here."

Shipley sighed and retraced her steps. "What?"

"Who is that?" Eliza pointed at a framed photograph on the wall.

It was the family, the four of them, on the beach in St. Croix during Shipley's seventh-grade spring break. Patrick wore a heavy black windbreaker even though it was ninety-five degrees.

His face was ruddy and marked with blond stubble. His long blond hair was wild and windblown.

"Oh, that's just Patrick, my older brother." Shipley yawned. "He's a little strange."

Eliza put her face up close to the picture. "When's the last time you saw him?"

Shipley shrugged her shoulders. "I don't know. He went to Dexter, but then he left. None of us have seen him since. I guess the last time was when we dropped him off for his orientation—a little over four years ago?"

Eliza nodded. "Well, you're wrong about him leaving Dexter. He's still there."

13

Nick lost his zen the hard way. It was taken from him. He flew into New York's LaGuardia airport from Portland, Maine, the night before Thanksgiving. Holiday backlog delayed his flight for nearly three hours. Then he couldn't get a cab. By the time he arrived home, the apartment was dark and his mother and his sister were fast asleep.

All the way home Nick had been thinking about how good his bed would feel when he finally crashed on it. For the past week and a half he'd been sleeping on the plank floor of his yurt. Tom, the asshole, had basically locked him out, insisting that he couldn't "work" when anyone was in the room. Home at last, Nick fumbled his way through the dark to his room and turned on the light. His bed was gone, replaced by a futon. A large black filing cabinet stood beside his desk, and on his desk was a Macintosh computer that was very definitely not his. The futon had been made up with fresh sheets and an old blanket. On top of the blanket was a note from his mom. *Welcome home, babe. Sweet dreams. I'll explain everything in the morning. xxoo Mom.*

Thanksgiving morning he awoke to the pungent smell of frying bacon and the sound of opera. A man was singing loud, obnoxious arias and laughing his head off. Nick got up and put on his cords and his Dexter sweatshirt. He opened his door.

"Mom?" he called, rubbing his eyes. "Mom?"

"We're in the kitchen, babe!" his mother called back. "Come and meet Morty!"

Nick went to the bathroom first. He suspected that Morty was not a kitten or a puppy or a goldfish; the pair of muddy running shoes in the bathtub confirmed it.

"Hi." Nick stood in the kitchen doorway scratching his head. His mom looked beautiful in her indigo-colored caftan, her blond curls spiraling down to her waist. His sister Dee Dee was in her lap, eating bacon—real bacon. A man in sweaty running clothes was at the stove, frying up more bacon. He wiped his hands on his T-shirt and strode over to Nick.

"Hello there." He held out his hand for Nick to shake. "Welcome back. Happy Thanksgiving. Have a seat. I've got more bacon coming up."

Nick stared at Morty's hand and offered his own limp-wristed one. "I don't eat meat."

"I do," Dee Dee said, stuffing bacon into her mouth. "I love it."

Morty was still holding Nick's hand. Nick pulled it out of his grasp. "So are you, like, living here?" he asked rudely.

"Morty and I have known each other since college." His mom pushed Dee Dee off her lap and breezed toward him, arms wide, the deep V in her caftan spilling open. Nick averted his eyes. She wrapped her arms around him and pulled him toward her. Nick had always allowed her to kiss him all over, nuzzle his hair, press his face into her bosom. He liked it. But this time he arched his back, trying not to get too close.

"There's my hug," she said, squeezing him even tighter.

"Hi, Mom."

She ran her hands over his chest and felt his arms. "Wow, babe. You feel all *muscular.*"

"Mom," Nick protested.

"I knew you were still growing! And don't worry," she murmured into his ear. "I'm making your Thanksgiving tofu."

Dee Dee ran over, a piece of bacon flapping from her lips, and wrapped her arms around their thighs. This would have been cute if Morty wasn't looking on with a smug, paternal smile.

He ruffled Dee Dee's curly blond hair. "This kid kills me," he told Nick. "I have another daughter out in California. Grows artichokes. She was never as cute as this one."

"I like artichokes," Nick said, trying to remain positive. *Another daughter?*

"There's no future in artichokes, especially not those organic ones with worms all over them," Morty insisted.

He was bald, Nick realized. He'd grown out the curly fringe around the base of his skull to give the illusion of hair. He looked like he was wearing one of those rubber clown masks—big nose, crab apple cheeks, and a ring of hair around a bald rubber pate.

"Morty's an accountant," Nick's mother explained. "Freelance. He's using your bedroom as an office."

That was only part of the story. His mom had left out the crucial elements, for instance where Morty had come from in the first place, where he was sleeping, and how long he planned to stay. Dee Dee still liked to get in bed with their mom in the middle of the night. Did she crawl in between Mom and Morty now?

A small white TV that hadn't been there before showed the preparations for the Macy's Thanksgiving Day Parade. Huge balloons hung in the air over the trees of Central Park. Clifford the Big Red Dog. Babar the Elephant. The Pink Panther. Goofy. Nick's family had always pooh-poohed the parade. It was too commercial, too crowded, too bridge-and-tunnel—not genuinely New York.

Dee Dee spun around and grabbed a piece of toast off her plate. She was five years old, but small enough to pass for three. "I can't wait, I can't wait, I can't wait!" she sang.

"Well, hurry up then," Morty said. "Get your coat on." He turned to Nick. "We're going to the parade. You coming?"

In the movie version of this Nick and Morty would bond over losing Dee Dee in the parade and then finding her again. Or Morty would choke on a parade-side pretzel and Nick would give him the Heimlich maneuver, indebting Morty to him for life. Nick would ask Morty to leave his mother alone, and in an effort to win him over Morty would get Nick tickets to Paul Simon's sold-out concert, or courtside seats at a Knicks game. Eventually Nick would embrace him as the father he never had. But this wasn't a movie.

"Mom, are you going?" Nick asked.

"I'm staying here to cook," his mother said. "But you should go. I could use the peace and quiet."

Nick bit his lip. "I think I'd rather just grab a bagel and walk around for a while. I'll give you a hand when I get back."

He walked around the corner to H&H on Broadway and bought a still-warm poppy seed bagel and a cup of black coffee. Avoiding the mayhem of the parade near Central Park, he headed over to Riverside Park and down to the Boat Basin, wondering for the millionth time what it would be like to sleep on a houseboat docked in Manhattan. Probably not the same as sleeping in a yurt in the woods in Maine. He'd wanted to tell his mom all about the yurt. He'd even brought pictures.

That's my babe, he'd imagined her saying. *You're the coolest.*

He didn't even know why he'd built the yurt anymore. He didn't like camping out. It hurt his back, it was cold, and there were noises—bats and raccoons and hunter's gunshots before dawn. There wasn't enough light to study by, there was no heat or toilet or running water. It was unpleasant.

Come to think of it, maybe he shouldn't have gone to Dexter at all. He could've gone to NYU or Columbia or even City College. That way he could've lived at home and kept his bed and prevented his mother from sharing hers with Morty.

He thought about calling his friends from Berkshire. Dewey and Bassett both lived in New York, and they were both big potheads. Dewey had gone to UC San Diego and Bassett was at UNH. Seeing them could go two ways: he'd either get majorly bummed out about how much things had changed, or they'd cheer him up. But his mood was far too gloomy for that even to be possible.

"Don't say anything about the election," his mother warned him when he got back. Morty and Dee Dee were still at the parade. She handed him a colander full of potatoes and a peeler. "Morty's a Republican."

"Jesus." Nick sat down and hacked at one of the potatoes. He sneezed violently. "Is there anything good about him?"

His mother looked up from the plate of tofu she was marinating. "I'm going to pretend I didn't hear that."

Nick's shoulders sagged. He picked up another potato and sneezed again.

"It would help if you could be nice. Morty might well be Dee Dee's father."

Nick put down the potato. "Jesus," he said again. He'd always known he and Dee Dee had different dads. Dee Dee knew it too. "I'm a free spirit," his mom would say with an easy laugh. It occurred to him now why she'd been so keen on his going to boarding school. She'd said it was because boarding schools had better sports, but Nick had never been very athletic. The truth was she'd wanted him out of the house so she could have men over and not feel awkward. His grandparents paid for it, and off he went.

"What?" his mom said. "Don't you think it's sort of nice that I've found someone?"

Nick peeled the potato very slowly. Peels fell on the tabletop like dead skin. Underneath, the potato was wet and slippery and rank. "I don't know," he mumbled, and kept on peeling.

When Morty and Dee Dee returned from the parade, Morty came up behind Nick's mom at the sink and put his arms around her waist. "You would have loved the new Goofy float," he told her. "It has great karma." He lifted up her hair and kissed the back of her neck. As if he knew anything about karma.

At dinner Nick learned that Morty had yearned for his mother ever since he'd laid eyes on her at U Maryland, their alma mater. "Corinne used to wear flowers in her hair every day. Drove me wild," he told Nick. "But she always had a boyfriend. I never even came close. Plus we had different lifestyles. Sure, I smoked dope, but your mother. Whoa."

Nick wondered if he should get out the gigantic red bong his mom kept stashed in her closet. He could have really done with a great big bong hit just then.

"We ran into each other about six years ago in a taxi of all places," Nick's mother said. "I was getting in and he was getting out. I didn't remember him, but Morty remembered me." She smiled at Morty, who responded by putting his hand over his heart. "It was nice."

"Your mother invited me back here for some wine. You were at a sleepover," he told Nick. "Of course within five minutes she's offering me—" He glanced at Dee Dee. She was busy making a hole in her mashed potatoes for gravy. Morty pinched his thumb and forefinger together and put them up to his lips.

"Morty!" Nick's mother exclaimed.

Nick pushed the tofu around on his plate. There was an unspoken rule between him and his mom that they did not talk about pot, they just smoked it, separately. He was pretty sure she knew he stole from her stash whenever he was home, but she didn't say anything about it, and he never mentioned it when the apartment reeked of the stuff. Now the secret was out, even though it wasn't a secret.

"Then one thing led to another and well—" Morty cleared his throat. "Your mom was pregnant with your sister. I wasn't in any sort of shape to be a dad just then. I'd already tried it and screwed it up. And your mom is such a great mom. I knew she could handle it."

"After you left for college and Dee Dee started kindergarten, I got kind of lonely." Nick's mom picked up the story. "I called Morty and he came by and cooked us dinner." She reached across the table and grasped Morty's hand. "And I just fell in love with him. I couldn't let him leave. And Dee Dee adores him, don't you, Dee Dee?"

Dee Dee picked up her caveman-sized drumstick and gnawed on it. "He's pretty cool," she said. Morty poked her in the ribs and she giggled. "Okay, okay. He's the best!"

Morty laughed. "And now of course I'm, you know—" He put his thumb and forefinger up to his lips again. "Every day." He rubbed his relatively flat stomach. "As long as I keep jogging and keep away from the donuts." He winked at Nick.

"Excuse me." Nick stood up and made a beeline for his mom's bedroom. Her closet had been rearranged to accommodate Morty's clothes. He retrieved the giant red bong, and an enormous Ziploc bag full of pot from her sock drawer, and took them to his room, where he stuffed them into his duffel bag. Back in high school he'd pinch only negligible amounts, enough for maybe two or three joints. But what could she do if he took her whole stash? He proceeded to troll his room for any books or personal belongings he'd be sorry to leave behind, sneezing over and over as he pillaged the dusty shelves. His *MAD* magazine collection went in the bag. *The Three Pillars of Zen* stayed on the shelf. His signed and framed Simon and Garfunkel poster was too big. He'd have to send for it later. Because after this weekend, he wasn't coming back.

"Thanks for cooking," he told his mom when he returned to the table. He sneezed again, making sure to aim it right at Morty's plate. Then he smiled with his mouth, not with his eyes, and raised his water glass, which was half-empty. "Happy Thanksgiving."

14

olidays are a state of mind. You spend all day preparing the meal, tolerating your family, and trying to be pleasant. Then, when you sit down to eat, that thing that's been nagging at you—that thing you thought was hunger—is on the tip of your tongue, and you just have to blurt it out. The inevitable result: tears or, at the very least, shouting.

Adam scooped another spoonful of stuffing out of the turkey that his dad had lovingly dressed and roasted.

"I'm thinking of transferring," he announced. "You know, to another college? In maybe even a different state?"

Shipley had continued to avoid him even after their kiss, and each hour he spent on campus was torture. Tragedy was right. He never should have gone to Dexter in the first place. He should have gone somewhere far away, where he never would have met Shipley and where he'd be too busy sightseeing and learning the language to feel as miserable as he felt right now.

"I hear it's very nice in Argentina this time of year." Tragedy pulled the platter toward her, picked up the carving knife, and sliced off four big slabs of juicy breast meat. She glanced up at her parents. "Don't try to talk him out of it."

"Watch it, baby," Eli Gatz warned, his drooping mustache drenched in gravy. "Don't cut yourself."

Ellen Gatz smashed her stuffing into her potatoes and swirled in some peas. Her frizzy salt-and-pepper hair was pulled back into the purple plastic clip she wore only on special occasions. "Where would you go?"

Adam poked his drumstick with the tines of his fork. He hadn't been very hungry lately. "I'm not sure. UMass? It's pretty cheap and not too far away. Or maybe I could try for a scholarship somewhere great, like, I don't know, Stanford?"

"Ha!" his mother exclaimed.

"Your grades are good, but not that good," his father said.

Adam glared at them. This from a guy who hadn't even finished college. "Well, it's worth a shot."

"Ev'ry morning, ev'ry evening, ain't we got fun? Not much money, oh but honey, ain't we got fun?" Tragedy belted out as she got up and dug around in a kitchen drawer for a plastic bag.

"Tragedy, what in the world are you doing? Get back here and eat your dinner!" Ellen shouted.

Tragedy returned to the table with three empty yogurt containers and a rumpled paper bag. "Waste not, want not," she said. "I'm taking some food to the hungry. That okay with you folks?"

"Our little Samaritan," Ellen trilled, although she didn't look too happy about it. Ellen had long given up trying to lose the extra fifty pounds she'd gained while pregnant with Adam. She liked to eat.

"Well, just make sure you leave us enough for turkey sandwiches tomorrow," Eli said. "And maybe give away those brownies you made yesterday. They gave me the runs."

"Thanks, Dad," Adam said, his mouth full of gravy-drenched mashed potatoes.

Ellen grabbed the turkey platter before her daughter could raid it any further. "Stop stealing our dinner and go get some beans. We've got frozen beans from the garden up the wazoo."

Tragedy put her hands on her hips. "Mom. Ellen. Frozen beans? What's a hungry person with no kitchen going to do with frozen beans? I'm sure they'd much rather have a Big Mac."

"Well, this is our dinner and we're still eating it." Ellen turned back to Adam. As was the way with so many parents who'd frittered away their own educations, she didn't want her son to fritter away his. "Seems to me you haven't given Dexter much of a chance, hon. They're giving you free tuition, and it's a way better school than UMass. What's wrong? You told me you liked all your teachers."

"I know," Adam said. "It's just . . . I don't know. It's hard to explain."

"What is it? Are the kids there not nice to you? You've always been a little shy." Ellen frowned. Then her face lit up. "I know! Why don't you have a party? You could throw one after the play next weekend. Invite the whole damn school. We don't care. We'll leave you to it. We can spend the night at Uncle Laurie's."

Tragedy pulled a bag of frozen beans from the freezer. She turned it over in her hands and sniffed it. Then she tossed it back inside the freezer and slammed the door. "A party? Rock on!"

"No one would come," Adam said quietly.

"Please," Tragedy argued. "All you have to do is make it very clear that there will be beer, and believe me, people will come."

Adam rolled a pea across the table. He flicked it at his mom. She flicked it to his dad, who flicked it back to Adam. "Go on, son. We promise to get out of your hair," Eli said. "And we'll get the keg. Heck, we'll get five kegs!"

Adam put the pea back on his plate. If he had a party, maybe she would come. And if she came, she might give him another chance. She might even kiss him again.

"We'll need to put up flyers," Tragedy advised. "But we have to make sure they're not queer. You know, so people will actually show up."

"We're having a party!" Ellen slapped the table with her pudgy, work-worn palms. She glanced at Adam. "Are you in, or what?"

"All right," Adam said. "I'm in."

Tragedy gathered up her containers and put them into the backpack she'd filled with warm clothes stolen from her father. Then she added a couple of bottles of home brew.

Ellen elbowed Eli in the arm. "She's running away again."

Eli tugged on his mustache. "Honeybunch, you're not, are you? You're not running away."

Tragedy cinched up the pack and slung it onto her back. For once in her life the thought hadn't occurred to her. "And miss the party? No freakin' way."

Patrick stood in front of Nick's yurt, admiring it. It was beautiful. Bent timbers, white canvas walls, and a high ceiling with a hole in it so you could see the stars. He'd been watching it all day. No one was in there. Almost everyone at Dexter had left campus, including his sister. But she had taken her car, and now he had no way to get around, no place to sleep, and nothing to eat. Last night he'd slept in the woods. When he woke up his limbs were so stiff he could barely stand. This big tent would still be cold at night, but he could use the sleeping bag the guy who'd built it had left behind and maybe build a fire.

Normally he went south at this time of year. Florida was always good, as long as he stayed away from Miami Beach. Sleeping on Miami Beach was like writing yourself a personal invitation to jail with no get-out-of-jail-free card. But he couldn't leave now. Not when things were just starting to get interesting.

He snuck into the tent, put down his copy of *Dianetics*, and scooted into the red sleeping bag, curling his legs around the pole that held up the roof. It was newly dark and the flap in the ceiling was open. He could just make out the handle of the Big Dipper, beginning to twinkle. The sky was a deep violet, enhanced by the purplish-blue light that shone atop Dexter's chapel spire. Vaguely he remembered a Dexter myth about that light. It was supposed to shine all the time, twenty-four hours, rain or shine, winter and summer. The light would only go out when a girl managed to graduate with her virginity intact. Back in the day, his goody-two-shoes sister might have been a contender, but not anymore. Now that she wasn't so good, he was even starting to like her.

"Hey, you hungry?"

It was that girl. She was standing in the doorway of the tent. "You better be, 'cause I brought a shitload of food."

She had turkey and mashed potatoes and stuffing and brownies and bottles of beer. Patrick hadn't eaten anything since yesterday morning. He wasn't sure where to begin.

"What happened to your Rolls-Royce, or whatever that car was you were driving?" the girl asked.

He grabbed a brownie and shoved it into his mouth.

"Man, I can't watch you eat." Tragedy glanced around the yurt. "It's pretty awesome in here, but you should close up the roof. It's getting cold."

Patrick didn't say anything. Why was she being so nice to him when he hadn't done anything to deserve her kindness? He unwrapped the turkey and devoured it. Tragedy grabbed the long pole that Nick had rigged to pull the roof flap closed, and wrestled with it until the heavy canvas flap covered the hole.

"There. Snug as a bug." She rested her hands on her hips, waiting for Patrick to speak. He was the worst conversationalist she'd ever met. "I put some blankets and some clothes in the pack. My dad's a little smaller than you, but a sweater is a sweater."

Patrick cracked open a bottle of beer and slurped it greedily. "Mmmm," he murmured.

Tragedy sat down and picked up *Dianetics,* paging through the book without reading it. Her hands needed to keep busy and she'd forgotten her Rubik's cube. "You don't care how I knew you were in here or why I'm, like, feeding and clothing you, or how come I'm even wandering around at night when I'm supposed to be at home eating drumsticks and dancing to *Saturday Night Fever?*"

Patrick watched her hands as they worked the pages of the book. "That's my book," he said.

Tragedy glared at him. "So?" She put the book down. "There, you happy?"

Patrick cracked open another beer.

"Did you know it was a leap year?" she demanded.

Patrick just sipped his beer.

"Freaky things happen in a leap year."

He shrugged his shoulders. Every day was pretty much the same to him.

She stood up. "Okay. Well, I guess I'm off. It's been real." She pulled the flap back in the doorway. "It's Thursday night, by the way. Thanksgiving. So relax. Enjoy. You've got, like, two or three more nights before the kids get back."

———

Not far from the yurt, Tom was locked in his room, painting. The Grannies had sold him enough E to last the weekend. He had six tabs left.

For a project of this size, floor space was key. He'd tipped both beds on end—he couldn't sleep when there was so much work to be done—but there was still hardly enough room for him to move around. The mini fridge in the corner was chock full of milk. That's all he needed. E and milk. Food and sleep and social interaction had become irrelevant, especially if the painting was going to be finished by next weekend.

He'd decided to do Shipley's portrait on small eight-by-ten prestretched canvases purchased at the college bookstore. He'd bought out their whole supply, all forty of them, and laid them on the floor on top of strips of double-sided tape to form one giant rectangular canvas. His aim was to complete the portrait exactly as he'd photographed it, head to toe, Macy's bag included. Then he'd shift around the canvasses and remove some entirely, so that the final product would look like one of those little puzzles where you move the squares around, after it had been scrambled up. So far he'd completed four canvasses—the two red squares that formed the lower half of the Macy's bag, and Shipley's breasts. Now he was working on her hair where it hung below the bag, spaghetti-length strips of plum and black and cream and tangerine.

"I feel it! I feel it!" he shouted, egging himself on. Naked, he squatted over the canvas and blotted his brush on his bare calf. "Nice and easy," he said, remembering that Nice 'n Easy was a brand of shampoo or hair color. He'd seen the ads on TV.

The phone rang out in the hall. It had been ringing all day. He was pretty sure it was his parents, but he couldn't very well talk to them when he had so much work to do. And he didn't trust himself to talk to Shipley. He was too excitable. Oh boy, did he want to kiss her! He'd already made out with her Polaroid.

He'd even tried to kiss his own penis, and found he wasn't flexible enough. Just this week of solitude—long enough to get the painting done—and he'd put the bed back where it belonged, let Shipley in, and show her how much he'd missed her.

He took a step back to admire his efforts, his jaw working as he gnawed the end of his paintbrush. Everything he'd painted before was bad because basically all he'd been doing was sending a big fuck-you message to Eliza, telling her to put some clothes on and stop annoying him. With this one he wasn't trying to make a statement or tell anyone anything. He was just showing what he saw. It wasn't about him, he was just the vehicle. On a journey. On a path to discovery. Of course he didn't know what he was discovering, but he'd know when he found it.

It was exactly like the Volkswagen ad when they used that crazy German word, *Fahrvergnügen*. It didn't really mean anything, but you knew you wanted your car to have it. *Fahrvergnügen* transformed the driving experience. When people looked at his painting, they would never be able to see things in the same way again. Everything would be imbued with color and beauty. Yellow would no longer be just plain yellow. Blue would no longer symbolize the sky or water. There was blue in Shipley's breasts and yellow on her thighs. The red Macy's bag wasn't a red Macy's bag anymore. It *was* the color red. He was going to change people's lives, or at least better them, one canvas square at a time.

He squatted down and smeared a tendril of grayish-purple paint on the canvas with his thumb. It might be nice, he thought, if she had a few tentacles mixed in with her hair.

15

ecember came, and it was as if Thanksgiving had never happened. The days were short. The nights were long. Students were getting nervous about midterms. Would cramming for Psychology damage their synapses? Was it possible to read *Moby-Dick* in one night? Would there be an essay or just multiple choice? Would exams be graded on a curve? The library was suddenly the most popular hangout on campus and the suggestion box in Coke's dining hall overflowed with pleas to *Make the coffee stronger!*

Nick still couldn't get into his room. Each morning after Nick showered, Tom was kind enough to toss some extra clothes out the door.

"It's only for the week," he promised. "And you'll be glad you made the sacrifice. You'll be *thanking* me."

Nick thought he'd go back to sleeping in the yurt, but it was too damned cold and dark, and he was already sort of over it. The honest truth was he'd built the yurt to impress his mom, and he hadn't even had a chance to tell her about it. He didn't really want to live out there anyway. Eliza had given him a camping stove, which was very thoughtful of her, but he hadn't even taken it out of the box.

He just had to face it, he'd never be like Laird Castle, no matter how hard he tried. Laird was hard-core, the type of guy Nick's mom would have shacked up with in college. She would have been delighted to sleep under the open roof flap, stargazing and toking up and expounding on the wonders of karma. But sleeping outdoors wasn't even safe—look what had happened to Laird. The common room had a TV, and the sofas were about as comfortable as the futon his mom had replaced his bed with. He could make do, as long as it was just for the week.

Tom stopped painting and left the room only for play rehearsal. He and Adam had the whole play memorized, and they were down to their last three rehearsals.

"I can't tell you how pleased I am," Professor Rosen gushed after their Wednesday night run-through in the auditorium. "Tom, I had my doubts about you at first, and I don't know how you've done it, but that was incredible. What'd you think, Nicholas?"

Nick was up on a ladder, adjusting the lights. He hadn't really paid attention to the rehearsal because he had absolutely no idea what he was doing. *The Zoo Story* was a one-act with only two actors who never strayed far from the park bench at center stage. He really only needed two spotlights. The problem was figuring out which ones. It didn't help that he was so high. The pot he'd stolen from his mom was pretty intense.

He sneezed once and then sneezed again. It was dusty up there in the rafters. "Great," he called back. "Definitely really great."

"I'm having a party after the play on Saturday," Adam told Tom. "You should come." He shoved his hands into the pockets of his wool pants. "There's going to be a keg."

Tom hadn't had a drink since he discovered ecstasy. He hadn't been to any parties either. Or eaten many meals. "Cool," he said, furiously working his jaw. His beltless, paint-spattered khaki pants hung a few inches below his boxers and his white undershirt clung to his half-starved stomach. His dark brown hair had grown out and stuck up in all directions. He looked nothing like the preppy Westchester boy his parents had dropped off in August.

"Are we done here?" he asked Professor Rosen. "Because I have a lot of work to do." He'd finished the top two-thirds of Shipley's portrait, but he still had the entire bottom third to do.

"Same time, same place tomorrow night and Friday. Don't forget," Professor Rosen reminded him. "And I like the disheveled look, but try to find something to wear without any paint on it," she called as Tom barreled toward the exit. "Jerry doesn't paint."

Adam remained onstage. "Shouldn't I wear a suit?" he asked. "Peter goes to the park from his job. He works in an office. Wouldn't he be wearing a suit?"

"Just wear whatever you have," Professor Rosen said. "He's sitting in the park. He'd probably take off his tie and his jacket. Just a nice white shirt and a pair of trousers and loafers would be fine. And maybe a suit jacket and tie to put down on the bench next to you."

The only suit Adam had ever owned was the Frankenstein suit he'd worn for Halloween three years running. And he'd never had any need for a tie. "Can't I borrow something from the costume department?"

Professor Rosen laughed. Dexter's theater department was tiny. Adam made them sound like the Metropolitan Opera. "You could ask your father," she suggested.

Adam nodded. His dad didn't wear ties either, but his mom's favorite store was called Family Clothes of Yesteryear, a used clothing store lovingly run out of a trailer beside the Baptist church in the next town. She could probably rustle up something there.

One of the doors in the back of the theater swung open. It was Shipley and Eliza, dressed all in black except for Eliza's hot pink earmuffs—long black coats, black boots, black gloves, and black wool hats. They looked like spies.

"Oh!" Shipley exclaimed when she saw Adam onstage. Her face flushed. "I'm so sorry. We were looking for someone else."

Ever since they'd returned to campus, she and Eliza had been fast friends. They dressed together in complementing colors. They ate together in the dining hall. They even peed together, giggling through the walls of the stalls.

It was Eliza's idea to make a game of finding Patrick. Of course it was Patrick who'd borrowed Shipley's car for days at a time, leaving those surly notes and storing food in the trunk. It was a wonder he hadn't left any books behind. He never went anywhere without a book—Carl Sagan's *Cosmos*, George Orwell's *1984*, *On the Road* by Jack Kerouac. He even carried around *Mein Kampf* for one long, scary week in Barbados. And he never took off his jacket. What a jerk. As a child Patrick was forever stealing Shipley's thunder. Now he was stealing her car.

Shipley found it completely infuriating. Patrick had always gotten all the attention with his hyperactive tantrums and need for specialists. He was ADD. He had sleep apnea. Chronic ear infections. Reflux. Doling out his medication alone took over breakfast and bedtime. And then there were the special private skiing instructors and running coaches because he was so good at sports. Five boarding schools, and he'd managed to get kicked out of every one. Meanwhile there Shipley was, the younger sister, trying not to cause any trouble or attract any attention.

Patrick didn't know her anymore. He'd never taken the time to get to know her. To him she was still the little girl he'd always ignored, teased, or outshined. More than anything, Shipley feared his presence would somehow cause her, out of sheer habit, to revert back to the demure simpleton she used to be. And her new life—the life she'd made for herself at Dexter—would be taken away from her.

They decided to lure him by displaying the clothes Shipley had bought for him on the front seat of the car. It didn't take long. They'd returned from Greenwich on Sunday night. Fifteen minutes later, the car was gone.

Tonight it was back.

"We'll just look everywhere until we find him," Eliza declared that night at dinner.

But Shipley wasn't so sure she wanted to find him. What would she do with him when she did? Still, she decided to play along because Eliza was so keen, and it was better than studying.

"Hello, Shipley," Professor Rosen called down to her from the stage. "You just missed a fabulous performance. But you'll be here for the real thing on Saturday of course."

"Definitely," Shipley agreed, blushing beneath Adam's steady gaze.

"Tom went back to the dorm," Nick called from atop his ladder. He sneezed. A shower of backlit germs rained down on the stage. "Hey, is he, like, lit up enough? Can you see him?"

Nick's earflap hat was askew. He looked very professional up on that ladder. Eliza stuck her chest out even though she was wearing her full-length black down coat. "I can see him fine." She turned to Shipley. "Hey, I forgot to tell you, Tom cut Portraiture today. He missed a good class too. It was so fucking awesome. I got to wear this snake they borrowed from the Bio lab. I felt like a fucking goddess."

Shipley was too busy staring back at Adam across the rows of seats to hear what Eliza was saying. His red hair shone in the hot white spotlight and his freckles danced around on his cheeks as he smiled at her.

"Hi," he said.

She opened her mouth and then closed it again. "I'm sorry," she said and spun around, using her entire body to force open the heavy black door.

"What the hell was that?" Eliza demanded, following Shipley into the Starbucks café. "Why'd you take off?"

"I don't know." Shipley put her hands on her knees and closed her eyes. She was out of breath even though she hadn't been running. She pulled a pack of cigarettes out of her coat pocket and lit one. "Patrick wasn't there anyway. Where else should we look?"

"Hey, you can't smoke in here!" the guy behind the counter called out.

Shipley tossed the smoldering cigarette into the trash. "I'd like a double shot of espresso," she told the guy. "You want anything?" she asked Eliza.

"Make that two." Eliza nudged Shipley with her elbow. "That guy Adam. You're boning him, aren't you?"

"No!" Shipley protested. She inhaled the pungent smell of freshly ground espresso beans. "Well, not really."

Eliza grinned. "I knew it! You're such a fucking slut!" She held up her palm for Shipley to slap. "I love that you're fucking Tom over. Put it here, Slutcakes."

Shipley grinned weakly. Eliza's distaste for Tom had become a constant joke between them. "I'm not fucking anyone over," she insisted. "I kissed Adam once. End of story. Tom is my boyfriend. You'll see. As soon as he's finished with his crazy top secret art project, we'll all hang out together."

"Motherfucking fuck!" Eliza pointed out the tall windows of the Student Union. Shipley's black Mercedes pulled out of the parking lot across Homeward Avenue and swept downhill toward the interstate.

"That's okay," Shipley said, relieved. She had enough to think about without having to worry about Patrick. "He can't go far. There's hardly any gas in the tank."

"You know if you really don't want him to take your car, you could keep the keys in your pocket instead of leaving them on the tire," Eliza suggested. "Then we could probably catch him."

"You're probably right," Shipley responded. Maybe this time Patrick wouldn't come back. He'd figure out a way to get more gas and just keep going.

They paid for their espressos and drank them on the spot. Shipley shivered violently. The rush of caffeine had given her the chills. She started toward the exit. "I need a cigarette. Come on."

They headed down the walkway toward Coke. The Dexter chorale was gathered on the steps of the chapel, singing Christmas songs. *"O little town of Bethlehem, how still we see thee lie...."* A steady stream of students trudged across the frozen quad, from the campus's three dining halls to the grand Greek revival–style library, to begin the age-old ritual of cramming for exams. Tragedy was outside Coke, taping a neon orange flyer to a lamppost. Dressed in her father's gray one-piece welder's suit and a red-and-white-striped pom-pommed ski hat, she looked like a character from a book by Dr. Seuss.

"Nice earmuffs," she called out. "Hey, Shipley, have you seen Adam?"

"He's in the auditorium. They're just finishing up." Shipley thought it best not to explain that she had barely spoken to Adam. Tragedy would not approve.

"Good." Tragedy smoothed down the flyer. "Then he can drive my ass home." She cocked an eyebrow at Shipley. "Unless you guys want to give me a ride."

Eliza snorted. Shipley glared at her. "Sorry, my car's . . . unavailable."

Tragedy slung her hand through the roll of tape like a bracelet. "Okay. Well, see you Saturday," she said. "And don't forget to bring a blanket. It's supposed to be warm as summer."

Tragedy's long legs propelled her toward the Student Union. Shipley stared after her. Eliza went over to examine the flyer.

"It's a party," she said. "Saturday night. The flyer's sort of old-fashioned. It's kind of cute. It says there's going to be refreshments and horseshoes and sheep-tipping." She giggled. "It also says to bring a date." She turned back to Shipley. "Who're you gonna bring?"

16

Even the most bucolic college suffers from bouts of nerves, when tension takes hold and rocks its pretty brick buildings on their foundations. This biannual occurrence is also known as review week. Students slog through cram sessions or camp out in the library in a vain attempt to acquire an entire semester's worth of knowledge in only seven days. If they'd cut class or slacked off and forgotten to read certain critical texts, this is their opportunity to catch up.

Clusters of students could be found huddled in Dexter's Starbucks café, madly quizzing each other and pumping themselves full of caffeine.

"Describe the events of D-Day."

"What is the area of the region bounded by the curves $y = x^2$ and $y = 1$?"

"Briefly describe one of Little Hans's dreams or fantasies from Freud's famous study."

"Define *Logos, ethos,* and *pathos.*"

"Which type of mineral deposits are segregated by density?"

Becky, Kelly, and Brianna, that inseparable threesome from the all-girls dorm, had promised each other to give up carbs until break. These unlucky girls had fallen prey to the dreaded Freshman Fifteen. Their pink sweatshirts clung to their newly fleshed-out forms, the hems stretched and frayed from being tugged down unflatteringly over the rear ends of their obscenely tight jeans.

"I could kill for a scone right now," Becky would moan, staring into the glass case at Starbucks.

"Be strong," Kelly would tell her loyally.

"Only one more week," Brianna would remind them. "Think how much better those scones will taste after exams are over."

"Think how thin we'll be," Kelly would add.

"Maybe Lucas will notice me then," Becky would say miserably.

"Quiet!" someone would shout. "Can't you see we're studying here?"

Apart from pastries, academics seemed to be the only thing on everyone's mind. Well, almost everyone.

Portraiture I's open studio began at 4 P.M. on Saturday, only an hour before curtain time for *The Zoo Story*. Most of the paintings hanging in the cavernous art studio were nudes of Eliza in all manner of erotic poses. Eliza had expanded her job description from model to wine steward for the occasion. Her heavy black boots resounded on the wood floor as she tromped around the studio pouring white wine into plastic cups.

Candace and Andrew Ferguson stood in front of their son's gigantic portrait of his girlfriend. They'd driven up from Bedford that morning and had arrived on campus only minutes before.

"Is that a squid in her hair?" Mrs. Ferguson whispered to her husband. "And why are her teeth blue? Or are those her fingers?"

Mr. Ferguson furrowed his bushy gray eyebrows. "Where's Tom?" he demanded.

"His play starts in an hour. I'm sure we'll see him after," Mrs. Ferguson soothed. "Here's his girlfriend now. Be nice," she warned. "She's probably embarrassed to have her naked body all ... *rearranged* like this. Especially in front of us."

Tom's mother was under the assumption that Shipley had already seen Tom's painting. Not so.

"Hello." Shipley kissed each of Tom's parents on the cheek before turning to the portrait. "Oh," she gasped and cupped her face with her hands.

She needn't have worried about her thighs, or even that she was naked. Except for the neat white card tacked beneath the painting—"Shipley, December 1992"—she was virtually unrecognizable. Nothing was where it ought to have been and nothing was the color it was in nature. Her belly button was a green eye lodged between her breasts. One breast faced forward, an overripe yellow gourd, the other lilted to the side, a shriveled plum. Her legs were black talons sprouting from her stomach, her hair a mass of purple tentacles. And, in the middle of everything, an inexplicable red Macy's bag—the only thing left unchanged.

"You made it!" Eliza bounded over and kissed Tom's mother and father on the cheek. She poured each of them a glass of wine.

"What do you think?" Shipley asked her roommate, nodding at Tom's painting.

"Well, it could be worse," Eliza said. "At least you can't see your cooter. Or maybe you can, but no one will ever know that's what it is."

"It's very different," Mrs. Ferguson offered.

"A major contribution." Tom's art teacher, Mr. Zanes, sidled up to them, sucking on a lollipop. Greasy tendrils of white hair clung to his drooping ears. "Shows you what can happen if you allow yourself to let go."

"So this is good?" Mr. Ferguson frowned at the painting.

Mr. Zanes nodded, the lollipop bulged inside his cheek. "I would say so."

"We should be proud?" Tom's mother asked.

"I'm proud," Shipley offered. Just because she didn't like the painting didn't mean it wasn't good.

Mrs. Ferguson touched her elbow. "We're going to the Lobster Shack for dinner after the play. We're hoping you'll come too."

The Lobster Shack was a Maine fixture where Dexter students took their parents to gorge on whole lobsters, baked clams, and French fries, and returned stinking of fish and grease. Shipley's mother wouldn't dream of going there. Too fattening, too smelly, too déclassé.

"I'd love to," Shipley said.

Meanwhile, Tom was getting ready for the play in the only way he knew how. The Grannies had run out of E. Stealing ether from the Chemistry lab was the next best thing.

"Ether is different," Liam warned. "It doesn't last. And you have to really go to town to feel the effects. It's a short-term out-of-body super-high."

"Sounds fine," Tom said. All he knew was he could not stand up in front of an audience, pretend to get stabbed, and smear himself with fake blood, without the aid of chemicals.

"The Robin Hood thing is what I like about it," Grover enthused on their way across campus. "Stealing from the rich and giving to . . . us."

"Don't worry, Geoff knows what he's doing," Wills whispered as the four boys tiptoed into Crowley, Dexter's science building. The building was unlocked, suggesting that there were other life forms on the premises.

Geoff Walker, ether-knapping expert, was waiting for them. Tom had only ever seen the pale, wasted, ponytailed Geoff jogging the five-mile loop around campus or scraping the wax off Granny Smith apples in the dining hall. It was almost incomprehensible that he ever did anything else.

Tom pressed the button for the elevator. Geoff shook his anorexic head gravely. "That is not your destiny," he said, leading the way to the fire stairs.

The ether was kept in a locked storeroom in the largest lab, on the fourth floor. Geoff had the key.

"I cut keys with my nail clippers," he explained.

"Can we hurry this up?" Tom said. "I have to be onstage in half an hour."

Inside the storeroom, two sizable brown glass bottles stood waiting on the shelf. The label read "Diethyl Ether," and beneath that was a picture of red flames with the word "flammable" in black.

"No smoking," Geoff warned. He removed one bottle from the shelf, unscrewed the top, and took a whiff. "Ah," he said, smiling for the first time. He recapped the bottle and handed it to Tom. The other bottle he wrapped in a spare white lab coat and placed gingerly into his backpack.

"If you want to feel it while you're up there, you've got to do it right before you go on," Wills advised as he led the way back downstairs. "Just pour some on a rag and inhale."

Tom held onto the bottle in his pocket. "Got it," he said. He'd been on edge all day. Hopefully this would help.

"Here, you can use this," Grover said when they were out-side. He removed the red bandanna from his shaved head and handed it to Tom. "Good luck, son."

Wills gave Tom a high five. "You're the shit."

Liam pulled Tom into a bear hug. "Break a leg."

"*Bonne chance,*" said Geoff.

Tom headed off on his own toward the Student Union. The setting sun looked like Tang-flavored crude oil, dripping from the treetops. It was already December, but the weather was freakishly warm. The quad was littered with tired, overcaffein-ated students sprawled on top of their discarded parkas, taking a break from cramming to enjoy the sunset. The day's last gun-shots resounded in the woods beyond campus as hunters all over Maine enjoyed the weather and brought in their seasonal quota of deer, quail, grouse, pheasant, fox, coyote, squirrel, rac-coon, woodchuck, and rabbit. At midday the thermometer had skyrocketed to seventy degrees. Around midnight the tempera-ture was set to drop, and a heavy snowfall would commence.

For his costume, Tom had settled on a plain white under-shirt, a pair of black suit pants without a belt, and his battered Stan Smith tennis sneakers with no socks. Jerry seemed like the kind of guy who would pick up a pair of suit pants from the Salvation Army because he thought they would last a long time and they cost only fifteen cents. Tom thought he looked sort of like Marlon Brando in one of his old movies—Brando with a big bottle of diethyl ether in his pocket. He quickened his pace. He'd have to hurry if he wanted to get thoroughly intoxicated before the curtain rose.

Out in the Student Union visitors parking lot, Adam leaned into the open passenger-side window of his parents' pickup and stole a french fry out of the greasy McDonald's bag Tragedy had been carrying around with her all day.

"I can't believe you said there'd be horseshoes," he muttered.

Tragedy rolled her eyes. "The party will rock. You'll see."

Eli Gatz switched off the ignition and pulled on his droopy gray mustache. His blue eyes were wide and excited-looking. Adam could tell his father was nervous for him. Acting in a play was not something Eli had taken on during his tenure at Dexter. In fact, he hadn't taken on much except Ellen and tab upon tab of LSD.

"Son, why don't you run in and get ready?" Eli said. "We'll stay here while your sister finishes her snack."

Ellen sat in the middle of the pickup's crowded cab, her stocky legs straddling the gearbox. "Her revolting snack," she said, holding her nose.

"That's what you get for raising me organic," Tragedy quipped, stuffing her face.

Ellen leaned across Tragedy's lap and admired her handsome son. Adam wore a gently worn charcoal gray 1960s J. Press suit, courtesy of Family Clothes of Yesteryear. She'd bought a genuine raccoon fur coat for herself at the same time, just for a hoot.

"You look very smart, hon. We're taking off for your Uncle Laurie's right after the play. So break a leg, and have a wonderful party, but try to keep it in the barn," she warned. "Or trash the house and get a girl pregnant—just don't come whining to me about it."

"Don't worry, Mom," Adam said.

A group of students headed inside the Student Union.

"Stay gold, Pony Balls." Tragedy made the sign of the cross in the air with a french fry.

"Okay, see you guys." Adam buttoned the middle button of his suit jacket and stepped away from the pickup, his body stiff with nerves. He and Tom really did have the play memorized, and Professor Rosen had been all smiles at rehearsal, but it was bound to feel different in front of a live audience—in front of *her.*

Oddly enough, their nightly rehearsals this past week had been almost therapeutic. Every night he got right up close to his jealousy and resentment instead of moping alone in his room. And each night Tom seemed more and more unhinged, muttering to himself and voraciously chewing gum, with paint all over his oversized, expensive clothes. Tom's behavior gave Adam just the tiniest smidgen of hope. Wouldn't Shipley prefer to be with someone clean and sane?

Professor Rosen was waiting for him backstage with two copies of *The Zoo Story* tucked under her arm. She wore a black turtleneck and pleated black corduroys. Her shiny short brown hair was parted on the side and combed neatly behind her ears. She looked very theatrical.

"Peter! You're here." The professor had gotten into the habit of addressing them by their stage names.

"Adam. It's Adam."

"Yes, well. Jerry is here too. So as soon as you're ready I'll go out and introduce you."

Tom was seated on the wooden park bench where Adam was supposed to sit throughout the play, holding a red bandanna over his mouth and nose. Eyes closed, he inhaled deeply.

"Are you okay?" Adam asked.

Tom nodded, keeping his eyes closed. He inhaled again. Adam thought he could smell paint thinner.

"I'm going to introduce you now," Professor Rosen said. She held up the copies of the play. "If for any reason you'd feel more comfortable reading from the text, that's fine too."

Adam and Tom shook their heads.

"Well, just know I have these, if you get into trouble." The professor blew them a kiss. "Good luck, boys."

Tom stood up abruptly and left the stage. Adam took a seat on the bench, his shoulders slumped. The lights went out. A single beam shone upon the red velvet curtain. Inside the glass-fronted lighting booth at the back of the modern, three-hundred-seat auditorium, Nick sneezed explosively.

Perched in one of the ergonomically designed front row seats, a beaming Professor Blanche sat with a sleeping Beetle tied to her chest with a yard of hemp fabric bought at the Common Ground Fair in Unity. There was a smattering of applause as Professor Rosen walked onto the black lacquered stage to greet the packed house.

"Good evening, ladies and gentlemen. Thank you for coming. It's my pleasure to introduce two very talented freshmen actors, Tom Ferguson and Adam Gatz, performing *The Zoo Story* by Edward Albee. I read the play for the first time in college—a hundred and ten years ago—and it's stuck with me ever since."

Body twitching and saliva oozing from the corners of his mouth, Tom peeked at the audience from offstage. His parents were sitting in the front row. Shipley sat next to his mom, holding his mom's hand. Eliza sat next to Shipley. The three of them whispered back and forth, giggling like nervous schoolgirls.

Professor Rosen bobbed up and down on the balls of her feet. Her hair was a helmet of copper beneath the spotlight.

"My seven-month-old has a thing for bubbles," she said. "I blow them for him until my mouth hurts and I can't take it anymore. He watches them, floating around in the air and bursting. Sometimes two bubbles bump into each other and float around together for a while until they both burst. This play is sort of like that—two totally separate bubbles colliding and floating around together, until they burst." She clapped her hands together. "Pop!"

The spotlight dimmed. Tom staggered against the closed curtain so violently there was a murmur from the crowd. He shut his eyes, blacking out for maybe three seconds, maybe three hours, maybe an entire week. The curtain opened. The play had begun.

Adam took off his suit jacket, folded it carefully down the middle, and laid it on the bench. He loosened his tie, waited a few seconds, then pulled it off completely and laid it down on top of the jacket. For a minute he just sat there, looking out at the audience as if it were a baseball game. Shipley was in the front row. He scooted back on the bench and looked up at the ceiling. He took a deep breath and closed his eyes. Then he picked up his magazine, which happened to be the December issue of *A Muse*, Dexter's literary journal, hot off the press. Shipley had written one of the poems. It was in the table of contents: "The Years Between Us," a poem by Shipley Gilbert, page 11.

Tom swaggered in from offstage, shoulders twitching, fingers flapping, knees all wobbly, and an actual river of spit gleaming on his stubbly chin. "I've been to the zoo," he slurred.

Adam was busy looking for page 11. He didn't even look up.

"I said, I've been to the zoo. MISTER, I'VE BEEN TO THE ZOO!"

Tom's voice was wet and throaty. His words were garbled and hardly intelligible. A few people in the audience tittered nervously.

Adam looked up from Shipley's poem. He was pretty sure he'd only understood what Tom was saying because he knew the play so well. "Hm? . . . What? . . . I'm sorry, were you talking to me?"

Tom did his best to keep his eyes open. He couldn't believe his parents were here. And Shipley, with her face showing and her body parts in all the right places. She looked sweet and unfamiliar, which would have added to her allure had he not been so completely out of his head. Ether was nothing like ecstasy. It was not a touchy-feely sort of drug. It did not arouse the senses. The only thing aroused in him was the screaming pace of his heart. He was *alive*—but barely.

He wiped the spit off his chin and waggled his head from side to side to keep from blacking out again. Honestly, the play gave him a hard-on every time he performed it. It was as if it had been written for him. He could feel it—he could feel it all *over*—and even though his mouth wasn't quite working right, the audience was fucking in love with him, he could tell.

The boys roared through the first half of the play, easy. Adam kept his eyes on Tom, forcing himself not to look at Shipley. During the funny parts, he could hear his parents' and Tragedy's hooting laughter coming from way in the back.

Tom hawked up a big ball of phlegm and spat it out right there on the stage before beginning his monologue.

"ALL RIGHT. THE STORY OF JERRY AND THE DOG. What I'm going to tell you has something to do with how sometimes it's necessary to go a long distance out of the way in order to come back a short distance correctly. . . ."

He went on to tell the story of how he, Jerry, had a problem with his landlady's dog. Jerry lived in a crummy boardinghouse in Manhattan, and this dog, who was black, all black, except for his constant red erection, growled at Jerry whenever he came and went. First, Jerry bought the dog hamburgers in an attempt to win him over. When that failed, he poisoned the hamburgers. The dog got sick but he didn't die, and their relationship actually changed for the better. Finally they understood and respected each other.

At one point during the monologue, Tom got to say the words "malevolence with an erection." Saying it felt awesome, like there were fireworks exploding out of his teeth. He couldn't believe he got extra credit for doing this. Extra credit for talking about erections out loud in front of an audience—fucking awesome.

From up high in his booth, Nick had a perfect view of the front row. He watched as Eliza picked the cuticles of both thumbs until they bled. She yanked at a thread in her black tights until it formed a large hole and then she picked at a scab inside the hole. She chewed on the ends of her dark hair. She clenched her fists together until her knuckles turned white. Sometimes she smiled. Eliza was a minor celebrity now that naked portraits of her were on display all over the art studio. Beside her Shipley looked very small and blond.

Tom was outrageously good. He stole the show, pacing and gnashing his teeth, spitting and gesticulating. Adam wasn't bad either. He was the perfect example of the status quo—someone who doesn't speak his mind and never steps outside the box. It was nice, how Peter was actually helping Jerry by sitting there, listening, just like he, Nick, was helping the creep who'd been sleeping in his yurt by not calling campus security.

First there was the pile of blankets and clothes. Then there was the book, *Dianetics*, which Nick had ignored. He was tired of seeking solace in platitudes. How could you get inner peace from an outer source? Then there was the stove Eliza had given him, which Nick had left unopened in its box. He preferred to eat in the dining hall, where he could fill his plate as many times as he liked, where there were croutons and eight different choices of salad dressing. He didn't even have to do the dishes. A few days ago though, he'd gone out to check on the yurt and found the stove all set up. A still-warm can of SpaghettiOs lolled on the floor. Well, at least someone was using it.

Tom had just finished his long dog monologue. Now he and Adam were fighting over the bench. Tom pushed Adam and Adam fell on the floor.

Shipley squeezed Tom's mother's hand. "Watch out!" she cried. "He's got a knife!"

Everyone in the audience craned their necks to look. A few girls giggled. Eliza nudged Shipley with her elbow. "None of this is real, stupid," she whispered in Shipley's ear. Tom was a surprisingly kickass actor. His voice didn't even sound the same. And Adam was pretty decent too.

The knife was on the floor. "Pick it up," Tom taunted Adam. "Pick it up and fight with me."

Shipley covered her eyes with her free hand. Her heart was racing. She peeked through her fingers. Adam bent down and picked up the knife. She began to shake uncontrollably at the thought of Adam stabbing Tom. She held her breath. Oh, it was perfect. It was just what she wanted! No, it wasn't. Oh, God, what was wrong with her? Her whole body trembled violently and she let out a yelp of nervous laughter.

Tom lunged forward and impaled himself on the knife. This was the scene he'd been worried about. A packet of fake blood was taped to his stomach. He felt the cold redness ooze out of the packet, staining his shirt. He gagged, staggered backward, and fell against the bench. Adam ran offstage. Tom was dying. The lights came up. The play was over.

The audience rose to its feet, hooting and applauding. Blanche stuck her pinkies into her mouth and wolf-whistled. From inside his hemp cocoon, Beetle let out a jubilant squawk.

Tom's mother squeezed Shipley's forearm. "He was marvelous, wasn't he?" she cried. "Oh, I'm so glad we came!"

"Bravo!" Tom's father shouted. "Bravo!"

"Atta boy!" Ellen Gatz yelled loudly from the back.

Up in the lighting booth, Nick sneezed his approval. His aim with the spotlight wasn't the best, but he'd managed to muddle through.

Tom lay where he'd fallen, having blacked out once more. Professor Rosen led Adam back onstage to take a bow.

Adam knelt down to murmur in Tom's ear. "Hey. Time to get up."

Tom remained where he'd fallen. Shipley covered her mouth with her hand. He never could handle the sight of blood. Had he fainted for real?

Tom could see himself as a baby, crawling around in his mother's flower beds. He saw the baseball his father had given him for his tenth birthday, signed by Reggie Jackson. He saw the French toast he and his brother made for his mom every Mother's Day. They put nutmeg in the syrup. He saw his driving instructor, with the ridiculous rack. He saw his cap and gown from graduation. They moved their tassels from the right side to the left after Principal Doogie Howser handed out the diplomas. Man, that dude was small. He saw Shipley take off her clothes and get into bed. She kissed his lips, his ear.

"Get up, Tom," Adam said again. "The play's over. We're done."

Tom reeled back to semiconsciousness. The crowd roared as he got on all fours and climbed unsteadily to his feet. His white shirt was stained red. His eyes were slits, his face ashen, his entire body drenched in sweat. He slung his arm around Adam's waist, staggered sideways and slung his other arm around Professor Rosen's shoulders. Supporting Tom on either side, the professor and Adam bowed together before dragging him off-stage.

Shipley was clapping so hard her hands hurt.

"That was pretty good," Eliza allowed. "Although I'm not so sure what it says about your taste in men."

"Bravo!" Tom's father called out once more. "Bravo!"

17

Second best to earning a lot of money and spending it is finding a lot of money and spending it. Patrick had taken the car three nights ago and still hadn't returned it. Lucky for him, his sister had left her wallet on the front seat with $135 in cash and her American Express card inside. Her name was unusual enough for people to think it might belong to a guy, and copying her signature was easy. She wrote like a sixth grader. First he bought a whole tankful of premium unleaded gasoline. Then he booked a room at the Holiday Inn. He'd dined on room service for the last three days, watching pay-per-view and eating chicken Kiev. But the Lobster Shack was legendary. He'd always wanted to try it. So he soaked in the tub, using up all the shampoo and conditioner and bubble bath the hotel provided, changed into some of his new clothes, drove to the restaurant, and snagged a quiet table in the back.

The Lobster Shack was an old salty dog of a place, with the requisite dark wood, fishing nets, ropes, and anchors. What made it unique was that the restaurant was perched on the bank of the Kennebec River, which rushed by the back windows with dark, liquid ferocity.

"You want baked potato or fries with that?"

"Baked potato."

"Salad or coleslaw?"

"Salad, please. And chocolate milk, if you have it."

"Yoo-hoo okay?"

Patrick munched his house salad with bleu cheese dressing and slurped his Yoo-hoo. One of the tenets of *Dianetics* was that simple pleasures like eating a good meal, kissing a pretty girl, enjoying a game of baseball are a necessity. One can survive without pleasure, but without pleasure life is not really worth living. To him that made a lot of sense. And it seemed to him that the Lobster Shack was full of simple pleasures.

He flipped through the pages of the magazine he'd found in the car. It was Dexter's literary journal. Shipley had written one of the poems.

The Years Between Us

My brother, the one in the looney bin,
Holds his arms raised up
to keep his balance, hands
in fists as he creeps,
crouching like a giant in a crawl space.

I imitate him as a joke to warn him.
I say, "You look funny."
He responds with secrets in his voice:
"I have traveled a thousand light-years today."

Funny that she'd chosen to write about a time devoid of simple pleasures, when he was only just barely surviving. It was after he'd been kicked out of boarding school again. This time he'd stolen a bicycle from one of the deans. Instead of taking him home, his parents took him to Mount Sinai hospital in Manhattan for a full psychiatric evaluation. He was there for two weeks, in a private room in the psychiatric ward. Each day he was interviewed extensively by doctors and put on various medications. He watched *Wheel of Fortune* in the TV room and ate his meals, family style, with the other lunatics. He couldn't open his window or wear shoes with laces.

He wasn't sure how long his parents intended to keep him there, so one afternoon he walked down the back stairs and out of the building. No one stopped him. He walked across Fifth Avenue and into Central Park, grateful that it was only October and still not too cold to be wandering around in only a hospital gown and bare feet. In the park, he found another bicycle and rode it out of town, all the way home to Greenwich.

He took the back roads, foraging for food and clothes in Dumpsters along the way, amazed by what people threw out and delighting in the freedom to take what he wanted and move about unseen in the shadows behind buildings. The first thing he found was a man's pink dress shirt, still in the plastic from the dry cleaners. He'd had a thing for pirates when he was a little boy. Pirates stole stuff to live and stay free, just like he was doing now. It was on that bike ride, wearing that pink dress shirt, that he became Pink Patrick. It wasn't a gay thing. It was his pirate name.

"Surf and turf medium well with a baked potato," the waitress announced, presenting him with a heaping platter of steak and lobster claws. In the middle of the table was a red plastic basket containing the metal tools used for cracking open the shells of lobsters, a plastic bib, and a pile of Handi Wipes. He was going to need them.

It was Saturday night and the restaurant was busy. "I just need to sit down!" a guy yelled from across the room. Patrick looked up from his dinner. It was Shipley's boyfriend, with Shipley and two middle-aged people who must have been the boyfriend's parents.

"Drink some water, Tom," Mrs. Ferguson told her son. "You're probably dehydrated."

"He's drunk," Mr. Ferguson countered. He raised his hand to signal the waitress. "I'll have a scotch on the rocks, and my wife would like a glass of white wine. Chardonnay, or Pinot Grigio, or whatever you have." He glanced at Shipley. "Make that two. And a glass of milk for the boy."

Tom put his head down on the table. "Oh wow," he moaned. "Wow!"

"Let's get some food in you," Mrs. Ferguson said as she perused the menu. "You always love a nice big lobster."

"Why don't we share one?" Shipley suggested, placing her hand on Tom's knee. She and Tom hadn't seen each other since before Thanksgiving. It was a relief just to be near him, even if he wasn't quite himself.

Tom flinched at her touch. His pant legs were damp with sweat. "I'm not really hungry," he slurred.

Mrs. Ferguson sniffed her wine and took a gingerly sip. "What is that dreadful smell?"

"It's fish, dear," Mr. Ferguson said, tipping back his glass. "This is a fish restaurant."

"No. It's a chemical smell," Mrs. Ferguson argued as she sniffed the air. "Like formaldehyde or paint."

Shipley could smell it too. She'd smelled it on the way over, in the backseat of the Fergusons' Audi. It was coming from Tom. She wondered if it were possible to do so much ecstasy that your sweat smelled like chemicals. In fact, she'd been so distracted by Tom's odor, and by his behavior in general, that she hadn't even noticed her car parked outside the Lobster Shack.

Tom's parents ordered two lobsters for everyone to share, a basket of fries, garlic bread, and fish chowder to start. Tom's head was still on the table. He appeared to be asleep.

"Tom?" Shipley leaned down to whisper in his ear. Her lips brushed his hair. "We're in a restaurant."

Tom turned his head and kissed her on the mouth. His lips tasted terrible, like salt and rubbing alcohol and bleach. Shipley pushed him away, blushing. "I think he's okay," she told his parents.

"Drink your milk, son," Mr. Ferguson commanded and gulped down his scotch.

Tom sat up and stared at the tall glass of cool milk. Milk had always seemed so appealing to him before—he couldn't get enough of it—but now the idea of drinking it seemed completely foreign to him. The idea of doing anything except breathing in more ether vapors did not excite him at all. The bottle was in his coat pocket, with Grover's bandanna. He could just slip off to the men's room and—

"I mean it now," Mr. Ferguson said firmly.

Tom did as he was told. The milk was lukewarm and felt furry going down. The waitress brought their chowder. Chunks of white fish floated in a gelatinous creamy stew.

"Now eat your soup," Mrs. Ferguson said. "It looks delicious. I don't know what they feed you up here, but you're wasting away to nothing." She shook her head. "We used to worry about putting on weight at college." She smiled at Shipley and took a sip of wine. "Just be sure to get your vitamins, both of you. You're still growing."

Shipley picked up her spoon and tasted the soup. "It's very good," she confirmed. She tied a plastic bib around Tom's neck, dipped her spoon into the bowl, and offered it to him. "Here, taste."

Tom's trembling lips parted and he allowed her to feed him the soup. It was salty and hot and he hadn't eaten in days. "More," he murmured, leaving his own spoon untouched. "Please?"

From across the room, Patrick watched his sister spoon-feeding her boyfriend like he was some kind of overgrown baby. It was sort of hypocritical of her to write a poem about how nutso *he* was when her own boyfriend couldn't even hold a spoon. The guy was like a giant version of a doll she used to have, the one that ate applesauce and then crapped it out into its little doll potty. Real Live Baby, or whatever the hell it was called. She looked happy, feeding him. So happy she had no idea she was being watched. Once he'd decided to veer off the usual get-up, go-to-school, play-sports, eat-dinner, watch-Carson, Monday-through-Friday, A.M.-P.M. path, he'd become completely invisible, at least to most people, most of the time. Definitely to his sister.

Half his surf and turf remained on the platter, untouched. That was the thing about eating a big meal when you're not used to eating much. He just couldn't get it all down. He signaled the waitress and requested a doggie bag. He thought about getting up and asking the boyfriend's parents for directions, pretending he didn't know his sister, that he was just some visiting dweeb from Connecticut. But then he chickened out. Spying on her was only fun when she had no idea he was there.

Or maybe she did know and she just wasn't letting on. He'd

found a whole bag of men's clothes from the Darien Sports Shop in the front seat of the car. He was wearing some of them right now. Not that he needed them. That girl who'd brought food and clothes to him in that big tent over Thanksgiving had pretty much set him up, although the stuff from the Darien Sports Shop was nicer.

He reread his sister's poem. What if she knew he was around and the poem was supposed to be some kind of message? He stared at her over the top of the journal, sending out telepathic messages the best way he knew how. *I'm right here, can you see me?* Without a glance in Patrick's direction, his sister wiped off her boyfriend's mouth, removed a drinking straw from its wrapper and stuck it into his glass of milk. Doggie bag tucked under his arm, Patrick stood up, put on his new black hat and gloves, and left the restaurant, brushing past the back of her chair as he went.

Mrs. Ferguson was trying very hard not to let Tom's odd behavior ruin the meal. "So how do you like school?" she asked Shipley.

Shipley wiped the chowder drool off Tom's lower lip and then offered him another spoonful. She took a sip of wine, wishing she could smoke.

"It's funny how you come to college and just sort of fall in with people," she mused. "People you never would have expected to fall in with."

"And have you two fallen in with a good crowd?" Mrs. Ferguson asked, frowning at her son.

Shipley crossed her legs and then uncrossed them again. She wouldn't exactly call Tom and Nick and Eliza a crowd. They were more like a focus group, although she wasn't sure what they were supposed to be focusing on.

"Yes. I have some nice new friends." She crossed her legs again and ate a spoonful of chowder with the same spoon she was using to feed Tom. It was hearty stuff. She licked her lips, gaining courage. "I just think it's strange how you wind up getting involved with people and, you know, pursuing different avenues than you ever would have otherwise, because of these early connections, the friends you make your first day here. I mean, what if I hadn't even signed up for orientation and met Tom that first day? Or what if I lived in a different dorm or was a day student?" She thought of Adam.

Mr. Ferguson had finished his drink and was trying to get the waitress's attention.

"But you're happy with the way things are?" Mrs. Ferguson asked. She seemed genuinely to care.

Shipley smiled at Tom. His eyes were closed, but he was still eating. "So far so good."

Mr. Ferguson had two more rounds of scotch. Then the fries and lobsters arrived with the nostril-penetrating odor of hot, fishy grease. Tom had eaten Shipley's entire bowl of soup and half of his own, although he still had not uttered a word.

"How about some claw meat, son?" Mr. Ferguson suggested. "You love the claws."

Shipley picked up the cracking tool and wedged a lobster claw inside it. She squeezed the tool between her fingers, cracking the shell. A geyser of clear juice spattered her plate. Using the tiny fork provided, she fished the meat out of the shell and dipped it into a bowl of melted butter. She held the fork up to Tom's lips. He opened his eyes and stared at the dripping, quivering, coral-colored meat with a dazed expression.

"It looks delicious," his mother said encouragingly.

"Just a little bite?" Shipley said.

Tom furrowed his eyebrows and wrinkled his nose, as if he were about to sneeze. Then he opened his mouth and vomited all over the table.

Mr. Ferguson pushed back his chair. "Jesus Christ, son," he sputtered.

Mrs. Ferguson ripped open a Handi Wipe and dabbed at her sweater. "Maybe he has food poisoning. We'd better get him out of here."

Shipley was already on her feet. "I think he's just really tired." All Tom needed was a glass of water with some Alka-Seltzer and some sleep. It occurred to her that once she got him tucked safely into bed she could drive out to Adam's party and spend the rest of the evening making connections with people she'd never had a chance to meet because she'd been too busy with Tom. And of course Adam would be there.

It was getting colder. Mrs. Ferguson drove them back. Adam's party must have been a success because the Dexter quad was deserted. Even Tom's dorm was quiet. A lone exchange student from Japan sat in the common room watching a videotaped episode of *Northern Exposure*. Everyone else, it seemed, was off campus. It was a good thing too, because Tom's trip from his parents' car to his dorm room was not a pretty sight.

Tom staggered and wrapped his arms around his mother's waist. Despite the bib, the front of the white dress shirt his mother had brought for him to put on after the play was tie-dyed with vomit.

"I love you, Mom," he mumbled.

"We'll have to throw his clothes away," Mrs. Ferguson commented as she staggered under her son's weight.

Shipley took hold of Tom's elbow. "Come on. Let's get you to you room." She reached inside Tom's pants pocket for his key.

"Hey, stop it. That tickles!" he gasped.

Mr. Ferguson held open the door. "You get him settled. I'm just going to buy him a cola from the vending machine. And I think I'll make a quick phone call while I'm at it."

The room was a mess of old paint tubes, coffee cans full of dirty water, empty milk cartons, and lolling paintbrushes. Nick's bed was still upended and the linoleum floor was tacky with spilled paint. Tom collapsed onto his bed. Shipley removed his sneakers while Mrs. Ferguson peeled off his soiled black pants.

"I've been to the zoo," Tom murmured with his eyes closed.

"Now your shirt," Shipley instructed.

"Come on," Mrs. Ferguson coaxed. "Help us out a little, Tommy."

They succeeded in stripping him down to his underwear and tucking him under his quilt.

"I'm glad to see he's using the bedding I ordered," Mrs. Ferguson said, standing back to watch her son sleep.

Mr. Ferguson pushed open the door and grimaced at the sight of the messy room. "I spoke to that professor. She said he's just plain exhausted. Said he's locked himself in his room all week trying to get that damned painting done."

He stood in the doorway, unwilling to walk all the way into the room. His mouth was drawn down at the corners, and his usually neat gray hair had sprung up on one side. He looked tired and disoriented, like someone who'd been through an ordeal—a storm at sea or a car accident.

He looked at his watch and then back at Tom. "We were

planning on waking up at the crack of dawn tomorrow to head back," he went on. He shook his head and stamped his loafered foot on the linoleum floor. "I've got to get back to the office, dammit. I don't know, darling," he sighed. "What do you think? Maybe we should stick around tomorrow and check up on him."

Mrs. Ferguson was that particular breed of Westchester mother who was not easily fazed. She'd raised two rambunctious, strapping sons and was married to a man who, on more than one occasion, drank so many martinis with his cronies at the Oyster Bar in Grand Central that he came home, passed out, and wet the bed.

"Oh, he'll be all right."

She went over to Tom's desk and sorted through the discarded paintings of Eliza's naked body parts. Frowning, she picked up the paint-smudged Polaroids of Shipley with the red Macy's bag over her head. "I'm certainly ready to hit the hay," she announced, placing the nude snapshots facedown on the desk.

Shipley stepped away from the bed and rummaged around in her bag for her cigarettes. "I think we should let him sleep," she said, leading the way out of the room.

She escorted Tom's parents out to their car and kissed them good-bye. Despite Tom's behavior, it was nice to have gotten to know them a little better.

"We're at the Holiday Inn," Mrs. Ferguson said. "Tell Tom to call if he needs anything."

"I will," she said, and waved them good-bye. It was only nine o'clock. Adam's party would just be getting going. She could drink a beer, maybe smoke a few cigarettes, maybe talk to Adam for a while. She might even try a game of horseshoes.

She walked across the quad to retrieve her car and found that it was gone. Tears sprang to her eyes as she stalked across the road again and into her dorm. Just inside the door was a white campus phone. She picked up the receiver, scanned the laminated campus directory that was nailed to the wall, and dialed the extension she was looking for.

"Dexter Security," a gruff voice answered.

"Yes," Shipley said evenly. "I'd like to report a theft. It's my car. It's been stolen."

18

The sun had set at five o'clock and the air was seized by the balmy stillness of an approaching storm. By seven the temperature had dropped to forty-five degrees. Now that it was past nine, it hovered just above freezing. Adam sat in the yellow rocking chair on his front porch, hands stuffed into the pockets of his ski jacket. That afternoon Eli had bought three kegs and put them on ice in the oversized watering trough in the barn. Hoping to keep their visitors away from the house, Tragedy wrote "KEG" in black marker on a fence slat, with a big arrow pointing to the barn.

Tragedy's hokey but suggestive promise of "refreshments and horseshoes" had worked. The lawn was littered with cars, and the barn was heaving. Adam liked the idea that the party was happening despite him, the invisible host. All anyone really needed was a place to go and something to drink. It was the guests who created the atmosphere, set the tone, kicked off the series of random events that would inevitably follow.

A lone black crow cawed its warning from the roof of the barn.

Then the tinkling sound of music filled the air. It was the Grannies, playing "Eyes of the World" from inside the barn.

> *"Sometimes we live no particular way but our own.*
> *And sometimes we visit your country and live in your home."*

Adam rocked in his chair, waiting with forced patience. She will come, he told himself, she has to come. Even if she was with Tom, she might steal a moment to talk to him. He could show her his room, his dad's welding shop. Girls liked stuff like that.

"Hey, loser!" Tragedy shouted at him from the open barn door. "What the fuck? You want a beer?"

The barn made Nick sneeze, but it felt good to be off campus, especially after the tedious hell of review week and the nerve-wracking job of managing the lights for Professor Rosen's show. He'd been so intent on doing a good job he'd even refrained from getting high—all day—which was a first for him.

Sea Bass and Damascus were manning the kegs. Eliza watched as Damascus lay down on the floor at his friend's feet and put the tip of a red plastic funnel—the kind used for oil or gasoline—into his mouth. Sea Bass picked up the long rubber hose and dispensed beer into the funnel.

"Hey, you know what I really want for Christmas?" Sea Bass said while his friend was furiously swallowing. "A blender. You know, so we can make cocktails and, like, fruit smoothies, right in our room?"

The keg glugged and sighed. Damascus swallowed and swallowed. Finally he smacked Sea Bass in the leg, indicating that he'd had enough. Sea Bass tossed the tap aside. Damascus sat up and let out an enormous burp.

"Your turn," he said, handing the funnel to Nick.

Nick shook his head. "No way, man." He picked up a plastic cup and filled it halfway with beer. Dust motes rose up from the barn floor. He sneezed, spraying snot all over the keg. "Can't lie down. Hay fever."

"Here, I'll take it." Eliza swiped the funnel out of Damascus's hands and lay down in his place.

Nick stood over her, watching. She was mad at him about something, he could tell. Now she was going to make herself sick just to spite him.

Eliza rested her head in Damascus's lap and slid the tip of the funnel into her mouth. Sea Bass picked up the tap and dispensed the beer. The cold liquid tickled her tonsils. She pretended she was at the dentist, except instead of asking her to spit, the dentist's orders were to swallow, swallow, swallow.

"All right!" Damascus cupped the back of her head in his hands. His fingers were warm and comforting against her skull. She closed her eyes and kept on swallowing. "Nice and steady."

She'd missed dinner, but now she was filling up with beer. It sloshed around in her belly and seeped down into her tights. It didn't even taste bad lying down. Perhaps if she'd eaten canned creamed ham lying down as a child, she would have been able to stomach that too.

"Nice," Damascus coaxed. "Nice."

Finally she made a little gurgling sound and Sea Bass released the lever on the tap. Damascus helped her into a sitting position.

"You okay?" He put a gentle arm around her. "You gonna hurl?"

Eliza wiped her mouth with the back of her hand. She shook her head, gripping her knees with her hands to steady herself. Her center of gravity had shifted. The barn was set at a tilt.

Nick gave her his hand. "Come on," he said. "Let's get some air."

He led her over to the barn door and propped her up against the door frame. Her black bangs hung over her eyebrows. She needed a trim.

"They're dancin', dancin' in the streets!" Grover sang and rattled his tambourine.

The Grannies had set up their instruments in the corner of the barn and were running through their playlist of Grateful Dead songs. All three Grannies had taken hits off Geoff's bottle of ether, and their playing was loud and sporadic, with spontaneous drum outbursts and random elated shrieks.

Eliza's now ever-present black down coat was unzipped. Underneath she wore black cutoff shorts over ripped black tights. "I hate this music," she belched. No one at Dexter besides the Grannies even liked the Grateful Dead. Everyone was into Nirvana and Jane's Addiction and R.E.M.

Occasionally the music was punctuated by the clang of horseshoes knocking against each other and the cries of some of the players. Tragedy had rigged a horseshoe throwing area in the lambing stall in the back of the barn, and a crowd of beer-wielding horseshoe enthusiasts had formed around it.

"Want to play horseshoes?" Nick asked.

Eliza shook her head, clapped her hand over her mouth, and took a few stumbling steps outside the barn. Then she puked in the grass.

"Oh God," she gasped, wiping her mouth. "That feels so much better."

A neatly coiled green hose hung from a hook just inside the barn door. Nick put down his beer, turned on the hose, and held it out to her. "Here," he said. "Drink."

Eliza took a few cautious sips, tipped her head back, gargled, and then spat. "There." She handed back the hose. "Good as new."

Nick turned off the hose and put it back on its hook. Eliza leaned against the door frame again, taking deep breaths of cool night air. He went over and stood beside her, looking out into the darkness. The kitchen lights were on in the farmhouse, and someone was sitting in the rocking chair on the front porch. "You know it's supposed to snow later," he said. "Like, a lot."

"Thanks, Storm Field." Eliza reached for his arm and tugged him toward her. She stood on tiptoe and pressed her mouth against his. Her tongue scraped against his teeth, prying them open.

Nick pulled away. "Hey! What are you doing?"

She scowled. "I just want to have sex with you, is that so much to ask? Think of it as a random act of kindness. And don't tell me you're saving yourself for someone, because that's bullshit. Obviously if the person you're saving yourself for doesn't want to do it with you now, they're not going to want to do it with you later. Capisce?"

Nick stared at her for a moment, enraged. Of course she was right. He'd been saving himself for Shipley, which was ridiculous. Shipley wasn't even there, and when she was there she was with someone else. Eliza was right here, and she wanted him. Besides, she was practically a campus sex symbol now that her naked portraits had been revealed at the open studio. Even Damascus and Sea Bass seemed to be into her.

He picked up his abandoned cup of beer and chugged the rest of it. It was probably a good thing he hadn't smoked any pot today. "Okay," he agreed and then sneezed. "Let's do it."

"I told you people would come." Tragedy handed Adam a cup of beer.

"Yeah." Adam took a sip. "There are definitely a lot of people here."

"Obviously not the right people though," Tragedy observed. She swiped her Rubik's cube off the porch steps and scrambled it up, shivering in her thin white sundress. "Brr." She went into the house and came back wearing Ellen's hairy raccoon fur coat. It looked great with her black rubber boots.

"If you want to, like, go forth and seek your fortune, I've got it covered," she offered. "You could just drive by the dorms or whatever. See if she's around."

"Maybe," Adam said. He looked up at his sister, his eyes bright and hopeful. "Are you sure?"

Tragedy worked her Rubik's cube. "Please. Just stop moping and get the fuck out of here. And don't come back until you find her."

The rocking chair teetered as Adam stood up. "You'll have to bring in the sheep." He zipped up his jacket and fumbled in his pocket for his car keys. "And don't forget the kittens. If it gets much colder, they need to go in the house."

"I'm not a moron," Tragedy said.

"Okay. I'm going." Adam smiled goofily at his sister. "Have fun."

She rolled her eyes and gave him the finger. "Yeah, you too."

The air was heavy and cold, the sky a low dark gray mixed with orange. The red taillights of Adam's VW disappeared down the road. Tragedy tossed her Rubik's cube onto the rocking chair and headed back to the barn.

It was a good party. The music was loud and everyone was already too drunk to notice how cold it had gotten. The clank of horseshoes resounded in the cool, hay-dusted air.

"Hey, beautiful." A guy with ridiculously large mutton-chops greeted her. He shoved a frothy cup of beer into her hand. "I'm Sea Bass," he said with a cocky smile. "And this is Damascus."

A stocky guy with a shock of dark, curly hair leered in her direction. "Wanna try a funnel?"

Nick followed Eliza up a rickety ladder to the hayloft. The boards were loose and bouncy, and they could see their fellow party-goers through the cracks. Four bare bulbs dangled from the barn's post and beam ceiling. Silvery dust motes rose up into the air, sparkling in the harsh yellow light. The impending snow was palpable now. People huddled around the water trough full of kegs as if it were a campfire, their shoulders draped in dusty woolen horse blankets someone had unearthed from the feed room.

"Wish we had a blanket," Eliza said wistfully. The hay was soft underfoot, but scratchy against her skin. The few times she'd had sex, she'd done it on her pink and blue Cinderella sheets back home, the ultimate defilement. She unzipped her down coat and laid it out on top of a pile of hay.

Nick watched her with his hands in his pockets. "You're not planning on getting completely naked, are you?"

"Pretty naked," Eliza said, laughing. She unbuttoned her cardigan. The blunt ends of her dark hair brushed the pale skin of her collarbone.

"You're actually really beautiful," he said.

"Actually?" She folded the sweater and placed it on top of a hay bale. Then she yanked off her top. "Is that supposed to be a compliment?" She stepped out of her cutoffs. In her red bra and holey black tights she looked like a circus performer.

Nick sneezed. Then he sneezed again and again. He wiped

his nose on the back of his hand. "Sorry. I guess my allergies aren't very sexy."

"Actually, they are."

His eyes were bloodshot and tearing and his nostrils were inflamed. There was a small pink scar between his eyebrows where he'd hurt himself at orientation, the day they'd first met. Eliza reached out and wiped the snot from his nose. She knocked off his stupid flap hat. "You're probably just allergic to your hat," she said, pulling him toward her so she could kiss his neck.

"You really are pretty," Nick said again and slipped his hands inside the waistband of her tights. Below their feet the Grannies lit into "Fire on the Mountain."

"There's a dragon with matches that's loose on the town. Takes a whole pail of water just to cool him down. . . ."

Eliza unbuttoned Nick's jeans and yanked them down around his ankles. She sat down on top of her coat "You need to take off your sneakers."

Nick stood over her with a big boner poking out of his Fruit of the Looms. He looked like a unicorn, sort of.

He squatted down to untie his laces. "I'm probably going to break out in hives."

Eliza hadn't expected him to be so dainty. "You're the one who built your own yurt," she accused, knocking him over onto his back. She tore off his shoes and yanked his pants off all the way. "Stop being such a wuss. I've waited too long for this."

Nick sneezed violently. "All right, all right," he said and rolled on top of her coat to escape the hay. It was actually pretty comfy, although he was allergic to feathers too.

"I brought condoms and everything," Eliza announced. "I got them at the health center." She fished one out of the pocket of her discarded shorts and examined the small print on the wrapper.

"You'll be glad to know they've got some kind of special sauce on them for extra sperm-killing power and glide. Oh, and ridges, just like Ruffles potato chips."

Nick sneezed again, even more violently this time. "They'll probably give me a rash too."

"Oh Jesus." Eliza tossed the condom at him. She took off her tights and threw them at him too. "Do you want to do this or what?"

Nick sneezed again and opened up his arms. "Come here," he said. "You must be cold."

Eliza giggled and dove on top of him, scattering an avalanche of hay out of the hayloft and onto the heads of the throng below. "Actually I'm getting warmer," she murmured. His boner pressed against her belly button. She reached down and took hold of it. "Warmer, warmer. Hot!"

"All right! I'd just like to congratulate whoever's up there getting it on!" one of the Grannies shouted. "Good times, man. Good times!"

Waiting for a snowfall is like watching a flower open. Scratch your nose and you miss the first flake's fall. Next thing you know, the horizon is as white as a plate.

It was almost eleven. The barn door stood open. Heavy white snowflakes fell from the sky like a chorus of paper angels. A few minutes ago the Gatzes' house, only one hundred yards away, was fully visible. Now it was obliterated by the whiteout.

"Guess we're going to be stuck here for a while," Geoff observed, waggling his bottle of ether in his skeletal hands.

"Time for a short break!" Wills flung down his guitar and knotted up his long yellow skirt as if he were preparing for a boxing match or a good game of tug-o'-war. Geoff poured some ether on the end of the knot, and Wills squatted down on his haunches to sniff it. Grover held out one of the straps of his overalls and Geoff daubed it with ether too.

"What is that stuff anyway?" Tragedy asked, swaying tipsily.

"You don't want to know." Sea Bass winked at her. "Stick with beer."

"Nothing worse than coming down from an ether high," Damascus observed. "Besides, it stinks."

"Ether is not cool," Sea Bass said definitively.

Tragedy didn't enjoy being told what was cool and what was not. She preferred to decide for herself. Horseshoes, for example.

She'd learned all about drugs in school. Home was so boring, everyone did them. Not her though. Her parents had done drugs to such excess back in college they were basically brain damaged. Drugs had always seemed pretty dumb. But ether was different. It wasn't a pill or a powder or some gross weed.

"Can I try some?" she asked Geoff.

Geoff appraised Tragedy's beautiful face, her lush dark hair, her curvy body encased in an inappropriately skimpy white sundress and furry raccoon coat. He appraised her black rubber farm boots and brown bony knees. "You look like a model," he said.

She held out her hand for the bottle of ether. "Come on. Just tell me what I have to do."

Geoff let her have the bottle. He reached in his pocket and pulled out a rag. "Just pour some on, hold it up against your nose, and inhale."

Tragedy did as she was told. Adam was going to freak when he came back to find her all fucked up. He was supposed to be babysitting, he was supposed to be in charge! She doused the rag in the clear, toxic liquid and held it up to her nose. Closing her eyes, she inhaled again and again, allowing the heady pulse of it to consume her.

The Grannies took up their instruments.

"It's a fucking blizzard!" Wills yelled before banging out the first few bars of a very up-tempo song that may or may not have been by the Grateful Dead.

Tragedy closed her eyes, falling into a blissed-out sort of trance. Every hair on her body vibrated intensely. Or maybe it was the raccoon coat, coming back to life.

"Are you okay?" Sea Bass asked.

"We told you ether was nasty," Damascus chimed in.

"You don't know what it feels like," Tragedy gushed, her eyes still closed. She could hear the kittens scratching away on the other side of the barn wall. She could hear the sheep milling around by the fence. She tipped the bottle back onto the rag and held it against her nose once more, loving the sharp clinical rush as it tore away at her nasal passages. *Scratch, scratch. Baa, baa. Scratch, scratch. Baa, baa.*

She opened her eyes. Outside, the landscape was a bright, fuzzy white like a white angora sweater. All those hours she'd spent poring over travel guides, imagining what it would be like to climb mountains in Nepal or dogsled in Alaska, and now her own backyard was completely spectacular and foreign. Geoff's face loomed in front of her, his hollow eyes gaping out of their sunken, hungry sockets. He stuck up his bony thumb in silent solidarity. Or maybe he said something that Tragedy couldn't hear.

Mesmerized by the whiteout, she stumbled out of the barn. White snowflakes drifted down from the sky and nested on her eyelashes. The sheep stamped and stared at her through the fence. They should have been brought in hours ago.

She held out her hands. The snowflakes screamed as they fell out of the sky and melted on her bare skin. The yard was already blanketed in snow. The house was a ghostly blur. Everything was white, white, white.

"I'm going out there!" she cried, making a run for it. She dashed across the yard, behind the house, and into the woods beyond. It was colder than she realized, and darker in the woods. Whorls of ice pelted her bare skin and skittered over the thick fur of her coat. All around her the tall trees swayed and shivered, leafless and unfamiliar. She'd roamed these pathless woods almost every day of her life, but tonight she couldn't see a thing. What a joke it would be if she got lost.

19

The average freshman course load at a liberal arts college such as Dexter looks something like this: Geology 101, The Romantics, English 100, Creative Writing: Poetry, Music Appreciation. An English midterm examination would involve two essays and four questions to be answered in a brief paragraph, such as, "Who wrote the lines 'When I behold, upon the night's starr'd face,/ Huge cloudy symbols of a high romance,/And think that I may never live to trace/Their shadows, with the magic hand of chance,' and what did he or she mean by them?" There would be an additional grammar section with witty, impossible questions, as in, "Write an ironic hortatory sentence in iambic pentameter using a gerund, a phoneme, and a conjunction. Please use proper punctuation." The Geology exam was all memorization, including the lab portion, which would require the identification of fourteen species of rock. Studying for Music Appreciation was almost pleasant. An entire night of Mozart, Bach, Chopin, and Beethoven concertos played at low

volume while you slept and you were bound to be able to distinguish them in the morning.

Shipley sat at her desk in her dorm room, listening to Chopin's
nocturnes and watching the snow fall with her Romantics an-
thology opened to John Keats's "When I Have Fears." It was almost midnight and the snow was falling hard. She was probably
the only one studying on campus. Everyone else was at Adam's
party, which had probably turned into a giant sleepover since no
one would want to drive back in the snow. Chances were, Adam
had already fallen into the arms of some pushy, overachieving
drunk girl who'd started studying for exams back in October. Of
course Shipley could have borrowed Tom's Jeep and gone to check
up on Adam herself. The Jeep would be better in the snow than
the Mercedes anyway. But Tom was not to be disturbed.

Through the aching strains of music she detected the inhar-
monious sound of someone knocking on her door.

"Hello?" she called, sitting up very straight.

The door opened a crack. "Shipley? Are you in there?"

For a moment Shipley thought she might be having one of her
daydreams—the pornographic ones she used to have before she'd
come to college. A tall, handsome stranger would walk into her
dorm room, mistaking it for his own, while she lay half-asleep in
her bed. He'd strip down to his boxer shorts and perform some
ritualistic football team stretching routine involving karate chops
and grunts and taut muscle flexes, completely oblivious to her
watching from beneath the covers. Then he'd slip into bed, and,
pleasantly surprised to find the bed occupied by none other than
Shipley herself, would proceed to make passionate love to her,
from behind. In the morning she'd wake up to find him stroking
her hair and gazing adoringly into her face. "What's your name?"
he'd say.

"It's Adam."

Shipley turned toward the door. "Adam?"

"I waited for you," he said, coming into the room. The shoulders of his blue parka were dusted with snow. "Finally I just decided to come look for you."

The truth was that Adam had been driving in circles around Dexter's campus for almost two hours, daring himself. The visibility got so bad he finally pulled over. Now he was here. And—miraculously—she was here too.

"It's snowing so hard," she said, closing her book. Chopin trilled away on the piano. Nocturne in G Major, Opus 37, Andantino. Or had the tape switched over to Beethoven?

Adam unzipped his jacket halfway. Taking it off all the way felt too presumptuous. "I was going to offer to drive you back to the party, but it's pretty bad out there. . . ."

"No, please. Come in. Sit down," Shipley said.

Adam took off his jacket and hung it on the doorknob. He sat down on the end of her bed. "Maybe in the morning we can ski," he said stupidly. He didn't even know how to ski, except cross-country, which didn't count.

"My father just bought a house in Hawaii," Shipley said. "Did you know they can ski there?"

"Skiing in Hawaii?" Adam exclaimed loudly. "I thought it was all volcanoes and beaches."

It was the most inane conversation either of them had ever had.

"You were great in the play." Shipley walked over to the bed and sat down next to Adam. His jeans were damp. His legs were very long. "But I—"

She wanted to tell him that she'd made a mistake. That she hadn't meant to kiss him that time, in Professor Rosen's kitchen. She wanted to tell him that she'd had a rough evening, what with

Tom being such a mess and throwing up everywhere, and Tom's mother seeing those pictures of her naked. Instead she found herself wanting to knock Adam down on the bed and kiss him again. The tape flipped over and new music came on. Violins and a cello. It was a Mozart sonata, or a Bach concerto. *Dolce ma non troppo* or *dulce de leche*. Oh, hadn't she learned anything?

"I don't want you to think I came here to—" Adam began and then stopped. It was pretty obvious why he'd come.

Shipley smiled. "I was beginning to feel like such a loser, studying on a Saturday. Everyone's at your party."

Adam wasn't sure if he was imagining things, but she seemed to be coming closer and closer. She smelled like fish and chips and cigarette smoke.

"Have you been to the Lobster Shack recently?" he asked, laughing. He'd been to the restaurant with his family on three occasions: Tragedy's thirteenth birthday, after his high school graduation last June, and once when Uncle Laurie came up to visit. They always came back smelling like a fish fry.

Shipley blushed. "I'm sorry. Do I stink?" The dorm was so quiet she hadn't felt comfortable taking a shower. It was too spooky.

"Kind of," he admitted. "But don't worry, it's not too terrible."

"I'm sorry." She moved away from him on the bed.

"No." He closed up the space between them. "It's really not bad."

Shipley allowed herself to look at him again. His face was only inches away. She could see his freckles now. "Someone stole my car," she told him. "Again."

"You have to be more careful," Adam murmured hoarsely. He couldn't stop smiling. They were breathing all over each other.

This was better than any daydream. Shipley didn't care what

she smelled like, she couldn't stand it anymore. She bowled Adam over on the bed and straddled his hips.

"I really wanted to go to your party," she confessed.

Adam kissed his way up to her lips. "It's better here."

Shipley slipped out of her shirt and unbuttoned her jeans. The sonata's final notes resounded from her boom box. Adam kissed her bare hip and slipped her jeans down over her thighs.

She fell back on the bed with an indulgent sigh. "I really need to learn the name of that song."

Patrick was glad he'd stayed in Maine for the winter. Winter there was so extreme. Sometimes there were warm days like earlier today—a balmy pre-Christmas offering, or a reminder of August. Then the snow came, piling up on the sides of roads and on the roofs of houses, whitening everything and making summer unfeasible.

Back when he was living at home, they'd spent Christmas in the Caribbean. Their parents liked undiscovered beaches on islands where they were the only white people. He'd played dominoes with the local boys on Salt Key. "Patrick, Patrick! Dominoes, Patrick, dominoes!" the boys shouted up at his window in the simple guesthouse where they'd stayed. None of the boys wore shoes, and the palms of their hands were pink like the inside of a fish. The local women made little sundresses for his sister. They went to a parade in the village, and she looked like a doll in her bright yellow dress, her blond hair braided with red beads. His dad took him spear fishing and he caught a barracuda.

The Mercedes skidded on the unplowed road. Up ahead was a nice-looking white farmhouse. Cars were parked willy-nilly all over the yard, and a small herd of sheep was clustered expectantly behind the barn, as if someone had forgotten to feed them. The kitchen lights were on inside the house, but the party was clearly in the barn. He could hear the thrum of guitar music even before he stepped out of the car.

"Bill Clinton is so freaking *hot!*" A girl's voice rang out through the chilly air as he trudged through the snow to the house. He mounted the porch steps and peeked through the smudged kitchen window. The house was still and quiet, as if it had been lulled to sleep by the snow. The door was unlocked.

Inside, the kitchen was messy. Patrick opened the fridge, which was covered with paper reminders—*Call vet for wormer. Sell manure. Cheese!!*—and all manner of crap. The contents of the fridge were even messier. Half-eaten brown apples. Moldy cheese. Hard bread. He was craving something sweet, but he could do a lot better at the Dumpster. A pint of yogurt looked promising, but when he pulled the top off the container, he saw it was filled with coffee beans. He went for a round Saran Wrapped ball of soft cheese that looked fresh and a bunch of green grapes in a plastic bag still tied in a knot from the store. He stuffed the whole ball of cheese into his mouth and then ran the cold tap to wash it down.

Eating the grapes three at a time, he pushed open the kitchen door and stepped out onto the porch. It was snowing even harder now. He could barely even see the barn. When he finally reached it, he slid open the big wooden door and poked his head inside.

Dexter students, looking so wasted their faces were sliding off their skulls, danced around a metal feed trough containing three kegs while the band played their way through their repertoire of Grateful Dead songs for the third time. Damascus and Sea Bass were playing horseshoes, calling out fouls and howling like it was the Super Bowl. Geoff lay on the ground, a skeleton on the barn floor, with his eyes closed and the funnel in his mouth. In the corner of the barn Nick and Eliza were slow-dancing, one body propping up the other. Eliza wore Nick's hat.

"I love you," she whispered into Nick's hair.

"Me too," Nick whispered back. "Actually."

Patrick thought he heard a mewing sound. He peeked through the dusty wooden boards of a nearby box stall. On the floor of the stall was a cardboard box housing a gray cat and her kittens. The cats stared up at him with accusing yellow eyes. *Have you been drinking?* they seemed to say. The kittens were shivering. Patrick opened the door to the stall and picked up the box. He carried it out of the barn and through the snow to the house, cradling the top of the box against his chest to keep out the snow. The mother cat was big. She must have weighed nearly twenty pounds.

He put the box under the kitchen table, filled up a bowl full of sheep's milk from the fridge, and placed the bowl next to the box. His parents had never allowed him a pet. It felt nice, providing for these little creatures.

"There," he told the wary mother cat. "See? I'm not so bad."

The gray cat continued to stare at him while he finished off the grapes. A minute or two went by. Then the cat stood up and stretched and hopped out of the box to lap up the milk. Patrick lunged for the box and scooped up a soft black kitten, carefully stashing it in his parka pocket. He headed outside to the car, ignoring the mother cat's accusing glare.

Tragedy buried her chin beneath the collar of the thick raccoon coat. The fur was warm as hell. Falling almost down to her ankles, it completely insulated every part of her body except her head, which was frozen raw. Pretty soon she'd be able to peel her head off her shoulders, like a wart that had been frozen off.

She liked to walk. No matter the weather, she'd always liked to walk. The woods around Dexter were connected by a trail that looped around itself like a giant pretzel, with the town of Home in the middle of one loop, and the college, up on its hill, in the middle of the other. She thought she knew the trail blindfolded—rain, shine, in sunlight, or in total darkness. One of her usual routes led from the top of the hill behind her house all the way to the field house at Dexter, on the other side of the Pond. This was the path she was on now. At least, she thought she was. Walking in a blizzard in the dark was like solving a Rubik's cube with only white squares.

The melody of the Bee Gees song she'd been named after moseyed through her mind like Muzak in a grocery store. *It's hard to see. With all this snow and no pants on, you're going nowhere...*

Her parents hoped that naming their beautiful baby girl Tragedy might provide some relief from all the ugly tragedies in the world. The personal is political. Make love not war. Think globally act locally. Those were their mottos. And she liked the way people repeated it when she said her name, rolling it around in their mouths and testing it out. "Pretty," they'd say, looking her up and down.

Where was the fucking field house? She'd been walking for hours, and there was not a building or a light in sight. The path she was on ended in a clump of uprooted trees. It looked like a car wreck. She must have gotten turned around somewhere. Maybe she'd walked over the state line into Canada, which might actually be all right. Her mom and dad would miss her, but she could write to them tomorrow and let them know she was okay.

"Fuck!" she exclaimed, remembering the sheep. She was supposed to put them in the back stalls and throw them some hay.

"Double fuck!" she shouted, remembering the kittens. It was

cold now and Storm, the mother cat, would be hungry. They should have been put in the house.

"Mom is going to kill me," she muttered, retracing her steps.

Adam would probably get home first anyway. He'd bring the sheep in. And if Storm was hungry enough she'd yowl her head off till he heard her. Tragedy could pay him back tomorrow by making his favorite peanut butter and jam yule log. But first she had to find a path out of the woods.

It was nearly 2 A.M. and still snowing hard. The haunting notes of Taps drifted underneath the door, the efforts of an ROTC student who had recently taken up bugling. Shipley lay under the sheet with her head on Adam's bare chest, drifting in and out of sleep. Adam was wide awake. How could he sleep? He felt like he'd just been born. He was finally alive!

"When you were a kid, what did you want to be?" he asked. "I mean, what did you want to be when you grew up?"

Shipley was just drifting into a dream. She was so tired, but she wanted to talk to Adam too.

"A train conductor," she responded drowsily.

Adam laughed, his rib cage jostling her head. "Seriously?"

"I loved the sound when they punched your ticket," Shipley told him with her eyes closed. "Greenwich is only a forty-minute train ride from Manhattan. I used to take the train into the city with my mother to go shopping. Saks, Bendel's, Bergdorf. Afterward we'd walk up Fifth Avenue next to Central Park. Mom liked to look at the buildings."

Adam waited for her to continue.

"I didn't really want to be a train conductor," she admitted with a yawn. "I always thought I'd get married and have two little girls and live in one of those buildings on Fifth Avenue.

They'd go to Sacred Heart so they could wear those adorable uniforms with the red-and-white-checked pinafores."

"Uh-huh," Adam murmured encouragingly. He had no idea what she was talking about. "Go on."

She inched closer to him so the top of her head was in the crook of his neck. Her hair smelled like seawater. "I have no idea what I'm going to do when I grow up. I guess I could be a poet," she mused. "Professor Rosen likes my poems."

"What else?" he prompted.

"What else?" She opened her eyes briefly and then closed them again. "I have this brother . . . ," she said, her voice trailing off as she fell back to sleep and into her dreams.

Her ice cream was dripping onto her skirt. The steps of the Met were crowded with tourists and schoolgirls. Only a few feet away from her a group of them sat smoking and gossiping.

"Here, use this," her mother said, handing her a Kleenex. "Don't forget we're meeting your father for dinner at seven."

A uniformed doorman pushed open the door to the green-awninged building across the avenue. He raised his white-gloved hand, his lips curled around a silver whistle as he hailed a taxi. A cab stopped, the doorman opened the door to the building, and out strolled Tom, wearing black Ray-Ban sunglasses and the same plain white T-shirt, black pants, and old tennis shoes he'd worn in the play, minus the blood. He looked like a movie star. No, he *was* a movie star.

Now she was kissing Tom and he didn't smell like chemicals, he smelled like Ivory soap, and his skin was so soft and—

Beep! Beep! Beep!

Orange lights flashed through the window as the staff of Buildings and Grounds plowed Dexter's section of Homeward Avenue. The sky was the pinkish gray of near-dawn and it was still snowing, although not quite as heavily. It was almost six o'clock in the morning. Adam was still awake. The bugler, who'd been practicing all night, burst into a rousing reveille.

"I don't know," Shipley said sleepily, picking up half from her dream and half from their conversation a few hours before. "I probably shouldn't have gone to college in Maine."

They were both quiet for a moment. Adam brushed his chin against her hair. "If you hadn't gone to school in Maine, you wouldn't have met me," he remarked pointedly.

The plows moved on down the road and the bugler paused for breath. For a moment the room was silent. Then a gunshot rang out, ricocheting off the windows and sending chills up their spines. The bugler recommenced his playing, this time a march.

Less than half a mile away, Tragedy lay bleeding in the snow. Whoever had shot her had broken the law; bear hunting season had ended just after Thanksgiving. Not that she was a bear. She was a person, wearing a coat, which wasn't even made out of bear fur. Raccoon hunting season might well have run all year, the little pests.

"At least I'm not fucking dead," she swore, attempting to stand. "Hey!" she shouted. "Hey! I'm fucking bleeding over here!"

Nothing. Snowflakes drifted prettily down through the white-washed trees. The storm was tapering off.

"Hey!" Tragedy shouted again, but her shout came out too hoarse to go anywhere. The bullet had gone right through her, somewhere near her belly button. She felt like she'd eaten a whole fucking pound of hot chili peppers. "Hey!" she shouted, even more hoarsely this time. Her voice was just a whisper, quieter than a snowflake.

She couldn't walk, so she dragged herself through the snow, scraping at it with her bare hands. A break in the trees and there was Dexter College, sitting prettily on its hill, the brick buildings all frosted with snow, the blue light shining from the chapel spire like a Christmas tree topper. It looked just like it did in the snow globes they sold at the campus bookstore. It looked like a fucking Christmas present. And just on the fringes of campus was that huge tent. She'd have to drag herself a hundred fucking miles to get there, but she'd get there. And then she'd yell her fucking head off until someone came.

"Shit," she whimpered. Her hands hurt. "Mom's going to kill me."

20

They say a pet can do wonders for your mental health. A pet is a source of comfort. Making a home for a pet gives you a sense of security and well-being. Providing for a pet is very satisfying and teaches responsibility for others. Pets appreciate leftover surf and turf from the Lobster Shack. Most of them do anyway.

Patrick hadn't thought of the right name for the kitten yet. Frodo was a good one, but once you named your cat after a character from *The Lord of the Rings*, you were pretty much done for—just you and your cat, living in your own little fairyland of magic and wizardry. Blackie was retarded. Jet was too gay. Raymond—so gay. Hugo was sort of theatrical. Or maybe Victor? No, gay again. Pink Patrick with a black cat named Victor. It was like something out of *Psycho*.

His Outward Bound instructors had written about the Pink Patrick incident in the report that went out to his parents.

"Patrick, are you gay?" his father had asked him after reading the report.

"What?" Patrick said. "Huh?" It was all he could think of to say. He'd never had a girlfriend, but he'd never had a boyfriend either. He was Pink Patrick. People avoided him.

"Here, kitty," he called, setting down a plastic bowl of surf and turf that he'd shredded into tiny scraps. The kitten scampered over to the bowl and sniffed it. Then it sat down on its haunches and began licking its asshole.

"Are you gay?" Patrick demanded of the kitten. He cracked a smile when it paused to look up at him with its big yellow eyes.

One of the thick wool blankets that girl had brought for him lay in a heap on the floor, right where he'd left it a few days ago. He lay down and rolled himself up in it, rubbing his palms against his thighs. The yurt's flaps were shut tight, but it was still freezing. He thought about lighting the little stove for the kitten's sake but he wanted to sleep, and it said in the directions not to leave the camp stove unattended.

"Here, kitty," he said again, but the kitten didn't move.

"Suit yourself," Patrick told it and rolled over.

He'd been driving for hours, hypnotized by the snow and the *flap, flap, flap* of the Mercedes's windshield wipers. He almost hit the same white car several times. Idiot, driving a white car in the snow. Eventually the kitten started mewing like crazy in the backseat and he decided it must have to poop. He couldn't very well let a cat poop all over a room at the Holiday Inn, so he'd brought it back to the yurt. He'd even dug away a place in the corner for it to use as a litter box, but the damn thing still hadn't pooped.

He dozed off. A while later he was awakened by a scratching sound. He sat up.

"You finally pooping?" he asked the kitten, but found that it was curled up asleep inside the red wool hat that girl had brought him on Thanksgiving. Its tiny chest rose and fell with every breath.

"*Hey,*" someone called from outside the tent. It was just a whisper, or maybe it was the wind. "*Hey.*"

Patrick stood up and untied the door flap. The girl who'd brought him things was lying at his feet, wearing what looked like a bear skin. A trail of pink snow led down the hill behind her and into the woods.

"Hey," Tragedy whispered to the toes of Patrick's boots. Then she passed out. The black kitten stalked over and lay down on her hair.

It wasn't snowing anymore. The sun was trying to come out. A few stray flakes drifted down from the trees. Patrick picked up the girl's cold, red hands and dragged her inside. She didn't stir. Was she dead? He knelt down and put his ear next to her mouth. A little puff of air tickled his earlobe. But man, her hands were cold, and her face was all shiny and red, like it had been power-washed. She was frozen stiff.

He flailed around in the half dark of the tent, setting up the little camping stove and lighting it with the wooden kitchen matches he kept sealed in a Ziploc bag. He turned the flame up as high as it would go and moved the stove as close to the girl as he dared. She lay stiff and cold in her mangy fur coat.

"Shit." The stove was pathetic. It barely gave off enough heat to defrost a mouse. He needed a bigger flame.

The tent was full of random crap—a metal cooking pot, a pair of mittens, a can of corn. He was suddenly reminded of *Quest for Fire*, the only movie he'd ever seen at a drive-in, and one of his earliest memories. His parents had taken him just after Shipley was born, and they had both fallen asleep in the front seat with the baby while he watched the movie from the backseat. It was all about cavemen looking for burning embers in old fires because they'd lost their original embers and didn't know how to start fires on their own. Man could not exist without fire. Man's evolution could be traced back to the quest. In the half-dark of the yurt he stumbled over *Dianetics* by L. Ron Hubbard. It killed him to burn it, but it was a nice thick book. Once it got going, the flames would be huge.

He opened the book and ripped out a few pages, crumpling them into tight balls and dropping them into the bottom of the cooking pot before tossing the whole book in. Then he turned off the stove and disconnected the little kerosene tank so he could douse the book with kerosene. Perching the pot on top of the stove, he lit a match, dropped it in, and poof, the book burst into flames. He rocked back on his heels, pleased with his work. It even smelled good.

One by one, the sage words of L. Ron Hubbard —"survival," "engrams," "audit," "clear," were singed and disintegrated as the book caught fire. Patrick placed the pot right next to the girl's shoulder. The girl slept on, except she didn't look like she was sleeping. She looked like a drowned person who'd been dredged out of the Gowanus Canal, just like on *Law & Order,* a TV show he'd watched in the truck stop in Lewiston where he hung out from time to time. The kitten mewed plaintively and pawed at the girl's limp hand. It seemed less afraid of her than it was of him. Patrick put one hand on the floor and reached out over her body with the other hand to pet the kitten.

"Go on, crawl inside her coat or something," he told it. "Warm her up."

The kitten walked around the girl's head and lay down on her hair, blinking its eyes in the firelight. Patrick sat back on his haunches. The hand that had been on the floor felt sticky. He examined his palm in the flickering light. It was matted with dark red stuff. Blood.

"Shit!"

The girl hadn't moved since he'd dragged her inside. He poked at her fur. Was that the source of the blood? Had she skinned an animal and put on its coat? No, the coat had buttons. He unbuttoned them all and pulled aside the lapels. Only the shoulder straps of her white sundress were still white, the rest of it was covered with blood. She was bleeding to death.

He buttoned up the coat, grabbed the kitten off her hair, and stuffed it in his pocket. Then he shoved his hands beneath the girl's back and thighs and did his best to lift her.

She was bigger than he was—tall. Her dark hair and big feet dragged on the ground as he staggered behind the dorms, skirting the fringes of Dexter's campus, to the parking lot across the road from Coke. The sun was getting brighter now, but it was still early, and the campus was quiet. Stumbling, he dropped the girl in the deep, powdery snow and opened the back door of the Mercedes. Her head bumped against the door frame going in, but she didn't even flinch.

The car sputtered to life. "Come on," he growled as the wheels spun in the deep snow. He backed onto the road and floored the accelerator, headed toward the hospital just outside of town. Back behind the dorms, the fire burned bright inside the yurt, causing it to smoke like a volcano.

Sea Bass was the only one with four-wheel drive and snow tires. "You'd think, coming to college in Maine, people would have more sense," he scoffed. Nick, Eliza, and Geoff were huddled in the back of his 4Runner. Everyone else was stuck at Adam's house, trying to dig their cars out with the two shovels they'd found in the barn.

"I've got chains," Damascus announced defensively from the passenger seat. "On my car at home."

"It's not about the tires," Geoff spoke up, his bony hands folded placidly in his lap as he gazed out the window. None the worse for wear after staying up all night and huffing an entire bottle of ether, Geoff couldn't wait to lace up his Nikes and head out for a run. "It's like running shoes. What matters is the distribution of weight."

Eliza was holding Nick's red, welted hand. They'd fallen asleep on top of each other in the hay. Now Nick's entire body was covered in an angry rash and his eyes were almost swollen shut.

"I think I need to go to the Health Center," he complained. "Get some cortisone."

"I think I need to sleep in a bed," Eliza muttered. She turned to examine Nick's profile. She expected him to look older, more manly, after last night. But his beard was just peach fuzz, not even worth shaving. "Sorry to be a buzz kill, but we have exams tomorrow," she reminded everyone.

"Fuck," Sea Bass moaned. "I'm so fucking screwed."

Nick wiped his nose on the cuff of his shirt. "Maybe I can get the nurse to write me a note." He looked down at his other hand, tucked inside Eliza's. He hadn't expected her to be the hand-holding type—more the whips and leashes type—but she was almost affectionate. He imagined her introducing him to one of her friends back home. "This is my boyfriend, Nick." He supposed that would be all right.

"Hey," he murmured into her ear. "Do you think I could go home with you for Christmas?" After all, he had nowhere else to go.

"Hell yeah," Eliza whispered back. She grabbed his swollen, drippy face and kissed him. This was what she'd always yearned for—someone who wanted to be around, someone who was hers. "Better not bring your bong though."

She imagined Nick smoking up right in the middle of the living room while her parents were out working in their real estate office over the garage. *Are you burning incense, princess?* they'd ask with their usual distracted cheerfulness.

"I was thinking of quitting anyway," Nick said. Something about the snow and staying up most of the night in a dusty barn without getting high had made him game for contest. Or maybe it was Eliza who made him want to stay on his toes.

The 4Runner barreled up the hill toward campus. Dexter looked like it was trying very hard to look adorable so the students would remember to come back after Christmas. Golden rays of morning sun shone gloriously down on the dapper redbrick buildings nestled in nearly two feet of fresh, white snow. A giant snowman wearing a Dexter baseball cap stood jauntily in the center of the quad.

Sea Bass rolled down his window. "Nice!" he called out to a pair of girls on cross-country skis. The girls turned their heads and gave him a cheery wave. It was that kind of day.

"Holy shit," Damascus cried, pointing. "What's going on?"

Black smoke erupted from Root's roof. The dorm appeared to be on fire.

"It's not the dorm." Geoff squinted out his window. "It's a forest fire out back."

Sea Bass put on his blinker and pulled into the driveway that led to the temporary parking lot on the other side of the quad, behind Root. Just beyond the parking lot, near the woods, was a gigantic bonfire. The flames were twenty feet high and dark orange. Sparks flew up into the air like firecrackers. The snow around the fire had already melted.

"It's the yurt," Nick said, feeling almost pleased with him-

self. It served that loser right, living in there without his per-
mission. "The yurt is burning down."

"No way," Eliza gasped. The whole damn thing was ablaze.
She squeezed his hand protectively. "Holy shit."

"Holy *fucking* shit," Sea Bass exclaimed.

"It's burning all the way the fuck *down*," Damascus said,
stating the obvious.

Everyone was quiet for a moment, transfixed by the flames.
Then Geoff opened his door. "Hey, come on, you guys," he said
with uncharacteristic enthusiasm. "Let's check it out."

They staggered out into the snow. The fire was magnificent.
And the authorities didn't seem to have noticed it yet. Swaying a
little from shock and lack of sleep, Nick raised his hand to shield
his sore eyes from the smoke. Just beyond the fire rose the chapel
spire, its blue light burning bright and blue and true as ever.

Patrick pulled the car up in front of the emergency room. He
flicked on the hazard lights and glanced into the backseat. The
girl lay in a pile of bloody fur on the plush beige leather, her dark
hair spilling onto the floor and her knees bent in a fetal position
to accommodate her long legs.

He stepped out of the car, wondering if he should notify
someone inside or if he should just carry her in. In movies they
just carried them in.

There were a few old people in the waiting room, sleeping.

"She's bleeding," Patrick told the woman behind the desk.
"She might already be dead," he added, although he'd seen the
girl's nostrils flare and her brow furrow when he'd dragged her
out of the car.

The receptionist stood up and peered at the girl in his arms.
She picked up the phone. "I have a bleeder. Possible NGMI.

I need wheels!" she barked into it and then slammed the phone down. She pushed a clipboard across the counter. "You'll need to sign in."

Patrick just stood there, breathing hard. The girl was heavy in her fur coat. "What should I do?" he said. "Put her on the floor?"

The receptionist took back the clipboard. "Is she your wife?"

Patrick stared back at her for a moment. "No. I don't even know—" He stopped, and then started again. "She's my friend."

"Name? Date of birth?"

"Who, me?" he stammered.

"No, her. What's her name?" the receptionist said impatiently. "When was she born?"

"I don't know," Patrick admitted. "She's young."

The receptionist picked up the phone again. "Where the hell are my wheels?" She slammed the phone down. "You can both have a seat until they get here," she told Patrick.

He staggered over to the nearest chair and sat down with the girl across his lap. Her face was purple and she smelled weird. She looked terrible. The weekend morning news played on the little television rigged in the corner near the ceiling. Just before the commercial, the camera flashed on the big Christmas tree in Rockefeller Center. His dad used to take him to see that tree, just the two of them. Every Christmas break, from the time he was about eight until he left for Dexter, they'd ride in on the train, go to Brooks Brothers to buy him a new pair of pants and a jacket, and then they'd visit the tree. They'd just look at it without talking. Sometimes they drank hot chocolate. Then his dad would say, "Better get you back home," and they'd walk back to Grand Central and he'd get on the train and ride back to Greenwich by himself.

A gurney arrived powered by two medics.

"Patient is female, name and age unknown! Trauma!" the receptionist shouted at them.

The medics helped Patrick lift the girl onto the gurney, smearing the white sheets with blood. "She's that girl from my sister's grade," one of them noted as they wheeled her away.

"Should I come back later?" Patrick asked the receptionist. "To see if she's okay?"

The receptionist didn't even look up. "That's not up to me."

The glass doors slid open and two burly policemen arrived wearing dark blue police-issue parkas and guns in their holsters. They were accompanied by the old ex-cop who managed Dexter Security.

"That your car parked there?" the Dexter Security guy asked. He pronounced "there" like "they-ah."

Patrick nodded. "Yeah."

"You're not a student up to the college, are ya?" the guy said.

Patrick shook his head. "Not anymore."

"He just brought a girl in," the receptionist spoke up. "She wasn't doing too good."

The policemen approached him from either side and clasped his arms. "That car's stolen," one of them said. "How 'bout you come with us."

21

The dorms were alive again. Everyone had returned from the party, or from wherever they'd been the night before—their girlfriend's dorm, skiing at Sugarloaf, a friend's house in Boston. It wasn't a noisy return, not with exams starting tomorrow. That bitter pill would have to be swallowed or chewed or crushed up and snorted, with no rush or high as a reward, just a blue book and two hours of tedious hell. Studying was advisable, and now was the very last chance to do it.

Shipley woke up with a start. Her hair was crusted to her cheek and she needed a shower. Someone was knocking on the door. Next to her Adam yawned and sat up too.

"Hi," he said, grinning.

The knocking began again. "Security," the knocker explained with a shout. "We found your car."

"Just a minute!" Shipley gathered the duvet around her shoulders and approached the door. Three months ago she'd arrived at Dexter a virgin. Now here she was, opening the door and talking to Campus Security with only a duvet around her while a naked guy lay sprawled on her bed. She opened the door and smiled pleasantly, like it was no big deal.

"You Miss Gilbert?" The security guy didn't seem to notice that she wasn't wearing any clothes. He didn't seem to notice Adam either. He'd probably seen it all in his day.

Shipley nodded and he handed over her wallet. "Car's parked in the lot across the way. You better go down to the police station when you get a chance. Guy stole the car is in jail. Claims he's your—"

"I know who he is," Shipley said curtly. "He didn't leave a note, did he?"

The security guy frowned. "Not that I'm aware of."

Behind them Adam cleared his throat. His red boxer shorts lay like a deflated balloon on the linoleum floor.

Shipley held out her hand. "May I have the keys, please?"

The man handed her the keys. "There's lots going on this morning," he said as he turned away. "You people was busy last night."

Just then Eliza came barreling down the hall, her bangs all tangled and bits of hay stuck to her coat. The security officer stood aside to let her pass.

Shipley slammed the door closed in Eliza's face and threw Adam his boxers. He scrambled into them while she put on her bathrobe.

"HELLO?!" Eliza burst in a moment later. "What the fuck did you do that for?" She took in the scene. Shipley's jeans were all wadded up at the bottom of the bed. Her ironed underwear lay where it had been flung, halfway across the room. "Fucking A, Slutcakes, you move fast!" She kicked off her sneakers and thrust her feet inside a pair of red rubber rain boots. "Hey, you guys have to come outside and see this. Nick's yurt is on fire. Come on, get dressed. I swear, it's amazing."

She waited outside for them while Shipley and Adam got back into yesterday's clothes.

"I can't believe I still haven't had a shower," Shipley said.

It was the only thing either of them said. Adam was embarrassed. Being alone with Shipley was one thing, but there was suddenly so much else going on—campus security, stolen cars, roommates, fires. It was a little overwhelming. And then there was the fact that he'd left his fifteen-year-old sister alone at the party. He had to get back.

Outside the air was clean and dirty at the same time. The snow was magnificent. It was everywhere. But the sky was filled with ash. At first it looked to Shipley as though Root's roof was on fire. Tom's in there, she thought guiltily. But as she drew closer, she could see that the fire was out back, beyond the dorm.

The yurt was a cone of fire rising thirty feet into the air. Sea Bass and Damascus and Geoff and the three Grannies and a crowd of other students fed the fire with sticks and newspaper, trying to make it last as long as possible—anything to procrastinate.

Adam kept his hands in his pockets as they approached. Indeed, this was news. This was excitement. But he needed to go home.

"Nick!" Shipley cried when she spotted him, gazing up at the fire with his flap hat on backward, eyes bloodshot from smoke and allergies. "I'm so sorry," she commiserated. "All your hard work."

Eliza slipped her arms around Nick's waist. "He doesn't give a shit." She lifted up one of his earflaps and licked his ear.

Nick swiped the hat off his head and threw it into the fire.

"Yes! Thank the lord!" Eliza cried. She unzipped her cutoffs beneath her long down coat and stepped out of them.

"No, not those. I love those!" Nick rescued the shorts before she could throw them into the flames.

"Aw." Eliza cupped his rashy face in her hands and kissed him.

"Wow," Shipley remarked. "That must have been some party."

"I think maybe—" Nick bent down and retrieved the gigantic red bong that was lying at his feet. "I think maybe this is the dawn of a new era." He tossed the bong into the fire and it exploded with a dramatic popping sound.

Grover threw his red bandanna into the fire. Then Liam took off his tie-dyed shirt and threw that in too. Next came Wills's skirt. All of a sudden everyone was taking off their clothes and throwing them into the fire.

"All right, all right," Mr. Booth, Dexter's president, shouted into a bullhorn from the front steps of the chapel. "The fire department is standing by, but I wanted to let you kids have your fun first. I know this is a stressful time, what with exams coming up tomorrow. You've got half an hour to go crazy around that bonfire of yours, and then I want you all in the library, studying."

If he hadn't won over the students before, he'd won them over now.

"And don't forget your coffee. The Starbucks café will be open twenty-four hours a day for the next week. The first coffee of the day is on me. Just show them your ID."

"Yeah, Boothy!!"

Adam cleared his throat. "Hey, will you be all right?" he asked Shipley. "I mean, would you mind if I just went home? I kind of have to clean up and everything, before my parents get home."

Shipley nodded, blushing. She wondered if Tom was watching from his window. "Good. That's good. Go home and I'll call you later, okay? I mean, I have two exams tomorrow, so I'm going to be cramming, but we'll figure something out." She couldn't believe how casual and distracted she sounded. "Okay?"

Adam was in too much of a hurry to even notice. He'd have to dig out his car. "Okay. So, I'll see you," he said, and strode away with his hands still in his pockets.

The fire burned with gusto. Students frolicked around it in various stages of undress.

"*Fire, fire on the mountain!*" Wills sang out in a high falsetto, making everybody laugh.

The house was just as Adam had left it except for the crisscrossing car tracks the party-goers had made on the snowy lawn. The porch steps were slippery, and he cursed Tragedy for not shoveling them and coating them with salt the way their parents had taught them to do when they were each about six.

"Hey, I'm home!" he called as he stomped into the kitchen, eager to tell his sister all about last night. On the drive home he'd imagined how he would quietly gloat at dinner that night while his mother and sister chided him about being in love. He imagined bringing Shipley home and fooling around with her in his room while his parents were downstairs drinking wine and dancing to "How Deep Is Your Love." He imagined his sister and Shipley becoming friends and trading clothes and hair bands and jewelry, or whatever girls did with their friends. But Tragedy didn't answer. He ran upstairs.

"Anybody home?

"Tragedy, you here?" he called, striding down the hall to her room. As usual her bed was made with perfect hospital corners. The floor was spotless. A neat stack of books far beyond her years sat on the desk. Advanced Latin. Calculus II. *One Hundred Years of Solitude. Tender Is the Night.* Chaos Theory. Fodor's *Greece.*

Michelin's *Brazil*. Her collection of Rubik's cubes adorned the bureau. One of the windows had been left wide open and snow had collected on the sill. It was freezing. He walked over and tugged the window closed, brushing the snow onto the floor. From where he stood there was a clear view of the driveway and the lawn. Except for the path he'd just taken from the end of the driveway to the front porch, and the dozens of tire tracks that looped around the yard, the eighteen or so inches of new snow was immaculate and untouched. No new footprints led from the house to the barn, where Tragedy should have gone that morning to hay the sheep. In fact, the sheep were standing out in the snow by the fence, baahing like crazy. He shivered violently and went into his room to put on a sweater.

Everything in his room was just as he'd left it too—bed hastily made with clothes pushed underneath it, desk chair askew. He whirled around and dashed downstairs again. Four pairs of green-gold cat eyes stared up at him from out of a towel-lined cardboard box beneath the kitchen table. Storm, the gray mother cat, got up and stretched, then leapt out of the box and trotted over to her empty bowl on the floor beside the woodstove. She meowed plaintively.

"All right, all right," Adam told her as he rummaged around in the cupboards in search of cat food. Where the hell was his sister anyway, he wondered, growing increasingly annoyed. After he'd fed the cat, he put on his good Sorel snow boots and went up to the barn to hay the sheep. The barn door stood open. He flicked on the light. The three spent kegs lay on their sides like abandoned carcasses. Plastic cups littered the floor like bones. He climbed up the ladder and threw two bales of hay down from the hayloft and carried them out to the snowy pasture. The sheep baahed eagerly when they saw him, crowding around the fence and butting their heads against their neighbors' woolly sides. They attacked the bales hungrily before he'd even cut the twine.

He watched them eat for a while, wondering what to do. How could he enjoy his feeling of elation at having spent the night with Shipley, his first real love, when there was no one there to share it with? Had Tragedy gone home with someone? Was she just out for a walk? Or had she finally done it this time, had she finally run away?

Back in the house he dialed Uncle Laurie's number and examined the contents of the fridge while the phone rang. Save for a piece of leftover shepherd's pie and an uncooked ham, the usually well-stocked fridge was strangely empty. There weren't even any grapes. Ravenous, he glanced at the counter, searching for the familiar containers in which Tragedy stored her daily baking endeavors. Nothing.

"Hello, this is Laurence," Uncle Laurie finally answered. Ellen's younger brother was the head of the History Department at the public high school in Lebanon, New Hampshire. He'd graduated from Columbia, cum laude.

"It's Adam. I was just calling to ask . . . to tell my parents something." All of a sudden he wished he hadn't called. If Tragedy was really gone, there was nothing they could do about it except wait for her to come back.

"They're on their way, son. They only just left," Uncle Laurie told him. "How are you, anyway? How's college?"

Adam closed the refrigerator and looked out the window at his car. "College is good. College is great," he said enthusiastically.

"Well, that's good. Your parents said you were having kind of a hard time," Uncle Laurie countered. "Said you were thinking of transferring."

Adam had forgotten all about transferring. He'd even met with

Professor Rosen to discuss his options. As far away as possible, he'd told her, and she'd suggested Dexter's brother school, the University of East Anglia, in England.

But after last night, all that was irrelevant.

"I think it's getting better now," he told his uncle. "Look, I had this party in the barn last night. I'd better clean up before they get home, okay?"

"That sounds like a good idea," Uncle Laurie laughed. "You take care. And say hello to your sister for me. I'll see you at Christmas."

"See you at Christmas," Adam said, and hung up.

It took a long time to clean up the barn and put everything back where it belonged. Someone had thrown up into the muck bucket and on one of the old horse blankets. Rusty horseshoes were scattered all over the place, and one of the shovels was missing. When he was finished, Adam lined the kegs up by the barn door, ready for his dad to load into the pickup and return to the liquor store in town. Then he dragged the heavy-duty trash bags out to the end of the driveway and returned to the house to shovel and salt the porch steps. Back inside, he lit a fire in the fireplace, stoked the woodstove, and walked from room to room, matching up stray shoes and neatening magazines and loose bits of paper. He was just sitting down to the reheated piece of shepherd's pie when the phone rang.

"Hello?" he answered, fork poised.

"This is Kennebec Regional Hospital. Is this Mr. Gatz?" said the person on the other end.

Adam put down his fork. "No. I mean yes. What's wrong? Is there something wrong?"

"We have a Tragedy Gatz here. In the intensive care. I assume she's your—"

"Sister," Adam answered robotically. Out the window he could see his parents' blue pickup make the turn into the driveway and amble toward the house with Ellen behind the wheel. He could see their innocent faces behind the thick glass of the windshield and wished they'd just keep driving, past the house, past Home, to a place with better weather and better news. "We'll be there soon," he said before hanging up.

He stood up and put on his coat. The shepherd's pie sat untouched on its plate. His parents were just opening the pickup's doors when he stepped out onto the porch.

"What the hell, Adam?" Eli shouted. "Didn't anyone bother to bring in the goddamned sheep last night?"

Ellen remained uncharacteristically silent, her mouth rigid and her cheeks pale. She seemed to sense that something was wrong.

"Shove over, Mom, I'm driving," Adam called, waving them back with his hands to indicate that they needed to stay in the car.

Ellen scooted over to make room for him behind the wheel.

"It's Tragedy," he explained as he closed the door and restarted the ignition. "She's been shot."

22

I t wasn't that long ago that Nick had waited outside his and Tom's room while Shipley and Tom fooled around, creeping back into his bed after they'd gone to sleep and leaving again before they woke up. It wasn't that long ago that Eliza had had to suffer through lunch in Coke's dining hall, pretending to be oblivious as she ate her peanut butter and jelly sandwich while Shipley and Tom felt each other up beneath the table. It wasn't that long ago that Eliza had considered joining the Woodsmen's team and becoming a lesbian, not necessarily in that order, or that Nick had considered signing up for "mental health" sessions with the nurse-practitioner to talk about his repressed anger toward his mother and his roommate. And it wasn't that long ago that Tom and Shipley had been one of those Dexter couples everyone assumed would marry soon after graduation.

Not that long ago at all—days.

Now the tables had turned. It was Shipley who sat alone at her desk, pretending to study, while Eliza rubbed cortisone cream all over Nick's mostly naked body beneath a flimsy cotton blanket.

"Do you shave your legs?" she heard Eliza whisper.

"No," Nick protested.

"But they're so unhairy," Eliza insisted. "Are you sure?"

Nick snorted and kicked his feet. "Would you like to inspect them more carefully?"

Eliza disappeared beneath the blanket. Shipley turned up the volume on Tchaikovsky and reread the same passage of Byron for the third time.

"Hey!" Nick squealed. "Stop it!"

Shipley scraped her chair back and yanked the earphones out of her ears.

"I'll see you guys later," she called out, even though neither of them was listening. Out in the hall she picked up the phone and dialed the Gatzes' number.

"Leave a message or be square!" Tragedy's loud, cheerful voice intoned on the answering machine.

"It's Shipley Gilbert calling for Adam," Shipley said. "There's no message," she added stupidly before hanging up.

She lingered in the deserted hallway for a moment, trying to decide what to do. She hadn't seen Tom yet—no one had—but she suspected he was still sleeping. A good girlfriend would have brought him a free cup of Starbucks coffee and a plate of toast from the dining hall. A good girlfriend would have spent the day with him writing out flash cards and testing him in Econ so he wouldn't fail his exam. But she'd already proven that she was not such a good girlfriend.

The midday sun was high and bright. Through the hall window she could see the black Mercedes, parked neatly by Dexter Security in a spot near the road. What was the trunk full of now? Donuts? Croissants? Cupcakes?

Four months ago she would have called home to tell on Patrick, but she was not the same person she'd been four months ago.

She was not as virtuous or as loyal or as discreet. She was not the good little girl her bad older brother had either teased or ignored. She was not the little sister Patrick had hated so much. She had no idea who she was or what she was becoming, but it was possible that going to see Patrick in jail would help move things along. Never mind Byron. She'd learned enough about Romance over the course of the semester to wing the exam.

Jail was a concrete addition to the Home police station, a low rectangular building with a wheelchair ramp leading up to the entrance. A steady stream of townspeople marched up the ramp and in and out of the door as if it were the post office. What reason did people have to visit the police station, Shipley wondered, unless they were visiting someone in jail?

"Parking tickets to your right," the uniformed woman behind the front desk told her.

"No, it's not that," Shipley faltered. "I'm here to see someone. In your jail?"

"I need your name, relationship to the detainee, and your ID, please," the woman said.

After she'd waited a few minutes, a male officer led her through the station house to the jail. There were no bars. The only indication of security at all was that once they'd gone through the door to the jail, the officer locked it behind them.

"You have a visitor," the officer said, knocking on another door in a narrow hallway before opening it with a key. "You okay with him in there?" he asked Shipley.

Now Shipley wished she hadn't come. It would be fine if someone else were there to do the introductions and most of the talking. But she was on her own.

"I guess," she told the officer reluctantly. "But can you leave the door open?" The idea of being trapped in there with Patrick was completely terrifying. What would they say to each other?

"That's fine," the officer said, opening the door all the way. "That's standard procedure." He stepped away from the door and drew up a folding chair in the hallway. "I'll be right here if you need me."

Patrick sat on a cot, holding a book, his blond hair and beard long and wild. He wore the wool sweater she'd bought him at the Darien Sports Shop, a pair of maroon Dexter sweatpants, and work boots without laces. His ever-present jacket had been removed.

"Hi," Shipley said. "Nice sweater."

Patrick looked down at the sweater and then back at his sister. "Thanks."

"Nice sweatpants too—anyone would think you were still a student."

Shipley's cockiness unnerved him. "Are you going to bail me out?"

She pressed her back against the wall. The only place to sit down was the bed, and Patrick was already sitting on it.

"That depends," she said, although she wasn't sure what it depended on. She couldn't remember the last time she and Patrick had spoken face-to-face. "Did you know Mom and Dad split up? Did you know Dad has a place in Hawaii? He's taking me there, after exams. Oh, and that big tent thing on campus caught fire. The yurt. It's totally wild." She put her hands on her hips. "What have you been doing all this time anyway? Where have you been?"

Patrick shrugged his shoulders. "I've been around."

He wasn't surprised about their parents. They'd always argued a lot. And he wasn't surprised about the tent either. He'd made a pretty good fire.

"So are you going to bail me out?" he repeated. He needed to see how that girl was doing. He didn't really care, he just needed to know.

Shipley glanced around the room. Now that she'd been in there for a few minutes it felt more like a cell. There was no window, and nothing in it except a cot, a toilet, and a sink. "What are you reading?" she asked.

Patrick turned the book over in his hands. "It's the Bible," he said. "I was reading something else, but it got ruined. And you know, the Bible isn't so bad."

Shipley waited for him to launch into some kind of sanctimonious religious lecture. Patrick had been known to delve into certain belief systems, like paganism or mysticism, becoming very devout and intolerant of anyone who didn't share the same beliefs, until he found something new to believe in. And there was always a book. The Bible was almost too obvious though. With his long hair and unkempt beard he already looked a lot like Jesus.

"Maybe I should read it sometime," she said, although she had no intention of doing so. They'd taken her bag at the front desk; otherwise she'd have lit a cigarette. "So what will you do when you get out of here?" she asked. "I mean, you can't keep on stealing the car."

Patrick shook his head. "I didn't steal it. I borrowed it. Besides, that car's mine too."

Shipley rolled her eyes. She really wished she had a cigarette.

"I have to see someone," Patrick told her. "Can you please get me out of here so I can do that, please?"

Shipley had never heard him speak in this way, like he actually cared about something. "Fine," she said. "You know I have exams tomorrow?" She poked her head out the door and beckoned the waiting officer. "What do I have to do to get him out?"

Because Shipley had not pressed charges, and there was no evidence that Patrick had done anything else illegal, all she had to do was get a cash advance on her credit card and post bail.

"Thanks, Mom," she said as she signed the receipt.

The same male officer led Patrick out to the reception area and handed him over to her, like a gift she didn't want. Again she thought of calling their parents, but it was more interesting not to. She would have enough of them at Christmastime.

"Okay, so who is this person you so desperately need to see?" she asked once they were outside.

It would have helped if Patrick knew the girl's name.

"Only family," the hospital receptionist told them.

"But I brought her here," Patrick protested. "She was wearing a fur coat and she was bleeding. Are you saying she's alive?"

Shipley wondered if maybe she should have called her dad after all.

The receptionist squinted at a piece of paper on her desk. "What'd you say your name was?"

"Patrick."

She squinted at the paper again. "Do you by any chance go by Pink Patrick?"

Shipley walked over to a chair. "I'll just wait here while you visit." She sat down and picked up the November issue of *Time* magazine with Bill Clinton on the cover.

"She's been waiting for you," the receptionist told Patrick. "It's upstairs. Tragedy Gatz. Room 209. Just got moved out of surgery."

Shipley dropped the magazine on the floor. Patrick was already walking toward the elevator. "Wait!" she called, rushing over to join him. "Wait for me!"

The receptionist scowled at her, but then the elevator arrived and there was nothing she could do about it. Shipley's heart beat loud and fast. Forte. Fortissimo.

The door to the room was open. Adam and two people who must have been his parents stood at the head of the bed where Adam's sister lay with a blistered face and bandaged hands. An IV drip was taped to her arm.

"You guys here for the ass transplant?" Tragedy joked hoarsely when she saw them. "You got the right room."

The guy who'd arrived with Shipley blinked his icy blue eyes. He reminded Adam of someone, but he couldn't quite think of who.

Patrick wasn't expecting an audience. And now that he knew the girl was alive, he wasn't even sure he wanted to see her. "I can come back later," he said, squeezing the kitten inside his pocket. Amazingly, the kitten had slept, curled deep inside his parka, the entire time he'd been in jail.

The color had returned to Ellen's cheeks. "You must be the famous Pink Patrick!" she crowed. "Our hero!" She raised her eyebrows at Shipley. "And who are you?"

Adam cleared his throat. "Mom, this is Shipley. The girl I was telling you about."

Ellen pursed her lips together, making it clear that she wasn't too keen on whatever she'd heard. "Let's leave Pinkie and Trag alone for a bit," she said, herding the rest of them out of the room. "That boy saved her life."

Shipley followed them out into the hall and closed the door behind her, still trying to reconcile the fact that Patrick was a hero.

"You wouldn't believe the morning I've had," she told Adam.

"A hunter shot her," Adam said. "She went for a walk last

night in Mom's fur coat and got lost in the snow. And then a hunter shot her."

"And if she'd died, I would have had to kill you too," Eli declared. "The both of you."

"The weather was so bad, the guy probably didn't even know he'd hit something," Adam went on, ignoring his father. "Anyway, it was an accident."

"But she's okay," Shipley insisted, glancing at Adam for assistance. His parents weren't exactly friendly.

Adam frowned. "That depends on your definition of okay."

"I'm so sorry," she said.

"Just so you know, Adam is grounded," Ellen interjected. "Until he's about forty-five. Although I don't suppose it makes any difference."

Shipley laughed. Then she stopped laughing. No one else was laughing.

Adam wanted to touch her, to kiss her, to tell her it was all right, but he'd already resolved something in his mind that had nothing to do with touching her or kissing her or talking to her ever again.

Ellen and Eli went over to the coffee station and poured themselves two Styrofoam cups of coffee and creamer.

Shipley leaned against the wall and closed her eyes. She needed a nap.

"My brother was always such a fuckup," she said to no one in particular.

Patrick had developed a hatred of hospitals when he was just a boy. He'd suffered from chronic ear infections and post-nasal drip, and when he turned six, the pediatrician ordained that his tonsils and adenoids needed to be removed.

His parents had lied to him. "You'll be asleep for the whole thing, and when you wake up you'll get ice cream," they said. But when he woke up, his head felt like an octopus whose eight legs had been eaten off by a shark. He didn't want any ice cream, and he refused to speak to his parents. It was about that time that he stopped taking off his jacket.

Shipley was only a baby then, sunny and silly. She sat on the floor, making puddles with his ice cream, while he watched back-to-back episodes of *The Twilight Zone*. He'd thought meeting up with her today would be a turning point of some kind, that he'd become something more than just the sketchy subject of a short poem. But he could see now that that would have been too easy. Turning points were hard to come by.

The room was full of beeping machinery. There were flowers on the nightstand and a TV was bolted to the wall. It wasn't anything like jail, although it sort of smelled the same.

"I brought you something." Patrick removed the kitten from his pocket and put it down on the bed. The kitten crawled onto Tragedy's chest and lay down.

She stroked its soft fur with her bandaged hands. "So, I'm still here, thanks to you." She glanced up at Patrick and then winced. "I don't feel so good though. Don't be offended if I conk out."

Patrick nodded. "I was in jail," he told her, trying to explain why he hadn't arrived sooner. "Not because of you. For something else."

Tragedy closed her eyes. "That's okay."

Out in the hall, Adam took a step toward Shipley and then stopped. "Look," he murmured. "I have two exams tomorrow and two on Wednesday, and then I'm done." His gaze met hers. "I'm transferring."

"What?" Shipley sucked in her breath. In her mind she'd already played out two separate scenarios. In the first, Tom challenged Adam to a bloody duel, with swords, and Tom won. In the second, she poisoned Tom with arsenic and then she and Adam ran off to Hawaii together. "Transferring where?"

"East Anglia. It's in England. Dexter has a sort of brother-sister exchange with them, so I was able to transfer my scholarship. I wasn't going to go, but now I think it's for the best. My parents are pretty mad at me. "

"It's for the best," Shipley repeated. She turned around to glance at Adam's parents, hugging each other by the coffeemaker. She'd wanted to meet them and make friends, but they didn't want to know her. Someone had to take the blame for what had happened and she was that someone. She was bad news.

Adam touched her arm and she turned around. Before he could say anything, Shipley grabbed his head and pressed her lips against his. He'd meant to give her a quick, sweet good-bye embrace, but something about rescuing her brother from jail and visiting a half-dead girl in the hospital had given Shipley a taste for the dramatic. It wasn't the fridge-slamming kiss from Professor Rosen's kitchen, but it was close.

"Adam?" Ellen interrupted from behind them. "We're going to head home in a little bit. Just as soon as Trag's friend comes out. We're going to make him some lunch and pick up some things for your sister. You coming?"

Adam grinned into Shipley's kissing mouth. He wasn't going to be the one to stop this. He could kiss her forever. Finally Shipley took a step back and smiled up at him. "Now you have something to remember me by."

Adam shoved his hands into his pockets. "I'll remember you," he promised.

"Nice meeting you," Shipley called to Adam's parents, but they pretended not to hear. It was pretty obvious she wasn't invited to lunch, and Patrick was probably better off with the Gatzes than with her. "I guess I should go and study."

Adam closed his eyes and opened them again. She was still there, although she had moved down the hall to the elevator. It arrived with a *ping* and the door slid open. Shipley lifted her hand to wave good-bye and stepped in.

Tragedy was too tired to talk. The kitten bathed itself in the crook of her arm, its small pink tongue dampening and flattening its black fur with impressive persistence. Patrick switched on the TV, but it was so loud and obnoxious he switched it off again. He opened the nightstand drawer and found another bible. The cover was bright blue with gold lettering and the line "King James Version" at the bottom. The one from jail just said "The Holy Bible" in white on a black background. He traded that one for the King James and closed the drawer.

"Well, I guess I'll go," he said. "I'm glad you're alive," he added without a hint of emotion.

Tragedy turned her head. "Doctor said I probably won't be able to have kids now," she told him. "Which sucks like a motherfucker."

Patrick smiled at her turn of phrase. "That's harsh."

She closed her eyes. "Don't think you're going anywhere either. I told my parents about you. They're taking you back to our house to eat good food and sleep in a nice warm bed. So suck it up, jackass."

Patrick wasn't so sure about that. He didn't know the Gatzes, and usually people didn't want him around. The worst thing about the yurt burning down was that he'd have no place to sleep, but he could always go back to his old winter haunts—a smashed-up windowless Winnebago on the banks of the Messalonskee Stream, an old shed next to a Busch beer warehouse, a truck stop in Lewiston, a homeless shelter in Augusta, and maybe after the students went home for the holidays, the overheated kitchen in the basement of Root.

"I'll see you," he said.

He opened the door and closed it quietly behind him. The Gatzes were waiting for him, all smiles and bear hugs.

"Yeah, see you, Pinkie." Tragedy yawned and fell asleep.

23

Sleep and wakefulness are active states controlled by specific groups of brain structures. The body does its repair work during sleep, restoring energy supplies and muscle tissue. If you happen to be recovering from an ecstasy and ether bender, there's lots of repair work to be done.

Tom had passed out facedown on his bed, in his clothes, just before nine o'clock on Saturday night. It was now four o'clock on Sunday afternoon. Deep within his cerebral cortex he detected a rhythmic knocking sound that was too loud and too fast to be the beating of his own heart. His toes twitched. He flexed his ankles. Then he rolled over and opened his eyes. Sun streamed in through the windows. The air smelled like burnt toast.

"Tom?" *Knock, knock, knock, knock, knock.* "Tom?"

He lay on his back, blinking up at the ceiling. His lips felt like they'd been caulked shut. His nasal passages felt like they'd been worked with a plumber's snake.

Knock, knock, knock, knock, knock, knock, knock, knock, knock, knock. "Tom?"

What day was it? he wondered. He remembered the play, which had gone well, he thought. His parents were there, or maybe that part had been a dream. They'd taken him and Shipley out to dinner to that fishy place on the river. He'd eaten lobster. He'd worn a bib. Right now his stomach felt hollow and sour. Maybe he was allergic to lobster.

Knock, knock, knock, knock. "Tom? Are you in there? I'm going to come in now. The door's not locked."

Professor Rosen opened the door and stepped into the room, looking like she'd just gotten back from cross-country skiing. Her gray wool kneesocks were pulled up over the legs of her brown wide-wale corduroy pants. Her red Gore-Tex jacket was tied around her waist, and she was still wearing her sunglasses and a purple ski hat. She took a moment to scrutinize the scattered paint tubes and brushes, the drying canvasses, the paint-spattered floor, Nick's upturned bed, and Tom's prone form.

"Tom," she said sharply. "Didn't you hear me knock?"

Tom pushed himself up on his elbows. "Where's Shipley?" He sat up and rubbed the sleep out of his eyes. "Man, what is that burning smell?"

One side of Professor Rosen's mouth twitched upward in a grim half smile. "Your parents came by to check on you early this morning, but they didn't want to wake you. They had to get back to New York. I promised them I'd stop by and see how you were doing later on. Your dad wanted me to be sure you got some studying time in before exams."

Tom blinked and looked at his wrist. His watch wasn't there. He'd taken it off for the play. "So it's Sunday," he said.

"And that burning smell is the smoke from the yurt your friend Nicholas built out back. It burned down this morning," she said.

"Holy fuck!" Tom glanced at Nick's upturned bed and frowned. "Nobody, like, burned up inside it or anything, did they?"

"No." The professor walked over to Tom's desk chair and picked up the blue bath towel that was draped over the seat. She tossed the towel at Tom. "Why don't you take a shower? I'll see if I can find Shipley. Meet me outside the dorm in twenty minutes. I'll take you guys out for some food."

Tom picked up the towel. "Isn't the dining hall still open for breakfast?"

The professor gave him another one of her half smiles. "Tom, it's after four. The dining hall won't be open until dinner at six."

Shipley burst into the room as Tom was staring out the window at the black ring of yurt ash in the deep, white snow. Water dripped from his freshly showered body onto the floor.

"Tom!" she cried, thrusting a gigantic cup of Starbucks coffee in his direction. She'd been lying on her bed, exhausted and dozing and pretending to study, when Professor Rosen called. "I got you a venti latte."

Her blond hair was scraped back into a messy ponytail and there were dark circles beneath her eyes. The cuffs of her jeans were damp and salt-streaked. Tom thought she looked wonderful. He held out his arms. The blue towel slipped from around his waist. "I love you," he said, fully naked.

Shipley put the coffee down on his paint-spattered desk and walked into his open arms. He hugged her tightly through her coat and rested his dripping forehead on her shoulder.

"I hope I didn't fuck up too much last night," he murmured.

She patted his damp back with her mittened hands. He was

so big and his room was a mess. *He* was a mess. But she loved him anyway. She would love him always. Adam too.

"You were fine. You were great," she said, and bent down to retrieve his towel. "Here, get dressed. Professor Rosen's downstairs. She says she's going to buy us donuts."

Outside, the setting sun was already drifting downhill. Professor Rosen's minivan was waiting for them. Stray flakes of snow drifted down from the trees and fluttered to the ground. Tom opened the van's side door. A baby was strapped into a car seat in the back.

"Hey, I didn't know you had a baby!" He thumbed his ears at the baby and stuck out his tongue. The baby seemed to be asleep with its eyes open.

"Hop in." Professor Rosen turned around and scraped the stuff on the backseat onto the floor. Diapers, maps, baby bottles.

Tom and Shipley got in. Nick and Eliza were in the very back seat, holding hands.

"Hey, Slutcakes," Eliza said. "What is this? Musical boys?"

Nick's cheeks were pink and shiny from so much cortisone. "You guys all ready for exams?"

Tom slid the door closed and settled into the seat on one side of the baby while Shipley sat on the other. "So who knew it was going to snow last night?" He caught the professor's gaze in the rearview mirror. "Did you know?"

Professor Rosen backed the van out onto the road. "The storm was on the news all week. People were buying up the whole grocery store. The turkeys were all gone. No potatoes even. Guess people thought the whole system would shut down."

They coasted down the hill toward town. Snow was everywhere. The entire campus had been transformed into a winter wonderland.

"Just look at it all!" Tom marveled, as if he'd never seen snow before. He turned his head to admire Shipley's profile against the white snowbanks outside the window. Then he glanced down at the baby. Its eyes were dark brown and its skin was the color of maple syrup. It was holding Shipley's finger.

"I can't wait for Christmas," Shipley murmured. Beetle's skin had reminded her of Hawaii.

"Me too," Professor Rosen agreed. "We're going to Sedona."

"I'm going to stay in my pj's till New Year's," Tom yawned.

Nick spoke up from the way back. "I'm going to Eliza's house."

"I can't wait for donuts," Eliza chimed in. She stuck her hand down the back of Nick's pants and kept it there. "Hey, is anyone else having major déjà vu?" She stared out at the snow for a while, then turned around and stuck her tongue out at Nick. He looked so much better without his hat, and his skin was beginning to calm down.

Nick pushed her bangs up off her forehead to see what she would look like without them. "Whoa," he said, and let the bangs drop. "Maybe you should start wearing hats." He kissed the tip of her nose. "I could knit one for you."

"Oh God." Eliza grimaced. "Please, someone just shoot us now and put us out of our misery."

Shipley undid her seat belt and crawled over Beetle's car seat to sit in Tom's lap.

"Oi!" Professor Rosen called out.

Nick and Eliza were all over each other now, the moist sucking sounds of their kisses muffled by the smack of the tires on the wet road. Tom put his arms around Shipley and pulled her in close. Through the very back window of the car she could see the blue light of Dexter's chapel spire, shining significantly on top of the hill, like a beacon. It was hard to believe it could ever go out.

Behind them, the road was a black river cutting across a glistening white field fringed with dark trees. A curl of smoke rose up from the chimney of a nearby farmhouse. She imagined Patrick and Adam and Adam's parents sitting around a fire, eating Tragedy's cookies and drinking wine. If Adam went to England, Patrick could drive his car instead of hers. Patrick might even move in with the Gatzes. It might work out for everyone.

She wrapped her arms around Tom's neck and kissed him in a roving, tentative manner, like a person trying to get into a house when they've forgotten the key. She kissed his forehead, his temples, his ears, his neck, his chin. He smelled like Ivory soap and Gillette shaving cream and Colgate toothpaste and Johnson & Johnson's baby shampoo—all the things she was used to. But there were other things she craved, things she didn't even know existed. Once you got a taste for the unexpected, it was hard to settle for anything less.

She paused for a breath. "Did you know they have snow in Hawaii?"

"That's why I went to college," Tom joked. "To learn shit like that." He tilted his head back and puckered his lips, eager for more of her.

Shipley slammed his head against the back of the seat and kissed him on the mouth, this time with conviction. Then, without another word, she pulled away and crawled back over Beetle's car seat. The van lurched over a bump and, for a moment, was airborne. One of Nick's Philosophy textbooks dropped out of his bag and slid across the floor beneath Shipley's feet. *An Inquiry Concerning Human Understanding,* she read upside down. Thank goodness she wasn't in that class.

She refastened her seat belt and gazed out the window. The sky was swollen and ripe. It would snow again, soon. There would be more snow, more kisses, more sex, more gunshots, more fires. This was what she had come for—what they had all come for. This was college.

Acknowledgments

I would be plagued by guilt and unable to write anything if I didn't know that my children were always having a good time without me, and for that I thank Marsha Torres, Erasmo Paolo, and my mother, Olivia. Thank you, Suzanne Gluck, agent extraordinaire, for being fierce, wise, sympathetic, and funny at all the right times; and Sarah Ceglarski, Elizabeth Tigue, and Caroline Donofrio for being wonderful. At Hyperion, thank you, Brenda Copeland, for your wit, keen insight, swift responses, and good taste in cheese; Kate Griffin for your professionalism; and Ellen Archer, for giving me a chance and then some. Thank you Barbara Pavlock for your help with Latin. Thank you Paragraph, where this book's beginnings were written. Thank you Karaoke Wednesdays. Thank you Ambien. Thank you Agnes and Oscar, my children and the teachers from whom I've learned the most. And thank you Richard, for reading this thing more than once, and for being a really good husband, despite being married to me.

Permissions